'I hope she'll be a fool – that's the best thing a girl can be in this world, a beautiful little fool.'

— F. Scott Fitzgerald (*The Great Gatsby*)

Part One

1

Maahi could have sworn the man standing behind her wasn't as close to her the last time she checked. He had been there when she first boarded the bus at Bangalore Dairy Circle. She had been running to catch it, and in her agitated state, accidentally brushed against his arm when she climbed in. He had looked up and smiled at her, a smile she returned hesitantly. Now she could feel him inching closer by the minute, towering over her. She shifted her weight on her feet and breathed out softly, deliberately. A few more minutes and she would reach her stop. She wished she could take a taxi, but she had to save from her allowance to buy lunch for Kishan. Her mother had sent her more money just over a week ago, and she didn't want to have to ask for more.

She was wearing a white chiffon shirt with a mandarin collar and loose sleeves that collected at her wrists. She had a beige tank top on underneath, an attempt to keep her stomach pushed in. Her mother called it baby fat—she thought it was adorable and assured her she would eventually lose it, that she was just a kid. But Maahi wasn't a kid, she was nineteen, and embarrassed about the slight bulge at the waist of her jeans.

Maahi raised a hand to tuck her hair behind her ear, and became aware of the man's eyes on her. She slowly pulled the hair back to her face, hiding as much as she could. She wasn't too fond of her round, chubby face either; it made her look younger. When the bus stopped at JP Nagar 3rd Phase, Maahi disembarked on impulse. She was supposed to get off at the next station, Bilekahalli, but preferred walking an extra kilometre to being around that man. The sunrays hit her face and she dug into her bag for her sunglasses. There wasn't much traffic, but it would soon be lunchtime and she wanted to surprise Kishan before he left on his break.

Born and raised in Ghaziabad, Maahi was having trouble adjusting to life in south India. She convinced herself that all she needed was time. She was halfway through her first semester at Christ University, from where she was getting her bachelor of engineering in IT, and she was yet to settle comfortably in this new city. There were a few people she talked to in class, but all her real friends were back in Vaishali, a township in the suburbs of Delhi. She called her friend Rohit every Sunday, and they texted each other throughout the week.

Maahi walked hurriedly towards Accenture, where Kishan worked as an associate software engineer. She still had to pick up lunch, and contemplated getting something from either Nagarjuna or Biryani Bowl, both of which were on her way. She knew Kishan missed north Indian food and would appreciate some butter chicken and garlic naans. Just the thought of it made her stomach grumble. She was coming straight from college and hadn't had a chance to eat. She felt guilty skipping the next two classes, but it was their anniversary. They first met exactly two years ago, and that needed celebrating.

Maahi saw a rectangular green neon board boasting 'Nagarjuna Andhra Style Since 1984' ahead on her right and decided to go there. Kishan always talked about how much he hated north Indian food cooked by south Indians. He didn't seem to mind this place though, when they came here a few months ago. He had brought her here for dinner when she had just moved to Bangalore. She walked into the dimly lit air-conditioned restaurant and the change in temperature made her sneeze. Covering her mouth with her palm, she walked to the reception.

'Can I look at the menu, please?' she asked.

'I'm sorry?' the middle-aged man in a white uniform at the reception asked.

Maahi was intimidated by his moustache. She cleared her throat and spoke again, louder this time, 'I have to get something packed.'

'You want the menu? Here, ma'am.'

Maahi felt weird being addressed as 'ma'am'. Her ears got warm as the man watched her read the menu. When he smiled at her, his teeth shone white—it was strangely appeasing and she smiled back, saying, 'Butter chicken and kulcha, please?'

'One kulcha only?' He pronounced 'only' as 'one-ly', and Maahi smiled wider as she scanned the menu again. The kulchas were Rs 50 each. If she got two, her total would be close to Rs 350, which would be too much for her. She shook her head, her stomach grumbling in protest.

'Wokay. One plate butter chicken and one kulcha, pack,' the man yelled towards the kitchen, before turning back to Maahi. 'Any sweet dish?'

'Oh.' She hadn't thought of that. 'Do you have gulab jamun?' she asked mechanically.

'Yes, two per plate.'

'One plate, please.' Maahi quickly dropped her eyes to the menu to check the price. Rs 65 for two gulab jamuns. It was their anniversary, she reasoned, and Kishan loved gulab jamuns. He would never think about money and she shouldn't either. He did have a job, to be fair, while she was a student. As she added up the amount in her head, the waiter handed her the bill. It was Rs 417.12. She had forgotten to take service tax and VAT into account. At least there would be no service charge since she ordered takeaway.

Maahi pulled out her wallet and counted the cash while trying to calculate how much money she would have left. A few hundred, to cover the next couple of weeks. It wouldn't be too bad; she had a meal plan at the college mess and her boarding was taken care of. She would just have to be extra cautious with spending until her mother sent her more. As long as she didn't run short and have to ask her for more, she would be fine.

While she waited for the food, Maahi observed the family having lunch at the table closest to her. They looked Punjabi and were speaking in Hindi. She realized how much she missed hearing people talk in Hindi. She stuck her tongue out at the little boy at the table, who giggled in response, but when his mother looked at Maahi, she quickly composed herself and diverted her eyes.

Her order was ready soon, and she thanked the waiter with one last smile before leaving the restaurant. She walked on the uneven sidewalk at the edge of the asphalt road, kicking up dry dust with her sneakers. It was close to 1 p.m., and Kishan's office was still about twenty minutes away. She walked as fast as she could without stumbling and falling on her face. She couldn't have another one of those. Kishan would make fun of her and call her a baby. She laughed quietly at the thought; he was always teasing her, but he knew better than anyone else that she was not a baby.

By the time she turned at Bannerghatta Main Road, Maahi was running short of breath, even in the pleasant September weather. The sidewalk got narrower and dustier. It was ten past one and she was afraid Kishan might have left for his break already, maybe even sat down and ordered food. If she had to call him and ask him to come back, her surprise would be ruined. She wished she were taller, just so she could have longer legs and walk faster. At 5'3" she found her pace quite restricted. She was thinking about how she looked next to Kishan—who was six inches taller, her skin pale against his—when she saw him walk towards her, right outside his office building. He was in conversation with a colleague, Payal, his head leaning towards her to listen. Maahi had met her a few times and wasn't particularly fond of her.

'Hello,' Maahi said, stopping right in front of them.

Kishan looked up. 'Oh, *Maahi*! Hey, what are you doing here?'

'Are you joining us for lunch?' Payal asked, her lips barely stretching in a tight smile. Her pointed nose was shinier than usual.

'Actually,' Maahi raised the takeout bag and said, 'I brought him lunch.'

'Aww, isn't she the *sweetest* girl!'

Maahi didn't like Payal's patronizing tone, but tried to be reasonable and shake it off. She felt better when Kishan said, 'I know, right?' and wrapped an arm around her shoulder. She blushed instantly. Kishan said to Payal, 'Sorry about lunch. Some other day?'

'Yeah,' Payal said. 'Yeah.'

'Bye,' Maahi murmured, before Kishan turned her away and they started walking to his office.

'I didn't know you were coming here,' he said, looking down at her sideways. He had recently taken to growing his beard. Maahi thought it was funny how it mostly spread around the edges of his face, making the V-shape of his jaw look rounder. The hair on the rest of his face, including his moustache, was scattered sparsely.

'That was the point—it's a surprise! Don't you ... *remember*?' Maahi asked, inspecting his eyes.

'Of course I do. Happy anniversary, baby,' Kishan said, rubbing her lower back.

The touch of his hand through the fabric of her shirt sent shivers up her spine. Maahi snaked her arm under his and rested it at his waist. As they walked to his cubicle, some people glanced their way and nodded. Maahi nodded back. She liked coming here, meeting Kishan at his workplace, around his colleagues. They were all nice to her and she enjoyed every visit.

When they reached Kishan's cubicle, he took the takeaway bag from her. There were two chairs. Maahi chose the one with his coat draped over the back. She could smell him on the coat, even over the strong aroma of butter chicken.

'Didn't you have class this morning?' Kishan asked, taking the other chair. He opened the bottom drawer and pulled out two Styrofoam plates and plastic spoons.

'I did. I'm not eating.' Maahi pushed away the plate Kishan was offering her.

'Why aren't you eating? Have you had lunch already?'

'Well, not really. But I'm not that hungry. I had a glass of milk before class.'

'With Bournvita?' Kishan chuckled. He loaded up one plate with the butter chicken before placing the kulcha on the other.

'What, it tastes good, and it's really good for you. More than that, it keeps milk from tasting disgusting and that's the point!' Maahi punched him softly on his arm.

He caught her hand and brought it to his lips. Looking her in the eye, he slowly kissed her knuckles before biting her skin.

Maahi inhaled sharply.

Kishan licked the bite, pulling her skin between his teeth, not breaking eye contact for a second. 'You know how I feel when you get aggressive…'

She tried to find her breath. He could take her to a different world in a second. That's all it took. From the first time she met him, he had held a certain power over her, something she could never understand. That night, two years ago, when her friend had introduced her to his cousin, and she had seen this man with dark eyes and even darker hair, she had felt something special for him. He wasn't like the boys back at school. He was more *man* than *boy*. He had two years left in his bachelor's programme in computer technology & applications at Delhi University. He had treated her as an equal. He looked smart, confident and interested in her—an awkward schoolgirl—and she was flattered by his attention.

That night, when they talked, and he asked her questions about her, she tried not to shiver under the sheer force of his gaze. No one had shown such interest in her life before, and she could see herself, as if from a distance, falling in love with this man. They exchanged numbers, and soon, their text messages became phone calls that lasted all night. She was in love and could feel it in every bone of her body, just as she did now, as he continued to hold her hand.

'There are people around,' she whispered.

'So? I'm not doing anything I shouldn't; you're my girlfriend.'

'Yes, but still…'

Kishan laughed and released her hand, kissing it before placing it back on her lap. 'You need to eat though. Here.' He tore a bite of kulcha and dipped it in gravy.

She leaned forward and ate it off his fingers. He looked at her as she chewed, which made her extremely conscious about the tiny acne scars on her face. She swallowed quickly and asked, 'How has your day been? Busy?'

'As usual. I'll have a more normal schedule by next month, I'm hoping. Once we finish this project.' Kishan nodded, more to himself. 'Tell me about your college. How are classes going?'

'They're okay.'

'Good. I hope you're not cutting classes. Why did you need to come here in the middle of a weekday? I don't want you to fall behind on your coursework.'

'I know. I'm doing fine, don't worry about me.' Maahi smiled. 'I went to the morning class and I'll get notes for the ones I've missed. I mean, it's not really all that difficult—'

'Maybe not *right now*, but it's going to get tough. You'll see. I've been there and I've done exactly that—that's how I know. You have to take this seriously. The initial classes will build your basics more than anything else.'

They ate quietly. Maahi took small bites, even as her stomach contracted with hunger. Back home, she could go without a few consecutive meals and still be fine, but recently she had found herself too weak to skip even one. She had no energy reserves to pull her through if she didn't eat.

'I need water,' she said.

Kishan passed her the bottle of water. 'I didn't mean to snap at you. I was only saying that for your own good.'

'I know. But it's our anniversary…'

'Yeah, I know. I do appreciate all this.' Kishan pointed to the food. 'And look, you got me gulab jamuns! How can I not love you?'

Maahi laughed as he ate one.

'I have a surprise for you too.'

'Really?'

Kishan nodded. 'You'll have to wait though. I have work to finish here, but I'll see you after that?'

'You'll come to my hostel?'

'If you don't mind.'

'Of course I don't mind! Around when? I'll have to check who the warden is and how to sneak you in, but we'll figure it out. We always do!' Maahi said, excitedly. She couldn't wait to see what the surprise was, but tried to contain her enthusiasm.

'I have to get back to work now. But I'll come to you as soon as I can, okay? If there's a problem with me getting in, I'll just take you back to my apartment. It feels like I haven't spent time with you properly in forever.'

'You've been so busy,' Maahi said, as Kishan kissed her lightly on the cheek.

'We'll make up for it tonight.'

That evening, Maahi took a second shower and changed into a light-yellow dress that fell in pleats just above her knees. She sat down on the bed with a book. Her room had ugly green bumpy walls. She was nearing the end of *Catching Fire*, the second book of The Hunger Games series. Rohit was reading the same book and she wanted to finish it before he could spoil it for her. She lost track of time as she fell asleep, her dreams and the novel meshing strangely.

Maahi woke up hours later, still holding the book, and looked around for her phone. It was almost ten and Kishan hadn't called. She texted him.

> Maahi: Where are you?
> Kishan: Stuck at work. Be there ASAP.

Maahi wasn't sleepy after her nap, and opened her novel again. She was getting to the climax and hoped to finish it before Kishan arrived.

A little over an hour later, when she finished reading the book and set it down, she texted Rohit.

> Maahi: Just finished Catching Fire.
> Rohit: Shit! I've got 4 more chaptersssss
> Maahi: Do you want to know what happens in the end?
> Rohit: OMG SHUT UP!!!
> Maahi: I'm just trying to help…
> Rohit: Turning off my phone NOW
> Maahi: Haha jk!

When Maahi didn't get a response, she figured Rohit had actually turned his phone off. Or chose to ignore her. She texted Kishan again.

> Maahi: Kishan!

Kishan: I'm on my way!
Maahi: Ugh. Come soon.
Kishan: Coming!

With nothing else to do, Maahi turned on the radio. Some regional music was on and she let it play. It sounded like Kannada, or maybe Tamil or Telugu. She felt quite embarrassed about not being able to differentiate between these languages, but she couldn't help it.

The song ended and another one started. She tried to guess what it was about, and judging by the upbeat tone, reached the conclusion that it could be about a crazed lover chasing after his new love interest, or a man singing at his friend's wedding, probably chasing the bride's friends and sisters. She laughed when she tried to analyse why she thought that the song had to be about a man wooing a woman in both scenarios.

The next song was milder, but she could hardly stand the one after that—the woman's screeching voice was disturbing. Even so, Maahi had no will to even pick up her phone and change the station. So she simply lay there that night, sleepless, listening to one song after the other, not understanding anything, but drawing her own conclusions about each of them, building stories to entertain herself. She eventually got hungry and drank water from the bottle by her bed.

She texted Kishan once or twice, and each time, he told her he was on his way. She resisted the temptation to call him, knowing it wouldn't make him come any sooner, since he was already on his way.

It was almost five in the morning when she got a text from him.

Kishan: Too tired. I think I'm getting sick. I'm just going to go home and crash. Sorry.

Maahi put the phone down and continued staring at the ceiling, listening to strange music, acutely aware of her breathing—slow and even.

2

When the sun came out, Maahi, for the lack of anything to do, took another shower. She got dressed for class and went downstairs to the mess. It was still early and she didn't see many people on her way there. She served herself some scrambled eggs and a slice of toast and took her plate to a table by the window. She looked out at the dirty blue sky waiting for sunlight to make it brighter. It looked dry and dead against the green grass.

'Oh, hey! You're Maahi, right?' a small, round man with square spectacles asked her.

'Hi, yes. Dev?' She saw him around all the time, but had only spoken to him once before.

'That's me. Can I sit with you?'

'Sure.'

'How's it going? Up so early,' Dev commented as he sat down opposite her, also looking out of the window.

'So are you.'

'Fair. I have to finish the assignment early; we're planning to go out for Prateek's birthday later in the evening. Are you coming?'

Maahi hesitated. 'I actually ... I don't know anyone.'

'Then you should definitely hang out with us. You'll meet everyone,' Dev said. He spotted someone entering the mess and called out, 'Hey Priyanshi, here!'

'Morning!' the curly haired girl called back, walking towards them. 'What's up? Hi, I'm Priyanshi.' She stuck out her slender hand to Maahi, flashing her electric-blue nailpolish.

'Maahi.'

'I was just telling Maahi that she should come with us to Prateek's party tonight.'

'Oh, yes,' Priyanshi said, visibly excited. 'You should totally come. It's going to be a lot of fun. I'm getting kind of sick of all these boys anyway. I'd love to have another girl around.'

Maahi smiled. 'I'll try to make it.'

Priyanshi brought her breakfast to the table and as they ate together, the rest of their friends joined in. Before Maahi knew it, an hour had passed and she found herself laughing with them. Her new friends. It was a strange group, with people from so many different states—Dev was from Bihar, Priyanshi from Gujarat, there were two boys from Uttar Pradesh and a girl from Maharashtra. Yet, for the first time since she had moved to Bangalore, Maahi didn't feel out of place, because they were all out of place, and being outsiders, they somehow gelled together. The thought was relaxing. She wasn't the only one lost, grappling to find a place for herself.

'Are you enjoying Bangalore?' Priyanshi asked her.

'I think so. The weather is much better than it is back home,' Maahi said, it was the only thing that came to her mind. She hadn't seen much of Bangalore yet, and found herself unequipped to comment on anything else.

Dev laughed. 'I know what you're talking about. It's a very

welcome change for me. If there's one thing I don't miss, it's the excessive humidity in Patna. In fact, every time I feel homesick, I remind myself of that. Works every time.'

'But it's no longer summer,' Maahi pointed out.

'Oh, it's always summer there. Except when it's winter—just these two extremes. God, I have goosebumps just talking about it. Look.' He pointed at his arm. Maahi couldn't spot any goosebumps. 'The terror.'

'He's just being dramatic, like always,' the girl from Maharashtra said.

'Don't worry, you'll tune it out after a while,' Priyanshi added.

Maahi grinned and said, 'I don't mind.'

'*HA!*' Dev punched the table with his fist. 'Not everyone is as judgemental as you guys, see? Maahi, will you be my new best friend?'

Maahi didn't know how to respond to that. She just sat there blushing while the others asked Dev who his current best friend was. Priyanshi pretended to be hurt when Dev refused to answer and the Maharashtrian girl said she knew it was her. Maahi could see herself being a part of this. She liked how childish they all were, and felt less burdened about appearing mature. She could be the awkward, shy teenager in the corner and wouldn't be forced to pretend to be confident and outgoing. She had only just met them, but she already liked them.

The guys from UP got up and Maahi checked the time on her phone. No messages or missed calls. She hated when that happened, particularly when she had kept her phone away for a few hours, expecting him to call or text. Maybe he was still asleep, she reasoned. He did go to sleep at five in the morning, and it was only ten. She missed him, but resolved not to call or text before he did. He had a long day at work the previous day and needed to catch up on his sleep. She didn't want to disturb him. She was also mad at him, but didn't want to admit it, even to herself. Being mad at someone when they couldn't help the situation was childish, and she was no child.

'Let's go,' Dev said, shaking her out of her thoughts.

Maahi got up, and the world swayed. She was more underrested than she had believed. She placed her palm flat on the table for support, staying very still, waiting for it to pass.

'Are you alright?' Dev asked, studying her face.

'Yes ... yes.' She didn't elaborate. She breathed out deliberately before picking up her bag. 'Ready?'

They walked out of the mess together, towards the IT building. Maahi didn't hear much of what they were saying at first, lost in her thoughts. But then she forced herself to be present and listen. She didn't speak though; they were walking fast and Maahi was losing energy. She missed her mom's cooking.

With three consecutive classes, the day went by faster than she had expected. She attended all of them, sitting with the same people in every class, for the first time since she'd been here. They were halfway through the third and final class of the day when she got a text.

Kishan: I miss you, baby. I want to see you. :*

Maahi didn't respond to it straightaway. She placed her phone face down under her book and looked up towards her teacher. But no matter how hard she tried, she could no longer concentrate on what he was saying. She didn't take her eyes off the green board, staring at it unblinkingly until a tear escaped the corner of her eye. She told herself it was fatigue, that she was having trouble breathing because she didn't drink enough water. Dehydration—that's what it was. She collected the sleeve of her shirt at her wrist and quickly wiped the teardrop with it. She shouldn't lose fluids when she was already short on them.

She got another text a little later.

> Kishan: I'm sorry. I know I messed up. But I'm really sick. :(:(

When the class ended, they met up with Prateek, the birthday boy. They decided to go back to their rooms to change and meet again in an hour to leave together. Priyanshi walked with her to their hostel.

'I like Nizami sir. I think he's a really good teacher,' Priyanshi said.

Maahi nodded.

'Maths is hard for me, you know? I'm not bad at it, but I don't like it either. To be honest, I don't really know what I'm doing here. Everyone was taking PCM after tenth class, so I took it too. I like chemistry, physics is okay too, but maths—ugh. I managed somehow. If not for group study, I would've failed. After twelfth, everyone was going for engineering, and I did the same. Now here we are.' Priyanshi sighed. 'Do you like it?'

'Hmm?' Maahi looked up from her phone.

> Kishan: Can you come over to meet me? Please? I need you. ;(

'Do you like maths?' Priyanshi repeated.

'I guess. It's alright.' Maahi shrugged.

'I don't know, man. It's not bad, but I can do without it. Nizami sir is making it much easier for me though. I really like him.'

'Yes, he's good.'

'Are you always this quiet? I feel like I'm talking too much.'

'No, no. It's okay.'

Priyanshi laughed. 'You're so sweet. You can tell me if I'm bothering you. I usually bother people. It's kind of what I do.'

'You aren't bothering me. I'm just ... not feeling that well.'

'Really? What's wrong? You do look a bit off. I was just telling Dev in class.'

'It's nothing serious. My head hurts.' Even as she said it, Maahi realized it was true.

'Oh, no. Do you think you can still make it to the party with us?' Priyanshi asked. 'Shit, don't answer that. I'm so selfish for asking that the first thing after you tell me you don't feel well.'

'No, it's okay. But I don't think I'll be able to come today.'

'Yeah, you don't look so good. You should rest. Some other time though?' Priyanshi kept a steady hand on Maahi's arm. They had reached the front door of their hostel.

'Yes, of course,' Maahi said weakly, feeling bad about lying to her and cancelling at the last minute.

Priyanshi patted her shoulder before leaving. 'Feel better.'

'Have fun.'

Maahi walked slowly to her room, her emotions oscillating. She was still angry at Kishan, but she couldn't help but worry about his health at the same time. She left her books in her room and locked the door behind her. She pulled out her phone.

Maahi: Leaving from hostel now.

Kishan: Can't wait to see you!!

Maahi took her time walking to the bus station. The evening sun was kind to her, and she enjoyed the fresh air. She had grown quite fond of her college campus and planned to walk more. Kishan went to the gym every day, no matter how hectic his schedule got. Maahi envied his determination to stick to this healthy routine and maintain his lean physique. She saw her campus as an opportunity for a fun workout, but hadn't had a chance to take out time for a morning jog.

When she reached Kishan's apartment, she felt much calmer than she had all day. She texted him from downstairs, so he was waiting at the door when she got out of the elevator. Kishan was wearing a pair of burgundy shorts with a checked shirt open down to the fourth button. His eyes were swollen and his hair was a mess.

'What's with your hair?' Maahi asked.

Kishan kept one foot behind the doorframe to keep it unlocked and leaned forward towards her. Maahi rose on her toes to give him a small hug, but Kishan kept holding her. He released a long breath into her short hair and pulled her tighter into his chest. Maahi arched her neck back in order to breathe. She closed her eyes as he held her, and felt the rest of her anger dissipate.

'I'm sorry about last night,' Kishan said. 'I feel so shitty about that.'

'No,' Maahi said quickly, placing her palm against his beard. 'No, it's okay. How are you feeling now?'

Kishan released her and shrugged. 'Not so bad, not so good.'

'You aren't warm. Do you have a headache?' Maahi followed him into his apartment and closed the door behind them. It was a one bedroom with lemon-yellow walls that contrasted with the orange ones on opposite sides of the room. Kishan hated those walls with an intensity that Maahi found amusing. He had chosen the apartment for its location and overall convenience, and had intended to repaint the walls from the very beginning, but hadn't had a chance yet. Maahi sometimes thought that even though he complained, he secretly liked them.

'Yeah,' Kishan said, looking around the small living area that was bare of furniture except the two plastic chairs next to the open kitchen, and a giant bean bag opposite his flat screen TV. The bean bag was the most disgusting thing Maahi had ever seen—brown, furry and smelling like stale potatoes. She liked everything else in his apartment. She was envious of Kishan because he got to live by himself. She had always wanted to live alone, but had to share her room at the hostel with a roommate. 'This hangover is killing me. I called out from work, but they still gave me shit to do. Been working from home all day. Sucks.'

'Hangover?' Maahi asked mildly. She followed him to his bedroom, which was in its usual state of disarray. 'Did you drink last night?'

'Mm?' Kishan ruffled the comforter on his bed and laid it back flat over the sheets. 'Better.'

'I asked if you drank last night,' Maahi asked again, watching Kishan as he climbed on the bed and rested his head against the headboard.

'Oh, yeah. Didn't I tell you? Yeah. Come here, snuggle with me.' Kishan wiggled two fingers at her. It reminded Maahi of how her mother used to tickle her as a child. She would curl her index and middle fingers inwards, like a hook, and tickle her from a distance. Even though she didn't actually touch her, Maahi would feel ticklish and giggle uncontrollably. It was strange how that particular memory flashed into her head.

'You didn't tell me,' she said calmly and sat down on the bed, facing Kishan.

'Really? Weird. After you brought me lunch, word got around that it was our anniversary. My colleagues insisted we go out for a couple of drinks after work to celebrate. So we went to this happy hour place on M.G. Road. It was a little far but they also serve north Indian food, so we had these amazing starters and in-house brewed beer—'

'You must've passed right by my college, going from your office to M.G. Road.'

'Well, yeah, actually. And I thought of you. I even told my friends that this is where you go to study,' Kishan said, smiling broadly. He slipped down under the covers, flat on his back. He patted the bed. 'Get in now!'

Maahi removed her sneakers and lay down on her stomach, on top of the covers. She propped herself up on her elbows and looked at Kishan sideways. 'You could've asked me to come with you.' Her voice was low. She managed not to let her displeasure show.

'But you can't drink. You're not legal yet, and trust me, this place wouldn't have let you in.'

Maahi kept quiet. The age difference between them bothered her sometimes. She wished she were just a couple of years older. You can't choose who you fall in love with, but there are all these rules you are made to follow, rules that come in your way. For the whole first year that they had been going out, they had to restrain themselves. She could never let go, let it happen, even when it felt natural. When it felt *right*. She had been seventeen, he had been twenty-one. It was true love for them, but it was a felony in the eyes of the law.

'Do you feel bad?' Kishan asked.

Maahi nodded. 'Kind of. I mean, it was *our* anniversary after all. You celebrated it with your friends, without me. I just think it's not ... I don't know. I don't mean to sound ... I don't know.'

'No, I totally understand. Hell, I wanted to spend it with you too, of course. I never intended for it to get so out of hand.'

'You kept telling me you were on your way!'

'Because I kept trying to leave, but someone or something kept holding me back. By the time I was able to get out, I felt like shit. Had to call a cab and go straight home and pass out, you know?'

Kishan was watching her closely. It made Maahi conscious about the pimple on her left cheek. She curled her lips inwards. 'Yeah,' she said. But she *didn't* know. She had lived with her family her whole life, in a protected and conservative environment. What did she know about going out drinking with friends, passing out and waking up with a hangover? 'I don't know why you have to be such a responsible grown-up and leave me out of everything.'

'What? Are you serious right now?'

'I don't mean it like that. But I also want to do these things that I never got to do in Vaishali, with my parents always around. Now that we're here, so far away from home, I thought I could try and see ... And you're here, so I know I won't get into any trouble.' Maahi wasn't sure if she should've said anything. She didn't find the look on Kishan's face particularly encouraging.

'Well, we can do something here, at my place. Or we can go out somewhere where you can get in. I didn't know you felt that way.' Kishan's tone was clipped and Maahi felt like a spoiled child asking her parents for things they didn't approve of.

'I just want to spend time with you, do fun things. That's all I want.'

'We're spending time together now … and I can think of fun things for us to do, if I *really* stress my brain…' Kishan winked.

'Like what?' Maahi giggled.

'Like, you know?'

'Nope.'

'Do you want me to spell it out for you?' Kishan ran his fingers up her spine.

Maahi sank her head into the mattress and hid her face. She could feel her ears get warm. Kishan's hand came to a rest at the base of her neck. He caught hold of a handful of hair and pulled. Maahi's face came up, and she met his eyes. He held her gaze and moved in, resting his mouth against her open lips. He swiftly turned her over on her back and moved on top of her, their lips pressed together.

'Do you still need me to tell you?' Kishan whispered.

'I thought you weren't feeling well,' Maahi breathed.

'Well enough for this. You.'

Her face split in a shy smile. She looked away from him.

'For *you*, always,' Kishan said. He placed his fingers under her chin and turned her face towards him. 'Look at me.'

As Maahi looked into Kishan's eyes, she forgot all her agitation from before. She was in the moment, loved and adored by the only man she had ever loved. The only man who made her feel like she was more than what she was, that she was better. It made her want to be *more*, to be better, for him.

3

'Ma, don't say that!' Maahi exclaimed.

'It's true! He never listens to me. I don't know what to do about it. If he keeps being friends with those boys and riding those fast bikes ... God knows he's going to end up in a ditch somewhere one day. I'm telling you, he never listens to anything I say. He never takes me seriously,' her mom cried.

The Internet connection wasn't very strong at her end, and Maahi could make out only vague, hazy expressions. But she hardly needed clear image quality to know what her mom's face looked like at that moment. She had seen that face uncountable times. Her younger brother Sarthak had a penchant for being a pain in their mom's neck.

'You need to relax, Ma. He's almost a grown-up now. He can—' Maahi began, but her mom cut her off.

'Don't you enable him!'

Sarthak appeared on the screen, shoving his head in between the camera and their mother. 'Yo, sis. What's up?'

'Why are you talking like that?' Maahi rolled her eyes.

'Like wha'?'

'If you're trying to be cool, you're failing miserably. You sound retarded!'

'That's offensive to people who're, ya know, retarded fo' real.' Sarthak snickered.

'Sure. I apologize to all retarded people in the vicinity who heard me and are offended. And by that I mean *you*.' Maahi laughed.

'Why you gotta be mean, yo?'

'Stop. Talking. Like. That.'

'You're no fun.' Sarthak's face disappeared and Maahi could see her mother again.

'Hey, come back!' Maahi said.

'Why?' Sarthak asked. 'So that you can lecture me too?'

Their mother shook her head, staying quiet. Every time she was tired of being a parent to Sarthak, she would delegate responsibility to Maahi for a moment, and take a step back. Even though Maahi was only two years older than him, and Sarthak pretended to not care about whatever she said to him, she knew he valued her opinion and was somewhat reluctantly grateful for it too.

'I'm not going to lecture you. Just come here. I want to talk to you.'

'Then talk. I can hear you.'

'Stop being a child, Sarthak. What is this I'm hearing from Ma? About these new friends you're going on bike rides with? You know you have to be safe, right? There's nothing wrong with making new friends and riding motorcycles, as long as you use your judgement. You wear a helmet, don't you?' Maahi asked.

'See? Lecture.'

'*Sarthak.*'

'What?' Sarthak let out an exasperated groan and appeared on the screen a moment later. Maahi could see the right half of Ma's face and left half of Sarthak's. She was struck by how similar they looked. Growing up, everyone always told them that Maahi looked like their father and Sarthak looked like their mother, but she never really saw it. But spending these past few months away from them, not seeing them every day, she began to see what everyone had been talking about. They had the same roundish face, the same straight nose, the same brown eyes. Anyone who saw them could tell they were related.

'You know what you're doing, right?' Maahi asked quietly.

'Yes. Stop worrying about me,' Sarthak said seriously, and those three seconds of seriousness were enough to reassure her.

'Good. How's everything else? How are studies?'

'How do you think?' their mother interjected. 'He never—'

'*Ma!*' Maahi and Sarthak said together.

'Fine, I won't say anything. No one listens to me in this house. I don't know why I even try. I'm just wasting my breath. Everyone here does as they please—'

Sarthak clutched her by her shoulders and pulled her into a bear hug. Maahi saw her mother's slight frame disappear into her brother's long arms. She couldn't help but feel a bit jealous.

'I can't breathe!' their mother yelped and Sarthak released her, laughing. 'I don't think you realize how big you've grown. Do you know, Maahi, he's taller than Papa now?'

'Really?' Maahi asked.

'Yep. I'm 5'11" now.' Sarthak smirked.

'Just one inch taller than Papa. Big deal.'

'You just jelly beans 'cause you just a little nugget yourself.'

'Oh God, you're not going back to talking like that again, are you?' Maahi shook her head.

'Yes, tell him how ridiculous he sounds when he talks like that,' Ma said.

Just then, Maahi heard a clicking sound on her door, and realizing that her roommate, Gunjan, was back, she plugged in her earphones. She nodded at Gunjan and mouthed *hey*, before resuming her Skype call. They talked for a few more minutes in a low tone, and when Gunjan left the room to go to the bathroom, Maahi quickly hung up and pretended to be asleep, pulling the covers over her head.

Maahi wasn't friends with her roommate, mostly because neither of them tried to talk to each other. The room they shared was tiny, with dirty green walls and two metal beds pushed against opposite walls, divided by one long study table between them. Their hostel was multi-storeyed, with small rooms shared by two girls selected at random. Maahi and Gunjan had started off on the wrong foot when Maahi arrived on the first day of college with her parents to find Gunjan hanging out with three boys and two bottles of vodka. Her side of the walls were plastered with Metallica posters and the corners of the room littered with cigarette butts. Maahi's mother asked her to stay away from *that* girl.

In fact, her parents were so bothered that Maahi began looking for other accommodations in areas near college. She hadn't realized how tough it would be to find a half-decent place and gave up after the first few days. Some off-campus hostels didn't allow girls to wear sleeveless tops, some had banned mobile phones with cameras, some didn't let outside food to be brought in and a few even forbid girls to pillion ride a bike, let alone own one. Maahi saw a hostel room that she got particularly excited about, before she found out that they allowed visitors only once a day, and only in the hostel lobby. They even had CCTV cameras installed and there were no male visitors allowed after 7 p.m., including fathers of the students. In the end, Maahi decided to accept her current living situation. Sure, her college required a fax from her parents three days in advance if she wanted a night out, but it wasn't as if she didn't have a secret way to sneak out.

Gunjan had been away the last few days. Maahi needed to keep their interaction to the minimum, as instructed by her mother, but she wasn't sleepy yet. She texted Kishan from under the covers for a while, before he went to sleep. She then texted Rohit and caught up with him. She heard Gunjan move around the room, and maintained a low profile until the lights were off and she heard no sounds for a while.

Maahi got up, shuffled her feet in search of her slippers and put them on before leaving the room. She stood outside in the balcony in partial darkness. It was quiet, and the light breeze held just a tinge of coolness. Maahi rested her arms on the cold metal railing and leaned forward to look up. She couldn't see the moon from where she was standing, but she could see some stars hidden behind the smog. And that was enough.

※

In the morning, when Maahi woke up to the sound of Gunjan's alarm, she couldn't go back to sleep. Gunjan, however, had no trouble falling asleep again. Maahi fetched her clothes and toothbrush and made her way to the shared bathroom. She felt a little disoriented; she had only caught a few hours' sleep. Priyanshi was by the sink brushing her teeth when Maahi entered the bathroom.

'Hey! Morning,' Maahi said, forcing herself to sound cheerful. She still felt slightly guilty about ditching them the other day.

'Hi.' Priyanshi's voice was muffled.

'I think I'm going to hop into the shower first.'

Priyanshi nodded.

Maahi entered a stall and put on the latch. She hung her clothes on the door and turned on the showerhead, which sprayed cold water on her. She jumped back and struggled with adjusting the temperature for a minute before getting it just right. She made out Priyanshi's voice over the hum of the water, but couldn't hear what she was saying. She turned off the shower.

'Did you say something?' Maahi asked.

'Just asking if you feel better now,' Priyanshi repeated.

'Yes. Yes, I feel much better now.'

'Okay, great.'

'Thanks for asking,' Maahi said, as she heard Priyanshi walk away. She struggled with getting the temperature right again, and eventually gave up, leaving the water a little on the colder side. She figured it was at least better than getting burned.

When she got back to her room, Gunjan was up, and so was the volume of her laptop, which was playing American rock music from the 90s.

'Morning,' Maahi said shortly and went about gathering her stuff for the day's classes. She intended to be out as quickly as possible, but Gunjan was in a chatty mood.

'Heard you were sick?'

'Yes, a little.' Maahi spoke loudly, to be heard over the music.

'Were you really, though? You can tell me. I won't judge you for lying to stay away from that group of losers. Freaking nerds, all of them.' Gunjan rolled her eyes.

Maahi felt disgusted. 'No, I didn't lie. And I don't think they are losers at all.'

'Fine. Don't tell me. But everyone knows you weren't *really* sick.'

'What does that mean? And how do you even know any of this?'

'They saw you at the bus station after you told them you couldn't go out with them because you were sick. That's how they know. And even the nerds talk, and others hear, and then they talk—do you really need me to explain to you how word goes around? Gossip 101,' Gunjan said and proceeded to laugh at her own joke.

'Crap,' Maahi muttered under her breath. She thought about how Priyanshi had behaved in the bathroom and saw it in a completely different light, given the new context. She felt worse than before about lying. She needed to clear the air. She rushed down to the mess, hoping to find Priyanshi or Dev there. She could try to talk to them, casually maybe, bringing up how she had to go out that day when she was sick.

Priyanshi wasn't around, but Maahi saw Dev at the counter with a bottle of flavoured milk. She walked up to him, but when he turned to her, she lost her courage.

'Hey, Maahi. How are you?' Dev said, showing no signs of anything unusual.

'Good morning,' Maahi said. She picked up a plate and walked around the counter to fill it. Her hands were shaking and she ended up making a mess of serving herself breakfast. To buy some more time for herself in order to calm her nerves, she walked over to the juice bar, and took a minute contemplating which one to get. She finally settled on mango milkshake and got a bottle. When she turned around, she saw that Priyanshi and a couple of her friends had joined Dev at a table. Gunjan's words rang in her ears. *Losers. Nerds.* But when Maahi looked at them, that's not what she saw.

She saw sweet people who had been kind to her and offered to be her friends. Maahi had somehow messed that up without realizing how and when it happened. She felt another pang of guilt. Talking to Priyanshi or Dev was one thing, but she couldn't face all of them together. Losing the courage she had been able to build, she walked to a table five tables away from where they were sitting, and ate alone.

※

A few weeks passed and Maahi got used to being alone again. She tried to mend things with Priyanshi, and on the surface, it appeared to have worked, but sometimes when she passed them between classes and made eye contact, Maahi felt there was still a hesitation, a distrust. It made her wonder whether there was something else going on under the surface. It was a small enough issue to be forgiven and forgotten by then, but maybe not. Maybe she really had hurt their feelings.

Or maybe Gunjan had said something to add fuel to the fire. The thought crossed Maahi's mind a few times, but she discarded it, convincing herself to stop being paranoid. In any case, Maahi found a rhythm in being by herself. She didn't mind eating alone, walking to classes alone, sitting with whoever had an empty seat next to them, walking back to the hostel alone. Sometimes she did wish she could have people to study with in a group, but she quickly learned to get over it.

Kishan had been busy the past few weeks, so they didn't get to spend much time together. They still managed to meet once a week, mostly on Sundays. Maahi didn't particularly mind the drop in the frequency of their meetings. The pressure of her coursework was rising and she was grateful for any time she got to study and finish her assignments. That didn't mean she didn't miss Kishan.

Maahi was rapidly approaching the end of her first semester, and when she thought about it, she was amazed by how much she had changed. From the cheerful girl who was always surrounded by her loving family, close friends and a boyfriend she couldn't go a day without seeing, to a solitary creature. Maybe that's called growing up. She couldn't help but feel proud of herself.

She was meeting Kishan later that day to help him pack. The project keeping him busy at work ended that week, and he was taking a weekend trip to Puri with his colleagues before it got too cold to go to the beach. Kishan had asked Maahi to come, but she knew her parents would freak out and not let her go. She thought about going without telling them, but chickened out. She kept imagining her parents landing up at her college to surprise her when she was over a thousand kilometres away. She also didn't have enough money for the trip and couldn't ask her parents for it without giving them a reason. Kishan offered to buy her tickets but she didn't feel right doing that. Having been raised in a middle-class family, Maahi had seen her parents work hard for their money and what trickled down to her was the idea that she had to earn her keep. She wanted to go with him, but it just wasn't feasible.

When she reached his apartment, she was exhausted from her day at college. She had an assignment submission deadline that day which had kept her up the past couple of nights. It was a Friday evening, she was mostly done with her week's coursework, and was ready to relax a little.

'Hey there!' Kishan said, holding the door open for her.

'Hey,' Maahi said, kissing him on the cheek before walking in. 'What happened here?' She gestured around the living room, which was in a mess. Maahi couldn't fathom how someone with such few pieces of furniture could create a mess of this magnitude.

'I honestly have no idea. I am as unorganized and dirty as you are organized and clean.' Kishan shrugged, looking around the room.

'Good thing I like it dirty!' Maahi said, tongue-in-cheek. She couldn't believe she actually said it aloud, but it slipped out before she could put a leash on her tongue.

Kishan laughed. 'Don't even go there right now. I'm all over the place. If we get into that, we'll get nothing done.'

'What do we need to get done?'

'Are you kidding me? Packing! I don't know if I even have clean clothes; my maid hasn't been here in a week. I'm so sick of wearing shirts and trousers to work, I can't even remember the last time I put on a pair of jeans.'

'Last week, when I was here,' Maahi said. She went to his bedroom and swung open his cupboard door. 'Don't be so dramatic about it. You're coming back on Monday morning. We only need to pack for two days.'

Kishan stood by the bedroom door, his head leaning against the wall. 'I don't even know where to begin.'

'You're such a spoiled baby! Okay, why don't you start by picking out two pairs of shorts and three T-shirts? I'll make a checklist of the things you need to take.'

'What if it's cold?'

'We'll check the weather then. Keep your swimming shorts if you're going to go swimming.' Maahi laughed. 'You really are hopeless, aren't you?'

'I kind of am.' Kishan nodded, sticking out his bottom lip.

Maahi eventually asked him to sit down on the bed, which was opposite the cupboard, while she packed for him. He sat there saying yes or no to clothes that she picked out. They were both surprised when she was done in under half an hour.

'You have a talent. A real talent,' Kishan said, pointing at the suitcase Maahi was zipping up.

'This is hardly a talent.' Maahi shrugged, but inside, she felt warmed by his comment. She pushed the suitcase against the wall and joined Kishan on the bed. They both fell on their backs, legs on the floor. Maahi sighed loudly.

'Thank you, baby,' Kishan said. 'Now if you could be a good girl and clean the rest of my apartment…'

Maahi giggled, her eyes closed, her lips stretched in a smile. 'Right.'

'I wish you could come with me.'

'Me too.'

'I'm going to miss you,' Kishan said, his tone sincere.

Maahi opened her eyes and looked at him. He was looking at her. She touched his beard. 'Me too.'

4

Maahi drove in silence, while Kishan reclined in the passenger seat, looking lazily out of the window. She was picking him up from the airport in his car. She had accompanied him to the airport when he was flying to Puri, and had taken his car back to her hostel. It was 5 a.m. on a Monday, but Maahi was glad for the opportunity to talk to him in person before they both got caught up in their week.

'How would *you* feel?' Maahi asked.

'I wouldn't feel anything. Because there *is* nothing to feel,' Kishan said. Maahi could sense the anger underlying his clipped tone.

'You didn't tell me she was going to be there.'

'Because I didn't know she was going to be there in the first place. I've told you this. Don't be unreasonable, Maah—'

'*Don't*. Kishan, no. Don't even pretend that this is normal and I'm the crazy one here.' Maahi tightened her hold on the steering wheel. 'You had several chances to tell me. I didn't have to find out on Facebook that you've been vacationing with your ex-girlfriend at the beach. That's not how it should be, and don't try to tell me otherwise.'

'She isn't my ex-girlfriend because she was never my girlfriend in the first place.'

'Right—my bad. *Fling*. Isn't that what you like to call it?'

'Don't make a big deal out of nothing. You're taking this way too seriously,' Kishan said.

'I'm not! You're taking it way too lightly. I would've been okay if you had just told me she was there, that's all. The fact that you lied—'

'I didn't lie—'

'Stop it!' Maahi shifted in her seat. She really didn't want to fight with him that early in the morning. 'Fine, you didn't lie. But you didn't tell me either. Withholding the truth is quite close to lying in my eyes.'

'It wasn't important enough to be mentioned. We bumped into each other and decided to hang out—that's all. It's not as if she's my enemy and I have to cut her out of my life completely.'

'And I'm not asking you to do that either. You can have whatever kind of relationships you want with your ex-flings.'

'Oh, thank you. I didn't realize I needed your permission, but now that I have it…' Kishan gave her a thumbs up.

'Kishan, I don't know why you're being so unreasonable about this. I'm just trying to tell you that I didn't like that I had to see this on Facebook. And I feel betrayed.'

'What is there to feel betrayed—' Kishan stopped abruptly and sighed. He turned away from her and spoke, almost to himself, but loud enough for her to hear. '… Exactly what we were talking about.'

'Excuse me?' Maahi was driving just around the speed limit, and finding it difficult to stay under it. 'You were talking about *what* now?'

'This. Dia and I were talking about this.'

'What, *me*? Why were you talking about me with your ex-fling?'

'Because you don't get it. You refuse to grow up and act like an adult,' Kishan said.

Maahi was appalled. She looked at him, trying to read his face, but couldn't find any emotion. 'And you thought it would be a great idea to discuss my immaturity with someone who doesn't know me at all?' she asked evenly, her eyes on the road. 'What did she say?'

'Nothing. That there is a four-year age difference between us that can't be overlooked. She said it'll get easier with time. To be honest though … I don't see how.'

'What do you mean "easier"? Is it tough right now?'

'Are you seriously asking me that? I mean, look at us. What do we have in common? What can we talk about?' Kishan asked. He looked at her expectantly. Maahi's palm got sticky.

'I talk to you about everything! I tell you everything. Isn't that enough?'

'For you, I guess. I don't know. There are things that I want to share with you too, but sometimes … you just don't get it. I mean, I'm not saying it's your fault, because it isn't. There's nothing you can do about it. Sometimes I just wish I could talk to you about things freely, without having to walk on eggshells, trying not to hurt your feelings.' Kishan reclined his seat further and leaned back.

He wouldn't meet her eye, so Maahi looked back at the road. She couldn't believe that he had talked to some random person about their private relationship and was behaving as if that was completely normal. She didn't hold anything against that girl, Dia. But seeing their pictures, both looking high and delirious, she hadn't been able to shake the feeling of betrayal.

Kishan clearly didn't see it, and if she tried to show him, he would somehow turn it around on her to prove his point about her being childish. She felt suffocated in the car with him and was glad that her hostel wasn't much farther away.

'Say something,' Kishan said, still looking out of the window with his eyes half closed.

'Say what?'

'Anything. Tell me what you're thinking.'

Maahi shook her head. 'I don't know, to be honest. I … never knew that you were unhappy and you felt like you couldn't share certain things with me. I thought we were okay.'

'We were,' Kishan said. He paused and added, in a voice much lower, 'We were okay.'

He didn't say anything after that, and Maahi's heart sank deeper. *We were okay.* We aren't anymore. *We were.* She stayed quiet the rest of the way, contemplating their relationship, wondering how Kishan really saw it. Did he see her as a burden, a weight he had to carry around with him, always being careful around her, watching his step? The idea was very unsettling. But it was probably true; he had more or less said that.

She pulled over outside her hostel and turned the key. 'Do you think we should talk about this more?' she asked casually, stretching her hand to pick up her bag from the back seat. Her face was very close to Kishan's. He looked at her eyes, dropped his gaze to her mouth and then met her eyes again. He held her hand lightly and rubbed his thumb over the inside of her wrist. The car was filled with his musty scent and she was overwhelmed by his sheer presence. Maahi got hold of her backpack, pulled it to herself and turned away from him.

'Yes,' Kishan said mildly. 'I think we should.'

'Okay. When?'

'Tonight after work? Can you sneak out?'

Maahi nodded and got out of the car. She heard his door open and close behind her, and then another door open and close a moment later. She heard the car start and drive away, but she didn't turn around. She kept her chin in the air. As she walked, blinking her eyes rapidly, breathing through her mouth, her steps were measured, confident. At least they appeared to be.

She skipped all her classes and spent the rest of the day in her room, staring incessantly at the ceiling. Gunjan wasn't there during class hours, and that gave Maahi plenty of time to think. She was used to seeing people around her breaking up, finding someone new and breaking up again. But she knew what she had with Kishan was different. There's a difference between being in love and being in a relationship. They were in love. They were meant to always be together.

She scrolled up her text messages and read every single text they had sent each other over the past couple of years. Right from the first one to the very last one from that morning. It was an eye-opening experience. For the first time, she was seeing her relationship with Kishan without rose-tinted glasses. Maybe it hadn't been all that great, after all. Maybe she had just built it up, turned it into something that wasn't there.

Her heart revolted against the idea. No. No, that can't be it. They had been through some bad times, it had been hard on occasion, but she never for a second doubted that it wasn't true love or they weren't supposed to be together. There was no barrier strong enough to separate them from each other completely. She knew he felt it too.

She found a message he had sent her after a fight, about a year ago. She had saved a screenshot. Every time she felt frustrated with him, she turned to that message. Reading it assured her that he was hers, no matter what. That he loved her and needed her, and no matter what stupid things they did to mess it up, they would still be together because it was real, it was magical, it was love. She read it whenever she needed proof.

> I love you. You're really smart and you get me. Well, you don't get me. But you get me much more than anyone else does and it's only you whom I want to get me. I am just bullshitting but I am scared. I want you and I don't want anything to go wrong. Please bear with me through my stupidities and don't leave me too easily. I am tough to be with but I hope someday it will all be worth it. I am sorry I shouted at you. After I hung up, I knew you would be sad. But I knew it was manageable. It got me scared. What if I piss you off one day and it's not manageable? That scared me. I am sorry for all the mistakes I might commit. Please never leave me.

Maahi's eyes filled up with tears. She let them flow freely into her hair. She knew they would make it work. She sometimes struggled with understanding what was going on in Kishan's head. He could get very distant if he wanted to and there was nothing she could do to get in. It was one of those times, when his reasoning about something was completely perpendicular to how she looked at things. She couldn't imagine how talking to an ex about your current girlfriend and your relationship troubles could be justified as normal.

A little after seven, when she knew Kishan would be home, she called him to ask if she should come over. When she got no response, she continued lying on her bed. Gunjan came a little later, but Maahi didn't move at all; she didn't even look up. Gunjan went about her business quietly, not interrupting Maahi's strange mood.

Maahi called him every ten minutes, for hours. Every time he didn't pick up, it got a little more difficult for her to breathe. She eventually got up and paced back and forth in their tiny room, trying to release some of her frustration, constantly calling Kishan. A hundred different explanations passed through her mind; none of them provided any comfort. Did he change his mind? Did he not want to talk to her anymore? Was he at work? Did something happen to him?

The more agitated Maahi got, the more frantically she called him. She wanted to believe he was just careless—the simplest and most obvious explanation. It was midnight, and there was still no response from him. Maahi sank into her bed and tried to hook up her phone to the charger. It took her a few attempts; her fingers shook wildly.

'You okay?' Gunjan asked.

Maahi shook her head.

'You don't look so good.'

'I don't feel so good,' Maahi cried. She tried to frame her sentences in her head before speaking, but her words slipped unchecked, out of control. 'It's just that ... my boyfriend. I don't know where he is and I've been calling him for the past five hours and there is no response. We had plans to meet tonight and he just disappeared. I don't know what to think or do. I'm so worried something happened to him. I mean, who does that? Do you think he's seeing my calls but deliberately ignoring me? We did fight in the morning and I know he's mad at me but *who does that*? I must've called him a hundred times by now.'

'Whoa. You need to chill, dude,' Gunjan said. 'I'm going to get you some water.'

'Thanks,' Maahi said, accepting the small gesture of support from an unexpected source.

'Now, as you know, I don't know shit about your boyfriend. Or, umm, you. But let me ask you this—do you want to be with a person who makes you feel like this?'

'Maybe it's not his fault! Maybe he got into an accident. Or lost his phone. These things happen, you know? You can't just assume it's him,' Maahi said heatedly.

'Whatever you say,' Gunjan said and zipped up her lips with her fingers. She sat back on her bed with her laptop and eventually plugged in her headphones. Maahi watched her. No matter how much the idea revolted her, what Gunjan said refused to leave her head. Did she want to be in situations like this all the time? How many more of these could she take before her knees buckled? She felt alone. That was the emotion that overpowered all the others she was feeling at the moment.

Deserted.

He was there. He was always there, but somehow, never there at all. She felt as if she was the only one who cared about their relationship and killed herself trying to work on it, when he couldn't be less bothered. The more she thought about it, incidents popped into her head, and added to her anger. He kept telling her he wanted the relationship, even needed it, but he never really did anything to fix it, or even sustain it.

She needed to tell him that. Maahi needed to tell Kishan that she needed his help, that he needed to work on their relationship with her. If he wanted to be with her, he needed to step up. He needed to treat her the way she deserved, to be respected, not taken for granted—the way she treated him.

He couldn't get away with being careless and self-absorbed all the time—that was an excuse Maahi was tired of. She was tired of making excuses for him. He couldn't just go around doing things like discussing their private lives with his ex and expect her to be fine with it.

Kishan had done things like that before. Stupid things, for which he later apologized, accepting that he was 'such an asshole' and promising her that he would 'try to be better' for her. Requesting her to not leave him too easily.

Her anger simmered beneath the surface, and when he finally texted her—'Oh fuck. I fell asleep. Coming over now'—she came dangerously close to hating him. He didn't even realize what time it was. Coming to her hostel at 1.30 a.m., when her roommate was there too, after being MIA for six hours … Either he didn't realize how difficult and inconvenient it would be for her to sneak him in, or he didn't care, he just assumed that she would do it for him, the same way she had been doing everything for him, never once putting herself first.

Maahi felt betrayed, short changed, as if he was breaking an unspoken promise. Somewhere in the back of her heart, she always knew that he wouldn't do for her even half of the things she did for him, but she never let that thought grow. She reasoned that he was different from her. His ways of expressing love were different and she had to accept that as a part of him. It was when she thought about how little *he* accepted *her* personality that her anger rose.

It was as if he had set standards for her—standards she could never match. It was never enough, no matter how hard she tried. Over the course of their relationship, she felt like she'd lost all her self-respect. *His* opinion, *his* wishes, *his* decisions—

they all came before her. But that was going to change. Maahi was partially glad he was coming over. She had to tell him how she felt; she couldn't bear to keep it with herself any longer.

When he finally arrived, half an hour later, Maahi sneaked him in. He gestured towards Gunjan and raised an eyebrow at Maahi.

'What? She lives here.' Maahi was annoyed. Her anger had reached tipping point and she struggled to keep it in check.

'Umm, guys?' Gunjan said.

'Do you mind—' Kishan began but Maahi cut him off.

'We can't ask her to give us privacy in the middle of the night. She lives here. Where do you expect her to go?' Maahi asked. 'It's not her fault you chose to be so careless.'

Kishan stared at her for a moment, then muttered, 'Fine.' He sat down at the edge of her bed. Maahi remained standing in front of him. Gunjan's eyes were glued to her laptop screen and her earphones were plugged in, but Maahi wasn't sure she wasn't listening.

'So, talk,' Maahi said.

Kishan didn't respond. He simply looked at his hands clasped together as he sat with his elbows resting on his thighs.

'Okay then, don't talk. I'll talk.' Maahi gulped, her throat dry. 'I am the closest person to you, but you can't talk to me about anything, even about us. You find it easier to talk to some random third person about it. What's that about?'

He sat there like a statue.

'I tell you everything. I share everything with you, but you say you feel like you can't tell me anything? Why is that? What are you so afraid of? I have been working on this relationship from day one. Even when you have treated me like a child, I have always been the grown-up in this relationship and I'm sick of it. I'm tired of working on it, I can't do it alone anymore. You have to take some responsibility.' Maahi paused to take a breath, and continued, 'You know what I think? I'm sorry for saying this and I'm sorry if it hurts your feelings, but it's truly how I feel. I think you are a coddled child who was never held accountable for anything in his life and that's why you can afford to be careless—because you've had everything easy, served to you on a silver platter. You've never had to work for anything, fight for anything. Well, I have been fighting for this, *us*, for two years now. And I can't do this alone anymore, Kishan. I just can't. I need your help. Do you want this relationship or not?'

Tears escaped Maahi's eyes, and she wiped them away angrily. As she gasped for air, she could feel Gunjan's gaze on her back. She felt her chest burning, and her face and her whole body. She didn't take her eyes off of Kishan, who didn't take his off his hands. He didn't even move. He sat there, not responding to what she said in any way, through words or action. And as Maahi studied him, it dawned upon her.

'Answer me.' An unknown force was pulling her down, not just her legs, but her whole body. She found it difficult to stand. She knelt down in front of him, looking up at his face. 'Kishan, say something.'

He continued hiding from her gaze.

'Do you want this relationship or not?' Maahi repeated, her voice barely held together, every word disjointed from the other. Her hands came together at her temples, rubbing them, trying to make sense of the situation.

Kishan looked at her. He met her eyes, his own glazed and hollow.

'Do you want this relationship, Kishan?' Maahi asked again. She couldn't look away from his eyes, those empty black shells, devoid of all emotion. Dead. She erupted. 'Fucking say something dammit!'

Kishan's nose curled up as he took big breaths.

It was the only sign of life in him that Maahi could see. Her body suddenly turned cold. She sat on her knees in front of him, their faces inches from each other. She had never felt further away from him. Her eyes pleaded his, her voice low when she spoke next. 'Just speak. Anything ... anything that would keep us together. Just say you love me...'

Maahi saw his eyes fill up. His lips remained pursed.

'ANYTHING!'

Later, after Kishan left without saying a word to her and Maahi found herself on the floor, with her face hidden inside a pillow to muffle her cries, their whole relationship flashed before her, piece by piece, digging harder on her wounds. She didn't notice Gunjan's hand on her back, her voice telling her how proud she was of her for speaking her heart out without fear. All Maahi could see was Kishan's hunched frame, sitting at the edge of her bed, his dead eyes looking at her. All Maahi could hear was silence.

Part Two

5

The smell of incense woke Maahi up. She sneezed once, and then again, before she got up and closed the door of her room. She hated when the maid forgot to close the door after cleaning her room in the morning. How hard was it to remember? Open the door, clean the room, close the door—that's all there was to it. What a great start to the day.

Maahi checked the time on her phone. 10.43 a.m. She was surprised her mother hadn't woken her up. Usually by this time, she would've stuck her head through her door a few times and yelled at her to get up. Maybe she had left for work without waking her up, which was something Maahi felt grateful for. She didn't get a lot of sleep the previous night, having stayed up late on her phone, scrolling through Kishan's Facebook profile—at least that's where she'd started. Hours later she'd found herself staring at Kishan's friend's sister's girlfriend's page, with no idea as to how she landed there.

She needed to stop stalking Kishan. It put her in a very bad mood. She had been like that ever since she returned home three months ago, right after her breakup. She couldn't bear to live in that city without him; he was the reason she had moved to Bangalore in the first place. She had called her mom and told her she wanted to come back immediately. Her dad had booked her on the next train, and she had boarded it with all her stuff.

When she arrived at Vaishali, her family was surprised to see that she had not come back to visit, she had *come back*.

They, especially her mom, had asked why on several occasions, but she couldn't tell them about her break-up. They didn't know she had a boyfriend to begin with, and now that he wasn't in her life anymore, what was the point in digging up the skeletons? Maahi did sometimes feel the need to share with her mom. In her darkest moments, she wondered how easy it would be to open up to her and ask for advice. But knowing her family the way she did, she suspected that more than anything else, she would get lectured about having had a boyfriend at all, because how dare she let her natural instincts as a young woman take charge of her and fall in love? Care about someone, feel emotional connection and physical attraction towards a man? That was simply unacceptable.

Maahi faced the lowest of lows of her life after her break-up with Kishan, and it changed her. The experience completely transformed the way she looked at love and life. The rose-tinted glasses were finally off. She could see her relationship with him for what it had been: her desperate attempt to keep holding together something that had no business existing in the first place. Maybe Kishan never wanted it. Maybe she never gave him a chance for an out, and when she did...

She looked at herself differently too. Kishan was right, she had been just a child. Maahi had taken to observing herself in the mirror every now and then. Nineteen, with nothing valuable to offer another person to make them want to stay with her. She looked through the recent pictures on his Facebook, with his female friends and colleagues, and tried to teach herself how to dress, how to do her makeup and hair. No one was interested in her boring jeans and sneakers. And there was much more to makeup than lip balm and kohl. Much more to hair than brushing it every morning and tying it back in a tiny ponytail. She learned all of this from the women on Kishan's Facebook, including Payal. She had no concrete evidence that there was anything going on between them, but she *knew*.

When she looked in the mirror, she was disgusted by what she saw. No wonder he didn't want her.

Maahi shook herself out of it before she sank deeper. It was too early in the morning for that. She had been good recently—reaching that level of depression only deep into the night. On most days, she could pretend nothing was wrong and survive without crying even once. She saw that as definite progress, compared to the first few weeks, when she faced existential crises every time she had a free moment. She was fine when she was watching a movie, but between the minutes of it ending and her deciding what to do with her time next, she had panic attacks. Her daily projects were to keep herself occupied every minute of every hour. She watched a lot of TV shows on her laptop. She tried reading too, but that didn't work out. She found that it was easier to watch movies than read books when your eyes had a tendency to well up every few minutes.

The house was absolutely quiet, which led Maahi to assume that Sarthak was at school, her parents at work, and the maid had already finished her work and left. She put her phone aside and got up. She didn't have a headache, which was a welcome change.

Maahi got into the shower, taking her time shampooing her hair. The warm water felt good against her scalp. After she was done, she wrapped her hair in a big fuzzy towel and mounted it on her head like a small hill. She put on a sweater over her T-shirt before going to look for food in the kitchen.

'Good morning,' her mom said, looking pointedly at the clock on the wall. Maahi followed her gaze; it was almost noon.

'Oh. I didn't know you were here.' Both her parents were sitting at the dining table. Her dad was reading the newspaper, an empty plate in front of him. Even Sarthak was home; she could see him through the cracked open door, in his room with his giant headphones on, playing a video game on his computer.

'Yes, it's a Sunday. Where else would we be?' Ma said.

'Are you done with this?' Maahi asked, pointing to her father's plate. She picked it up and placed it in the sink.

Maahi sensed the tension in the air. She wondered if they had been talking about her again. She had heard them do that a few times before, expressing concern over what she was doing with her life, what the neighbours were asking and how she had lost all focus and was overall useless. She wasn't ready for another one of those conversations with them, but there was nothing she could do about it. She sat down at the table opposite her mom, with her father on her right, in the head chair.

She served herself an aloo parantha and was filling up her bowl with raita when her mother spoke.

'What's going on, Maahi?'

'What do you mean?' Maahi asked evenly.

'Papa and I are worried about you. You're not showing interest in studies or anything. What do you want to do? Have you thought about going back? You are still enrolled.'

'No, I can't go back!'

'But why? It is such a good college. You have a great career ahead of you, a future. How can you give that up?' Ma asked.

'We have talked about this, Ma. I can't go back now—they're starting finals in two days. I won't pass any of the exams.' Maahi looked from her mom to her dad, who was still reading the newspaper. 'Papa, I told you I don't want to do engineering.'

'Then what do you want to do? You're just wasting time right now—dropping out of college, staying at home, doing nothing.' Her mother was easily agitated and tended to be extremely outright in the way she spoke, and Maahi had never been bothered by that before she came back from Bangalore. It could've been because she never really gave her mom a chance to complain about her the way she complained about Sarthak all the time. She had been a good kid, scoring good grades, getting into a good engineering college, on her way to secure a bright future for herself, until she gave all that up and came back home.

And now she had to decide what she wanted to do with her life. And it terrified her. What terrified her even more than knowing she didn't want to be an engineer, was not knowing what she wanted to be instead. She had to first figure that out and then convince her parents. 'I'm not sure yet.'

'What do you mean?' Ma started.

Papa interjected, 'Let her be. She still has time to decide. She doesn't want to go back to Christ, so this academic year is lost anyway. That gives her plenty of time to make up her mind about what she wants to study.'

'What does she know? Who doesn't want to do engineering? Why would she let such a great career go? I don't understand—'

'To be fair though, Christ isn't all *that* great,' Sarthak said, coming out of his room, his neon-green headphones resting on his shoulders, the wire coiled around his neck. 'And literally every second person on the street is an engineer, so it's not that great a career anymore, Ma.'

'Don't interrupt when elders are talking,' Ma snapped.

Sarthak snickered. 'You're on your own, Sis.'

If only Maahi could tell him how right he was.

Ma didn't pursue the subject any longer. Maahi kept stealing glances at her and Papa and felt something tighten in her throat when she saw how disappointed and worried they looked. Papa was better at hiding it, but she could tell. She had disappointed Kishan, failing to match his expectations over and over again until he was so disappointed he couldn't be with her anymore. And she had disappointed her parents by coming back from Bangalore with nothing to show for her time there.

She thought about the months she had spent there, trying so hard to feel at home, and failing. She hadn't even made any friends. Such a waste of time. She always sensed that she wasn't supposed to be there. But maybe it had nothing to do with the city, maybe she didn't feel at home there because she wasn't at home with Kishan. She wasn't supposed to be with him. The thought made her feel better and worse at the same time.

Since it was a Sunday, which she hadn't realized until her mom told her, Maahi decided to call Rohit to see if he wanted to hang out. Rohit said he was free to come over and he didn't have to ask her where she wanted to meet. They always met at her home now, because she never went out.

'I can't stay long. I have a date later,' Rohit said when Maahi opened the door for him. Maahi thought of Rohit as her hottest friend. He was 6'4" tall and lean. That, along with his hooded hazel-coloured eyes and thick, unruly hair, fetched him quite a lot of modelling offers. He didn't take them seriously in the beginning, but once he started walking ramps and getting attention from women, it got hard for him to turn back. He was studying architecture in college and was very focused on his studies, but he modelled on the side; it was easy money.

Maahi remembered having a small crush on him back in school when he'd just joined in tenth grade. But he was the cool sporty boy and she was the quiet, chubby nerd—she knew that would've gone nowhere. Prospective relationship angle out of the way, she had been much more comfortable talking to him, helping him out with notes when he missed classes to play cricket tournaments. She was surprised to find them becoming good friends.

'Oh, that girl you were seeing? What's her name, Ruchita?' Maahi asked as they walked to her room. She sat down on the bed and Rohit rotated her study chair around and sat down facing her. He had the whole man-bun thing going—all of his hair pulled back low on his neck, tied in an untidy mess. He was also wearing horn-rimmed glasses to complete his sexy nerd look, when he was the exact opposite of a nerd.

'Close. Ruchika. I really like her, but I kind of get the feeling that she's not that into me.' Rohit shrugged. 'I wouldn't blame her; she's the smartest girl in my college. Why would she go out with *me*?'

'Come on! Don't underestimate yourself. Like, have you looked at yourself in the mirror recently?'

'No, seriously. You don't get it. She is amazing.'

'Why do you feel like she's not into you?' Maahi asked. She had never questioned Kishan's love for her after the first time he professed it. From then onwards, she had simply assumed that it was forever—never considering a scenario where their feelings might change. But his feelings did change. Maybe her feelings changed too, but she refused to see it and continued lying to herself.

'She said she's really caught up in her studies right now and doesn't have time to hang out that much and maybe she's being honest, but I don't know. We'll find out soon enough, I guess.' Rohit shrugged again.

'Why don't you ask her?' Maahi suggested.

'What am I supposed to ask her? No, man, I can't. What if she says she doesn't want to see me anymore? That is a possibility. No. I prefer being with her for however long she agrees to. I'm not doing anything to prompt a sudden death scenario.'

'If that makes sense to you, great. What do I know about relationships anyway?'

'You know enough. Don't you dare let that asshole make you doubt yourself. You know what, I don't even want to talk about him. No. We're not doing this,' Rohit declared. 'New topic.'

'I don't have anything new. Just, been here, doing nothing.' Maahi gestured around her room. 'Ma's getting really agitated now. I need to figure out what I want to do soon.'

'Do you have any ideas?'

'Not really. I think I'd enjoy studying art. English literature, maybe? But I'm not sure yet. Plus, Ma's going to freak out. Anything non-technical is a hard sell for her.'

Rohit laughed. 'Your mom's hilarious. Last time I was here, she asked me to convince you to go back to Christ. But she'll come around. If you find something you really want to do, I'm sure she'll back you up.'

'But I don't. And in any case, I do have to spend the next seven to eight months here at home, with nothing to do. I can't believe I wasted a whole year.'

'Consider it a long vacation. Watch movies, read books. You'll miss all this free time when you're neck-deep in your course and workload next year.'

Maahi let out an elaborate, frustrated sigh. 'This is the furthest thing from a vacation. I have all this time and with nothing to occupy me, I'm literally driving myself crazy.'

'I didn't realize it's that bad. I mean, if you need something to do, why don't you look for like, a part-time job or an internship? It's only going to help your résumé.'

'A job right after school? Who's going to hire a twelfth pass girl? I have no experience in anything and I'm pretty sure I'm talentless too.'

'No, you're not. Now who's underestimating themselves?' Rohit pulled out his phone and scanned it. 'In fact, I think one of my friends could have something for you. Let me see…'

'What do you mean?' Maahi asked. 'And how many friends do you have?' She was always surprised when Rohit casually mentioned new people in conversation. They could be talking about anything under the sun, and out of the blue, he would bring in a friend she had never heard of before. In the past year that he had started modelling, his social life had blown up multiple times.

'I walked with this guy, Prasoon, in a show once. He is starting his own company with a friend—they're developing apps that predict certain things … I'm not exactly sure. I think Prasoon sent me the details,' Rohit said. He looked into his phone for another second before giving up and putting it away. 'I'll find it later and forward it to you. Anyway, so they're either launching soon, or have already launched. I'm sure they could use some help. They asked me, but I'm already struggling with finding time to do the modelling thing on top of college, so I couldn't do it. Maybe they have something for you if you're interested?'

6

'Hello! Fourth Eye Apps, this is Maahi,' she sang into the phone. Her voice was cheerful, her face deadpan. She was glad they couldn't see her. Her pretension had its limits. 'How may I help you today?'

'I had a question about one of your apps,' a man's voice said. 'The one that predicts shit?'

'You must be talking about The Poop App.'

'Yeah, that one.'

'What's the question, sir?' Maahi asked, dreading the response.

'I wanted to ask if it actually does predict shit. Because it told me I was going to shit this morning, but I didn't. Yesterday neither. Not for the past three days, actually. And now it says I'm not going to shit in the next seven days, which is a concern. But I'm not sure if it's actually a concern because this shit app is shit and doesn't know shit, and if I go by the shit track record of the past three days I didn't actually shit, does that mean I shouldn't believe this shit when it says I'm not going to shit this whole week?' The voice grew louder towards the end of the monologue.

'Sir, the app works on a unique algorithm that takes your information—'

'That's bullshit! Your shit app doesn't *work* at all.'

'What I'm trying to explain to you, sir, is that the algorithm predicts the next bowel movement on the basis of the information you enter. The results may vary—' Maahi spoke in a calm, robotic tone that she had no trouble maintaining, but was cut off again before she could finish.

'I am sick and tired of this bullshit shit app. For three days it has been misleading me. I ate a whole plate of chicken chowmein last night, with a plate of chilli. If that doesn't make me shit, what will!'

'Sir, I don't think I'm qualified to answer that question. I would recommend seeing a doctor at this point, instead of worrying about the app—'

'You don't tell me what to do! Don't you dare tell me what to do! Let me talk to your manager!' The man was screaming at this point, but Maahi was hardly bothered. She actually preferred the call going to Prasoon; she wouldn't have to deal with it.

'Sure, sir. Let me forward your call to the manager. If you could please hold while I connect you—'

'NO!' the man yelled. 'Don't put me on fucking hold. I know what you're trying to do. You will put me on hold and then make me wait for a long fucking time and then hang up on me. When I call back, someone else will pick up the phone and then I will have to start over and explain the situation all over again.'

There was literally one customer service number you could call Fourth Eye Apps on, and literally one person who answered all the calls made to that number. Maahi sighed at her life. 'What would you prefer then, sir?'

'I want someone to fucking tell me when I'm going to shit next. Have you ever been constipated for four days in a row? And then have an app tell you you're not going to shit for seven more? Fucking bullshit this shit—'

'Sir, I would request you to not use that language with me,' Maahi said mildly, but with authority.

'Didn't I fucking tell you already to not tell me what to fucking do?'

'I am going to hang up now, sir. Have a good day.'

'Don't you—'

Maahi had already disconnected the call. She leaned back in her chair and stretched her neck. The plush leather chair was her favourite thing at Fourth Eye Apps. That and the fact that she could stay away from home where her family was driving her nuts about making a decision about her future. The pressure had risen. The past six months had gone by really slowly, and Maahi had struggled through each day.

She heard stories about how people took up jobs they thought they would be interested in, and soon find out they weren't really. Eventually, the dislike turned into hatred and took over their lives and made it a living nightmare. That didn't happen to her. She hated this job from the first day, and the feeling didn't intensify over time—she hated it the same amount.

Maahi had started this job knowing it had an expiration period. She needed to be here only until she joined college. What she hadn't realized was that after six months, she would be nowhere close to deciding what she wanted to study. She expressed her interest in English literature, but her mother revolted against it aggressively. She couldn't believe her daughter had lost all ambition and was considering such a non-technical, unprofessional stream. She asked Maahi what she wanted to do after she graduated with a bachelor's in English and Maahi said the first thing that came to her mind—teach.

Maahi was lectured every day for six consecutive days about how the profession she chose needed to align with her personality. Her mom told her that a girl who was too shy to talk in front of a few new people would have no success in a career that required public speaking. Maahi didn't resist the logic.

She was comfortable amongst her friends and family, but she had always been that girl in the back who was too shy to talk to new people. In her time working at Fourth Eye Apps, she had learned to talk to strangers, over the phone, one person at a time. Teaching a class was an entirely different world. Ma had a point, but Maahi would've appreciated her having a little faith in her daughter, however undeserved it was.

Maahi was thankful her mother had at least made peace with the idea that she wasn't going to be an engineer. She made Maahi fill out several admission forms for colleges in Delhi University, from programmes ranging from computer science and physics to business economics and political science. Her hope was for Maahi to figure out what she wanted by the time the results came in and she had options to choose from.

When they did, Maahi was glad to find she wasn't offered any colleges in physics. And she somehow convinced her mother to not force her to do computer science again. She had a few options in business economics and political science, and she had to make a final decision. Maahi considered having turned her mother from BSc to BA a feat in itself. But she wished she had done that a little earlier when the option of studying English literature was still available.

'Hard call?' Prasoon appeared in front of her desk and asked.

'I guess.' Maahi shrugged. 'I had to disconnect.'

'Language?'

'Yep.'

'Ugh, good then. Don't engage the a-holes.' Prasoon looked around her desk. There was one spreadsheet open on her computer with a list of things she could say to the customers, and a calendar with all meetings and appointments listed. Apart from the computer and the telephone, there was nothing to see. 'How is everything else going? Good?'

'Yeah, all good,' Maahi said.

'Great. I'm going to head out now; I'm done for the day. Give me a call if you need me, okay?'

'Sure, thanks.'

'Cool.'

Prasoon left, and Maahi watched him walk away, wondering about his life and what it would feel like to be in his shoes. Graduating from engineering college, starting his own company—if you could call two app developers and one office manager, who Maahi was, a company. They were making apps that predicted ... things. Weird things. Most of these apps were quite unconventional. Apart from The Poop App that was supposed to predict people's bowel movements, there was The Sex App, which would essentially tell people the next time they were going to get laid. The secret algorithm worked on a simple permutation and combination technique, first asking the user to input their existing data, and then projecting it on to the future, 'predicting' it.

Another popular one was The Breakup App. It would ask the user to enter their entire history of love interests and tell them how long their existing relationship was going to last.

Maahi once overheard Prasoon telling his partner to change the app to predict longer or lifetime relationships. Based on the past, the app tended to end relationships more realistically. Apparently, people didn't want to hear the truth.

Then there was The Death App, which, as the name suggested, predicted the user's death, based on their family history. The names of these apps were truly uninspired and obvious, as was the algorithm and predictions. Maahi didn't understand why anyone would make this their career and concentrate all their energy on it. She wondered how Prasoon's parents must have reacted to his decision to not take a campus job but start up a wacky app-developing business. And somehow, some of these apps worked, and even though all of them were available for free to download on iOS, they still seemed to be making money. Maahi always got paid on time. It wasn't an amount to speak of, but she did earn every paisa of it, taking all the strange calls she got.

She only used The Period App. That one was quite obvious and uninspired too, but she thought it was handy. She was bad at remembering dates—except when it came to Kishan's birthday, their anniversary and every other time he had done anything sweet for her—and at the very least, the app saved her period-math, so it wasn't such a bad thing to have. Also, Prasoon had asked her to test it since she was the only woman in their 'office' and laughed, but it did get weird real quick and he changed the topic.

There was another one she thought was funny—The Hunger App. Prasoon had asked her to test it, as a way of changing the topic from The Period App. This one, Maahi thought, was especially inaccurate. It kept telling her she was supposed to be feeling hungry when she wasn't. She would leave home after having breakfast, and the app would tell her she would be hungry again at lunchtime, then again in the evening around the time she left work, and then again at night when she got home. Sometimes, it also predicted that she should be hungry in the middle of the night when she found herself unable to fall asleep.

Maahi thought it was hilarious. Normally, if she ate in the morning before leaving for work, she was good until she got back. Sometimes, she would go to a coffee shop near the office during lunchtime to get a cookie, just so she had something to do. Also, because she really liked the place. Just thinking about it made her want a cookie. She checked the time—it was 4.14 p.m. She got off work at 5.00 p.m., but since she hadn't taken her lunch break that day, she texted Prasoon to ask him if it would be okay if she left early.

Maahi picked up her pen and notepad from the table and shoved them back into the drawer. She put her water bottle back in her handbag and was ready to go. She sighed at her life again. She got out of breath climbing down the four flights of stairs and was glad she took her break at the end of the day and wouldn't have to climb back up. She dreaded the stairs and all kinds of physical work. Life was easy but boring at her nine-to-five desk job, answering calls, talking to weirdos, arranging meetings for two people and maintaining their not-so-packed calendars.

By the time Maahi reached Cozy Coffee, she was in a much better mood. She even began to think of the shitty call as humorous. She walked in through the door with handles shaped like coffee mugs and looked up at the menu displayed above the counter. She didn't need to; she already knew what she wanted.

'Can I have a chocolate chip cookie, please?' she asked Naseer at the counter. He was short and fair and the kind of skinny that didn't look healthy. He had the face of a child and his lips were pinker than Maahi's.

'Sure. That would be twen—'

'Ask her to get the one with almonds,' a voice said. A second later, Maahi saw a messy bun tied on top of a head emerge from under the counter, followed by a heart-shaped face with a small, sharp nose and a pointed chin. Maahi was struck by how big her eyes were, how bright they shone under perfectly arched eyebrows, and how upbeat her attitude was. 'Get the almond one. It's the *cookie of the day*. I baked it myself.'

Maahi's eyes dropped to the girl's nametag. Laila. Maahi had never met person with that name. She had never seen her around, but then, she had never been to Cozy Coffee in the evening. She didn't know how to respond. 'I, umm…'

'Go for it, girl. You've got to trust me on this.' Laila winked.

'You can't force customers to get what they don't want to—' Naseer interjected, but was cut off by Laila.

'Don't. I'm just recommending the *cookie of the day*. Like *you* were supposed to.'

'I wasn't. CJ said there's no such thing as *cookie of th*—'

'Ugh, whatever.' Laila rolled her eyes and her petite frame disappeared under the counter again. She seemed to be just a couple of inches taller than Maahi, but much skinnier. Maahi heard her shuffling under there, but couldn't see what she was doing.

Naseer turned to Maahi. 'I'm sorry about her. That will be twenty-one rupees.'

'Actually…' Maahi hesitated, and then continued, 'Could I have the one with almonds? The one she recommended?'

'Oh, no, no. You don't have to. Don't let her bully you into getting something you don't want.'

'No, it's not that. I always get the same one. Why not try the *cookie of the day*, right?' Maahi chuckled nervously. This was the longest interaction she had had with Naseer in all the months she had been going to the coffee shop.

'There is no such thing as *cookie of the day*. She made it up,' Naseer said, pointing accusingly at Laila, whose bun—with curly hair spilling out unchecked—was all Maahi could see.

'I'll still get it.' Maahi laughed nervously. She just wanted to get her cookie and leave. There were three people waiting in line behind her.

'Seriously? Because you really don't have to,' Naseer said and Maahi felt as if he was bullying her into not getting the one with almonds.

'Seriously.'

Maahi heard a 'Ha!' from under the counter and smiled to herself. Laila appeared a moment later. She heated up her cookie for a few seconds and served it on a plate. Maahi wanted it in a paper bag, to go, but didn't want to ask. So she thanked Laila, picked up her warm cookie and sat down at a tiny round table by the window.

She felt strange sitting alone to eat. It reminded her of her time in Bangalore, when she used to eat by herself every day. Surrounded by people, but alone. Remembering that time also reminded her of Kishan. She wished the couple sitting on her right would stop holding hands under their table.

She was surprised at how delicious the cookie was. She turned towards the counter and saw Laila watching her. Catching her eye, Laila raised one of her perfect eyebrows. Maahi smiled and nodded. Laila took a small bow.

Maahi blushed and turned back to her cookie. That was all she had going for her in life. She chuckled at the thought. When did it get so complicated?

She didn't want to acknowledge it, but these rude calls bothered her. She had learned to easily tune out and not let them affect her mood, but it wasn't exactly something she wanted to be doing with her day. She was better than that. She was slightly relieved that she still thought that she was better than something. That she wasn't desperate enough to settle yet.

Maahi got up and started walking to the Metro station. The commute from her workplace in Gurgaon to her home in Vaishali took over an hour by train. She had expected to hate it, but it didn't bother her at all. She found herself squished in the ladies' compartment every morning and evening, and somehow it made her feel like she wasn't alone. Admittedly, she knew nothing about these women and their lives, but taking the train ride with them made her feel like she wasn't the only one struggling.

7

A few weeks later, Maahi woke up with a final decision. At breakfast, she told her mom that she wanted to study political science. Her mom said no, it didn't offer great career opportunities. Maahi asked her about her only other option—business economics, which her mom seemed fine with, so they made the deal. At that point, after having stressed over it for months, Maahi was just glad it was done and over with.

It also meant that now that her college was starting in a couple of months, she would have to quit her job at Fourth Eye Apps—a prospect she was looking forward to. She would miss the fifteen grand a month she made there. It wasn't much, but it was the first time she was earning and she didn't have many expenses anyway. She would hate going back to taking pocket money from her parents.

She got off the Metro at M.G. Road and walked towards the office. Even though she hadn't been particularly fond of working at the place, Maahi found herself trying to absorb everything on her way there. The routine she had followed for the past half year was coming to an end. She realized that no matter how bad her job was, she did learn a lot. She had earned experience when people called to know when they were going to have sex next, but it was experience regardless. Maybe someday she would look back at her time at Fourth Eye Apps—her wacky first job—and laugh. She told herself she was being too dramatic about it, that there was nothing to get sentimental about, but allowed herself the drama nevertheless. Just deciding her college and major was a big load off her shoulders, and she found it much easier to walk without it.

She passed by Cozy Coffee and made a mental note to get a cookie on her way back home. She greeted Prasoon as she walked in and took her seat at the plush revolving chair. The office was basically a big L-shaped storage box—with a high ceiling and a metal garage door at the front. They had two desks close together in one corner, separated from the other end by a plywood partition, and there was a desk at the front for Maahi. She sat down and pulled out her notepad and pen from her bag.

She had some more time left there, but she thought it would probably be good to let Prasoon know she would be leaving them soon. A warning is always good when you're going to leave someone. She thought about how Kishan had never talked about breaking up, or even being unhappy with her, and suddenly, one day when she asked him if he wanted the relationship ... he hadn't spoken. He still hadn't spoken.

In almost a year since they broke up, Maahi hadn't heard from Kishan. She visited his Facebook page on occasion. Some of his pictures were with Payal, but it didn't bother her anymore. She thought she was finally getting somewhere with her plan to forget about him. Her initial goal had been to forgive and forget, but that was harder to achieve since he never asked her for forgiveness.

Maahi answered calls all morning, not hating it as much as usual. She attributed it to the load she got off her shoulders that morning. Everything was lighter, easier without that. She was even hungry at lunchtime, which had never once happened in her time working there. The Hunger App was right this one time—Maahi found her stomach cramping with hunger.

She walked to Cozy Coffee, reading their menu in her mind. There was a 'help wanted' sign on the door she pushed open. She had decided on a coffee with a butter croissant. Laila was at the register.

Maahi had to stand in line to let two people in front of her order first. When it was her turn, she told Laila what she wanted. Laila didn't ask her to get something else this time. While she served her coffee, the silence felt a little weird and Maahi tried to think of something to say to her. 'Naseer not here today?' Maahi asked.

'Nah, he's gone,' Laila said, pointing at the 'help wanted' sign next to the cash register.

'Oh, yeah. I saw that outside too.'

'Yeah, we need someone to take over, like, today. I can't keep doing this shit by myself. I can handle it in the interim, but they need to bring someone soon.'

Maahi nodded and looked back at the sign. 'How long has this been up?' she asked.

'A week? Eight days—feels like forever. Don't tell anyone, but CJ, our manager, is an asshole. He's an ideal customer service guy on the outside, but when it comes to his own employees, ugh,' Laila ranted on.

'Who would I tell?'

'What?'

'Nothing. I was just…' Maahi felt her ears get warm.

'Speak up, girl! Who are you afraid of? It's just you and me!' Laila laughed. 'Ah, you remind me of me from like ten years ago. I was quite a shy fifteen-year-old. And then I turned sixteen and everything changed.' Laila mimed an explosion with her hands.

Maahi struggled to respond to that, mentally calculating that Laila was five years older than her. She seemed mature and well put together too, which intimidated Maahi. Her eyes rested on the wanted ad again. 'Umm, no, it's not like that. I was…'

'Oh, are you interested in the position?' Laila asked, following Maahi's gaze. 'It's a really chill job. All you have to do is take money from people and give them food or drinks in exchange—whatever they want. And spend the whole day with me—which could be a deal breaker, but everything else is quite alright. Scratch that, I already mentioned CJ. He's not that bad. I mean, as managers go, he tends to be a pain in the ass, but you can take him.'

Maahi thought about that for a second. She somehow found herself considering it. She was starting college soon and already had a job in the interim. Why was she considering a job at a coffee shop, especially when she didn't need a job at all?

'Okay.'

'Okay?' Laila raised an eyebrow at Maahi.

'Yeah.'

'Cool. Let me see if CJ is around. Actually, you know what, never mind. He delegated it to me, so I'm just going to interview you. Hi, I'm Laila—I'm the baker and service manager. I basically do everything around here. I'll be your supervisor. We're looking for someone for the counter. Don't worry, it's not much. You don't even need to be good at maths, really. But you will need to speak up, because you'll have to talk to the customers, okay? Are you fine with doing the interview right here?'

They were standing on either side of the tall counter, Laila resting her elbows on the cool granite and leaning towards Maahi, who was shuffling on her feet.

'I can't leave the counter unmanned. Unless you prefer coming in later or you want to wait till the end of my shift or until it cools down a bit so that we can talk for a few minutes? But we do need someone soon, and you are already here and like I said, it'll only take a few minutes, it's just a formality. Our requirement is to find someone who can stand on their feet and do things that most humans are easily capable of. Unless they are dum-dums,' Laila said, then added softly, 'like Naseer was.'

Maahi blushed.

'Okay, let's do this. So, how educated are you? Are you in college?'

'No, but I start this academic year.'

'Cool. What and where?'

'DU. Indraprastha College, business economics,' Maahi said. If asked one day ago, she wouldn't have been able to answer.

'Oh, you're so young. I graduated a while ago—in mass communication, can you believe that? But then I shifted gears—I'm about to start a diploma in bakery and patisserie from IICA. Have you heard of it?'

Maahi shook her head.

'It's the International Institute of Culinary Arts. I'll need to find a big-girl job once I'm done, but this is good for now.' Laila looked around at the bright purple interiors of Cozy Coffee. 'But you're good, you have three years till you graduate.

I'm sorry, I digress. It's just that I haven't had anyone to talk to all day and now I can't seem to control my verbal diarrhoea. So, anyway, I come in late—around 2 p.m., and I close the shop at around 8 p.m., so it'll be perfect if those timings work for you. Right now our schedules are all over the place because I work more hours over the summer, but once college starts, there'll be a lot more consistency. Unless you want to work longer hours over the weekend?'

'I don't know…' Maahi said. She asked herself what was happening and how she ended up there.

'Sure, of course. We can figure that out later. By the way, where do you live?'

'Vaishali.'

'Oh, that's a commute. Will you be okay taking the closing shifts with me? We could go up to Rajiv Chowk together. You'll be on your own from there. But those are details we can furnish later. The pay isn't much to speak of, but it's not bad at all as a student. In fact, over the summer, I've been able to save a little too by working extra hours.' Laila winked at Maahi again.

They talked for a few more minutes—Laila spoke and Maahi listened, after which Maahi found herself shaking Laila's hand, accepting a job at Cozy Coffee. She felt like she had entered an alternate reality where things got out of her control and chose a path for her that she hadn't imagined before. And in that moment, she didn't mind.

'Do you still want me to get that coffee and croissant for you? Or do you prefer getting it yourself, now that you have access to this side of the counter. *And* we get employee discount,' Laila said.

'I'm good,' Maahi said, and turned around. She had to go back to Fourth Eye Apps and tell Prasoon she was quitting.

She felt bad about not giving him a notice, but in her defence, she hadn't exactly had a notice either.

'One last question—when can you join?' Laila asked.

'Monday.' Maahi didn't know why she said that; it was the first thing that popped into her head.

'Perfect. I'll send you the offer letter and you make sure you print a copy and sign it. Bring it in on Monday and … that should be it.' Laila gave her a wide smile.

'Sounds good,' Maahi said, meaning it. As she walked back to the office, she wondered what it would be like to work with Laila every day. Would she ever get a chance to speak? She felt drawn to her flamboyant, dramatic, fun personality. Maahi thought it was strange how her personality was the exact opposite of the way she dressed. Admittedly, Maahi had only seen her twice, but both times, under the Cozy Coffee apron, Laila had a grey top, black jeans and black sneakers on. Her hair had been pulled on top of her head in a messy bun again, some strands falling loose against the taut skin of her face— the soft curls quite a contrast against the rest of her. She came across as an independent, confident girl who could take care of herself. Maybe even beat someone up if they troubled her, even though she was skinny.

Maahi chuckled as she entered the office, soon to become her old office. She couldn't decide how to approach the subject with Prasoon, so she waited for him to drop by, which he did a few times during the day, more out of boredom than anything else, Maahi suspected.

Sure enough, within half an hour of her returning from lunch, Prasoon came to her desk. 'Hey, how are we doing today?' he asked.

'Good.' Maahi smiled.

'Great! No difficult calls?'

'Nope.'

'Perfect. That's always good.' Prasoon looked around her desk, as he always did during their brief, awkward interactions every day. 'Anything I need to know?'

'Umm, actually…' Maahi began, losing confidence fast.

'Yes?'

He was looking at her, and as Maahi felt the full force of his eyes on her, she tried not to crumble. It wasn't that he had a personality that intimidated her. She was just easily intimidated, especially when she felt as if she was in the wrong. But she couldn't work two jobs at once, so it needed to be said. 'When I first joined, you knew that it was temporary, right?'

'Yes. Until your college started, of course. You told me before you started,' Prasoon said. 'Oh, is it already time?'

He seemed to be quite okay with it. Maahi saw that opening and took it. 'Yeah.'

'Do you start college soon? I didn't realize you'd even picked one yet.'

'It's a … recent development. I'm going to take business economics at IP.'

'DU?'

'Yes.'

'Cool. Congratulations!' Prasoon said and offered her a handshake. He seemed to decide against it and went for a hug, which got awkward when Maahi had to get up and return his half-hug with her desk and computer between them. He looked a little embarrassed and Maahi felt bad. He had been a good boss. He tried to maintain a healthy, professional work environment, and it always felt a bit like make-believe because, no matter how hard Maahi tried, she couldn't see Fourth Eye

Apps as a real company and the office as a real workplace. They might be making profit and slowly becoming a rage amongst iPhone owners, but Maahi just didn't see it that way. She reflected that it was a good thing for them that she was leaving. She got the job done, but she wasn't an employee who believed in the vision of the company—whatever the hell that was.

'Thank you,' Maahi said.

'Until when can you work? Or do you have to leave us immediately?' Prasoon asked. Maahi wasn't sure how to feel about him not being affected at all by her quitting. On one hand, she was relieved that a possible awkward conversation had turned out to be easy. On the other, having worked there for some time, she hadn't expected them to not blink an eye when she left.

'I can work until the end of the week, if you prefer?'

'Sure, that works.'

'Do you need me to help with interviewing people and training whoever fills this position? We could post an ad on the website and see if candidates can come in sometime this week for interviews?' Maahi suggested, trying to make the transition easy.

'Actually, we don't know if we'll hire someone else immediately. All our apps are doing okay, but iPhones are still quite expensive around here … We'll mostly be working on making these apps available on Android. That should keep us busy for the next few months. We'll probably look for someone after that,' Prasoon explained.

'Oh, sure. I understand.' Maahi suspected that the 'company' wasn't generating a lot of profit, and they were probably glad they no longer had to pay her. She wondered if they had been keeping her just because they didn't know how to begin a conversation about letting her go.

After lingering around her desk awkwardly for a few more minutes, Prasoon bid her a good day and left for a 'meeting' somewhere. Maahi realized she should've just told him she had to leave the same day. There didn't seem to be a point in her staying and working till the end of the week except for answering angry calls by constipated or sexually frustrated people and engaging with them for no apparent reason. She wondered where these weirdos would go to vent once that option became unavailable 'for a few months' after she was gone.

She couldn't care less about it. She turned back to her computer screen, scrolling through the list of responses to choose from, thinking about how she was going to tell her parents that she quit her desk job to work at a coffee shop. She was quite sure Ma would be disappointed. Maahi had managed to extend the disappointing streak against her mom and the aunties in her colony. Maahi knew that most of these aunties would actually be happy to get another opportunity to show concern and judgement on the outside; they didn't actually care about her future. For a fleeting second, she wondered how different her mom's attitude towards Maahi's life would be if she didn't have all those voices constantly whispering in her ears. She didn't brood over that for long.

Having made two important decisions in her life that day, she got home after work and decided to suspend the conversation about the day's developments until the next day. She was in a happy mood, feeling calm and settled. Normally, her days ended with anxiety and restlessness—so she welcomed the change.

Her mom made idli-sambhar for dinner, which was Maahi's favourite. In all the months that she had been back, this was the first time Maahi got special treatment. Knowing that it was because she had done the 'right thing' by choosing a field of education her mom approved of, she didn't want to stir the calm waters by announcing that, come Monday, she would be serving coffee to strangers. There were jobs that were respected, and then there were ones that were looked down upon in the Kothari household. The Kotharis simply did not believe in customer service jobs.

If only her parents knew the nature of her desk job at Fourth Eye Apps.

8

Maahi hadn't realized how long she'd have to postpone the conversation about her new job. She began with a temporary excuse—telling her parents her office timings had changed and she was needed from two to eight instead of nine to five. Ma was worried about her commute from Gurgaon alone at night, but Papa convinced her, saying it was only a matter of a few months.

Maahi hadn't intended to lie about it. It saddened her to lie to her parents. She figured that since it was only a matter of a couple of months, it wasn't crucial that they knew. It was only once those months were over and her time to quit her job and start her classes came that she realized she didn't want to quit.

She enjoyed working at the coffee shop, and she didn't want to leave. She understood that college was important too and she was willing to work fewer hours at the coffee shop to accommodate that. It was better than quitting altogether. Her job might not look like much to an outsider, but she loved everything about it. She loved the long rides on the Metro she took every day to Gurgaon and back, she loved walking from the M.G. Road Metro Station, surrounded by shopping malls, to the Cozy Coffee, which was just five minutes away—she was fascinated by how much quieter things got in a matter of minutes, and she got calmer with it.

Cozy Coffee was located on the ground floor of a five-storeyed building. It was small, cosy, as the name suggested, with six round tables with three chairs each, and two couches lining the front windows. Everything was bright purple and white—the walls, the floors, the ceilings, the countertops, the cups. That could've been the only thing Maahi didn't like about her job—being surrounded by things so violently purple.

When it was time to quit, she couldn't imagine leaving this place behind, and she talked to Laila about it, who talked to CJ and they came to the conclusion that they could survive with her working fewer hours. She would need to go there after her classes and stay until closing. It would be a hectic schedule, but Maahi didn't see this as just a job. It was more like therapy. Laila had become a close friend and confidant, a fact that surprised her, since their personalities were exact opposites.

Somehow, somewhere, something had clicked. Staying together in a confined space for hours left minimum leeway; they didn't have any other option but to become friends. Soon, Maahi couldn't imagine going through her days without talking to Laila. Laila's parents were divorced and she lived with her mom. She had been working at the coffee shop ever since she started college, and she needed that job to support herself. But what Maahi admired the most about her was her passion for baking cookies. She was always inventing recipes using the weirdest ingredients and she was always trying to force CJ to let her put them on the menu. CJ was used to rejecting her ideas, but never asked her to stop trying new recipes. Laila said it was because her cookies were awesome and he loved an excuse to eat them. She believed that, one day, she would bake a cookie that would be 'The awesomest of all awesomes and CJ's heart would melt with the cookie in his mouth' and finally, after all these years of tears and sweat, her own recipe would be on the menu.

When college started, Maahi told her parents that the people at Fourth Eye Apps needed her to work until they found a replacement. Things went smoothly for the first five weeks. Her lies worked, until one day, her neighbour Mishra aunty's son happened by her shop with his girlfriend and saw Maahi working there. Even then, Maahi thought she would be fine because he wouldn't risk telling anyone anything when Maahi had seen him with his girlfriend. Always a great blackmailing tool.

She even confirmed it. She walked over to him casually and said, 'So, my parents don't know that I work here.'

'Okay…' he said, exchanging a look with his girlfriend.

'I'd appreciate it if you don't tell anyone before I tell them myself, please?'

'Sure.' He smiled, but Maahi wasn't convinced.

'What's wrong?' Laila asked when Maahi went back behind the counter.

'That guy over there lives three houses away from us. I hope he doesn't tell my parents I work here,' Maahi said, stealing a glance at him. For the life of her, she couldn't remember his name.

Laila laughed. 'Are you serious? Of course he's not going to tell your parents! What is this, fifth class?'

'I don't know. I'm getting a weird vibe from him.'

'You need to chill.'

Maahi hadn't been able to chill and for good reason. That

evening when she went home, both her parents were waiting for her in the living room. She instantly knew.

'He told you,' Maahi said. She closed the door behind her and sat down on the sofa in front of her parents, putting down her handbag.

'Did you think we would never find out?' her dad asked.

'It's not like that—'

'How long has this been happening? Ever since your office timings changed? When was that, three months ago?'

'Papa, let me explain. I didn't intend to lie to you. I just didn't know how to tell you in the beginning and then I thought…' Maahi tried to explain, but couldn't find a legitimate reason, other than her parents' disapproval. If she brought that up, it would show that she knew they wouldn't approve and did it anyway.

'What did you think? How could you do this, Maahi?' her mom asked.

'I can't believe this. My daughter working as a waitress… I don't understand why. What is the need? Don't your mom and I give you enough?'

'It's not about that, Papa!'

'Then what? What happened to the other job—the one with the app developers? Did they fire you? Is that why you took this job?'

'No! They didn't fire me. I quit.'

'But why!' both her parents asked together.

'Because I wanted to do this job. I like working at Cozy Coffee. I like the environment, the people—' Maahi tried to explain but was cut off by her mom.

'You can't be serious!'

'What do you do there?' Papa asked.

'I work the register.'

'Is that what you want to do with your life?'

'Who said anything about life? This is something I enjoy doing now—'

'What do you enjoy there? What could you possibly enjoy working at a coffee shop?' Mom interrupted. 'Do you realize what people are saying about us now? Mrs Mishra's son told her and she told me. You know how she is. She must have told the whole colony by now. Everybody must think we're too poor to take care of our children and our children need to serve coffee for money.'

Angry tears filled Maahi's eyes. 'I'm sorry, Ma. It's just something I want to do and I knew you wouldn't let me. So I decided to keep it from you.'

There was silence in the room.

'Do you realize how much you are hurting us by doing this?'

'Think about it, Ma. Am I hurting you or am I hurting your image in front of all these aunties from the colony who have nothing to do with us? I don't understand how they get to decide what we do with our time.' Maahi hadn't intended to say it, but in the heat of the moment, she couldn't stop herself.

'Don't talk to your Ma that way!' Papa said.

'No, let her. Let her say whatever she wants. At least then I will know why she did this. Why she is intent on ruining our family's reputation,' Ma said.

'She isn't anymore.' Papa turned to Maahi. 'From tomorrow, you're going to college and coming straight home. Let them know you're quitting and that's the last I'm hearing of this place.' He got up. His was the final word. There was nothing she could do about it. That's how it always worked. Ma would raise questions about every small thing the kids did and it wasn't to be taken that seriously. Papa came in only in extreme situations and whatever he said had to be done. There was no explanation, no reasoning—nothing was going to change his mind.

Ma got up too, shaking her head. Maahi looked from one disappointed parent's face to the other's. In that moment, she came to the realization that no matter what, they would always be disappointed in her. There was nothing she could do to impress them. In a matter of a year, everything had turned upside down, she had fallen in their eyes completely when she dropped out of engineering college and came back home. She would never be able to redeem herself.

Maahi waited five minutes after her parents left the room, to collect her thoughts. She was going to college every day, she wasn't missing any classes, she was submitting all her assignments on time. And she was doing all of that for her parents' happiness. Wouldn't it be only fair if they can let her do what made her happy with whatever time she had left in the day? She was simply asking to be allowed to do an honest day's work and earn her money. It was hardly prostitution. And yet, they made it sound like it was. As if she had to give up her self-respect and honour to do what she was doing. The worst part was that they thought she was doing it only for the money.

She picked up her phone.

> Maahi: My parents found out about the coffee shop. They're making me quit.
>
> Rohit: Oh, shit. How do they know?
>
> Maahi: Mishra aunty told Ma. Her son saw me at the coffee shop today and told his mom.

Rohit: Wow. What a loser!

Maahi: What should I do now, Rohit? I don't want to quit.

Rohit: Do you think you can convince your parents?

Maahi: I don't know. But I can't imagine the next 3 years of my life going to stupid college and coming back home. To disappointed parents. Every day.

Rohit: It can't be that bad. You'll get involved in classes and new friends once you start.

Maahi: It is bad! You don't know. I feel worthless. It's like if I don't go to class or submit my assignments, it would make no difference. The world won't fall apart.

Rohit: What do you mean?

Maahi: My role at Cozy Coffee isn't much, but at least I'm needed. If I call in sick and they can't find someone else to cover my shift, they would have trouble keeping the place going.

Rohit: So the world would fall apart at least a little bit, for a little while.

Maahi: Yes.

Rohit: I get that. You want to feel useful.

Maahi: I just need to feel NOT worthless.

Rohit: Tell them that?

Maahi: They won't understand. You know how they are.

Rohit: But you've got to try, right?

Maahi: Right.

Maahi kicked off her blue converse shoes, unwrapped her scarf from around her neck and breathed for a few minutes, letting herself cool down before padding to her parents' bedroom in her socks. Ma didn't like them to wear 'outside shoes' inside the house.

Ma and Papa looked up at her.

Maahi stood at the door and spoke evenly, looking at the TV screen. *Big Boss* was on; she cringed. 'I know that this makes you unhappy, but I can't help but feel like *anything* I do always makes you unhappy. I don't want that, and I try, I really do. But I'm sorry. This is the one thing that I need to do, and I'm sorry that I'm such a disappointment to you, but I hope you won't take this away from me.'

She looked away from the TV and at her parents, neither of whom said anything. This time, she couldn't stop the tears. She could barely stay audible as she said, 'I won't let you take this away from me.'

When her parents didn't speak in the next whole minute, Maahi went back to the living room. People she loved needed to stop doing that to her—being silent when she needed them to speak, and tell her that they would be there for her.

'Whoa, what's up?' Sarthak asked when he came home and bumped into her in the living room.

Maahi shook her head, picked up her stuff and went to her room. She stayed there for a while. She couldn't stop crying. Beyond the obvious reasons, she felt that there was something else, something big that was being taken away from her. She hadn't been confident as a child, but there's a certain amount of confidence a person tends to have until it's snatched away from them. She had lost all of that when Kishan didn't want to be with her anymore, and with that she had also lost her purpose, her ambition and her desire to do something, *be* something. She was only now beginning to get that back.

There was a knock on her door. Maahi sniffed and wiped her tears on her sleeves. She sat up on the floor and looked for something to check her reflection on. She didn't want her parents to see her cry. She didn't want to hurt them like that.

She took a second to compose herself before opening the door. It was Sarthak. She turned around and sat down on her bed. Sarthak turned on the light and closed the door before sitting down next to her. He didn't say anything.

Maahi couldn't handle more silence. 'They don't get it,' she said, choking on the words.

'I know.'

'They just don't. I mean, I don't know what else I can do.'

'There's nothing you can do,' Sarthak said.

Maahi paused. 'What do you mean?'

'You can't. Once they've decided you're not enough for them, you're not enough for them. Trust me, I've lived that for years, I've experienced that all my life, as far back as I can remember. I've never been good enough for them.'

'No, it's not like that!' Maahi said. The thought was too sad to comprehend. 'You know Ma. She just makes a big deal out of everything. Everything's dramatic to her. She likes to complain a lot, but she doesn't mean it. You know that. We all know that.'

'Yeah? Then why are you crying?'

'I'm not. I've had a hard day and it's getting to me. That's all.'

'A hard year,' Sarthak said, and she looked at him. 'I've been right here. I've seen it. It's made my life easier—all the attention being directed at you. You being the disappointment for a change doesn't mean I don't see that you've been sad this whole time.'

Maahi's lips trembled. 'I shouldn't have come back. I should've stayed there ... no matter how hard it was.'

'No. You've got to stop doing things because others want you to. Why the hell are you studying business economics?'

'The same reason you're studying PCM. The same reason you'll study some kind of engineering once you're done with school.'

'It's different for me. I'm lucky I actually like PCM, and I actually want to be an engineer. But you're right—I would've been doing it even if I hated it,' Sarthak said. When Maahi looked at him, she noticed how much he had grown. He wasn't just taller, he had started shaving. He wasn't the chubby boy she was used to seeing. Ma had raised two chubby kids, but for different reasons, neither of them had retained it. Sarthak was losing width and gaining height. And he seemed more ... stable somehow. More grown-up than child. Maahi wondered if he was popular in school. He must be. He was quite good looking, with those broad shoulders, and stupid hair—short on the back and sides, with a long layer on top, sweeping over his head, tapering to a tip at the front. He was quite fond of his hair, spending a lot of time in front of the mirror with a tube of hair gel that Ma said was going to leave him bald one day.

'Do you want to get out for a second?' Maahi asked.

'Out where?'

'I want to show you something. Let's go.'

'Right now?'

Maahi nodded, already putting her shoes back on. She pulled a jacket on in case it got cold on their long ride to Gurgaon.

Maahi was glad to find that Sarthak was a very responsible driver. He followed all the rules, never went over the speed limit, and seemed to have complete control over the bike. It took them less than an hour to reach Cozy Coffee. Once there, Sarthak parked outside and they walked to the entrance. Maahi took out the keys and unlocked the door.

'This is the place I've been hearing about the whole day?' Sarthak asked.

'Yep,' Maahi said.

'Cool. I like it.'

'Me too.'

Maahi showed him where she worked, what she did. She told him about the customers, the strange things that sometimes happened. She told him about Laila, whom he already knew about, but she had been using different contexts when she had talked about her day at the dinner table. She was glad she didn't have to watch what she was saying anymore.

They kept all the lights off, except the one in the kitchen. Maahi pulled out some cupcake recipes she had collected from magazines, YouTube and some she had 'invented' the way Laila did. With Sarthak as a helper—which meant someone who passed things to her and ate the half-done batter—Maahi set to baking. She prepared enough batter for half a dozen vanilla cupcakes and handed it over to Sarthak for whipping. She took another bowl and prepared the batter for chocolate cupcakes.

As they whipped, they talked about all the things they hadn't talked about in ages. They used to be really close growing up. When Maahi thought back, she realized that it was around the time she got involved with Kishan that she lost her bond with her brother. They recreated it over baking.

Maahi timed the oven carefully, trying not to mess up the end result. She had enjoyed talking to Sarthak, but she knew he would be expecting some cupcakes at the end of all the work. She wasn't about to be a disappointment yet again, not that day.

When Maahi pulled the trays out, she was relieved to see that the cupcakes were baked right, maybe a little too much, but she would take that—it was better than burning or being undercooked.

'Oh shit. That looks awesome!' Sarthak jumped off the counter and walked towards her.

'Careful. They're hot. And you have to wait for the toppings—that's the fun part.' Maahi was giddy as a child with a candy. She couldn't wait to decorate them. She pulled open the cabinets on her right and inspected their contents. 'Let's see what we've got here.'

Maahi pulled out some toppings she liked and Sarthak followed suit. 'How do you not get fat working here? I would just eat it all.'

'It's a struggle.' Maahi laughed. 'Okay, so for the vanilla cupcake, how about frosting and sprinkles?'

'Sounds good to me.'

'Try caramel and cinnamon dust on vanilla too. And for the chocolate—we can try marshmallow frosting. It'll take some time. You can have the vanilla ones till then.'

Sarthak gladly agreed.

Maahi found a tutorial on YouTube and began making the frosting. She put eggs, water and sugar in a bowl and began beating. 'Is that good?'

'Yum,' Sarthak said. He spoke a lot less once he started eating.

It took Maahi a good half hour to make the marshmallow frosting, but she was happy with the result. As the last of the marshmallows melted, she brought the bowl to the chocolate cupcakes and poured the topping on one of them. Sarthak picked it up even before she stopped.

'So good,' he said after taking a bite.

Maahi laughed at his enthusiasm. She felt a warmth spreading through her as she watched him eat. She didn't feel quite as worthless anymore.

'You bake?' a voice said from behind, startling both Maahi and Sarthak. Laila was standing at the door, chewing gum, inspecting the crime scene.

Part Three

9

'Did you tell him? Go tell him!' Laila prodded.

'No, stop,' Maahi muttered. 'That's not how life works. You can't just make up rules and make others follow them.'

'That's exactly how my life works. We need to enforce *cupcake of the day*. Trust me, once we start getting good testimonies from customers, CJ's going to bend. Now *go*.'

Knowing that Laila wasn't going to let it go, Maahi went under the counter and emerged on the other side. 'If he complains to CJ, it's on you,' she said.

'Everything's always on me.'

'Because you're the one always coming up with these ideas!'

'You're the one who bakes these cupcakes. I'm just trying to help you get out there. Establish yourself as a baker!' Laila threw her hands in the air in frustration.

'Right, of course.' Maahi rolled her eyes. She loosened the strings of her apron as she walked to the man in a white lab coat at the table by the window. He was sitting, but Maahi could tell he was tall and possibly had a good body. That was also because, when he had come in earlier and she took his order,

Laila had whispered 'I can just tell he works out', eyeing him with barely concealed appreciation. Maahi's ears grew warm remembering it, but before she could turn back, he looked up from his phone and right at her. Maahi nodded towards his screen, which had a bright pink and purple maze with pillars strewn randomly in and around it, over fake green grass. 'Clash of Clans, huh?'

He laughed. 'If you can tell from five feet away, you know it too well.'

'My brother plays that stupid game all the time. Gets on my nerves,' Maahi said. Under the soft sunlight reflecting off the window, his eyes shone. They were brown like hers. Maybe a shade or two lighter. They were intense; she found herself unable to break contact.

'Umm, *sorry*, I guess?' he said, placing his phone face-down on the table.

'No, no, you can play it. I mean, if you want. You don't need my permission, of course. I was just trying to make conversation and then I went ahead and made a fool of myself and now I can't stop blabbering.'

'That's quite alright.' He laughed. Maahi couldn't get over that laugh. It changed his face. She thought he was attractive, but his laugh was the real game changer. The crinkles that formed near his deep-set, perfect eyes and on the bridge of his nose were adorable.

'I just wanted to tell you about the *cupcake of the day*, if you're interested. It's a spice cupcake filled with caramel, with vanilla frosting and caramelized apples on top, sprinkled with cinnamon.'

'Whoa.'

'Yep. It's quite good; I made it myself,' Maahi said, and then blushed. 'Which means I would totally understand if you don't want to try it. Cool. So now that I've told you about it, I'm going to go hide behind the counter and wish for invisibility as my superpower.'

Maahi turned around and shuffled away without giving him a chance to speak. This place did something to its staff—they could never shut up. She remembered the time when Laila had interviewed her and wouldn't stop talking. Maybe it was something in the air. Or the icing sugar.

'So? Does he want it?' Laila asked when Maahi got behind the counter.

'No, of course he didn't want it. Why would anybody want my cupcakes?'

'Why not? The cupcake has spices in it *and* caramel filling. On top of that, there's vanilla frosting and caramelized apples and cinnamon sugar powder,' Laila said. She paused for a second and asked, 'Do you think we went too deep?'

'A bit, yes. There's too much in there,' Maahi said, dejected.

'Well, hey. It's not just a cupcake—it's an experience. Don't get it if you're not ready for it.'

The seriousness with which Laila spoke made Maahi laugh. 'I guess he wasn't ready for it then,' Maahi said.

'Then he didn't deserve it. What a waste. I thought he was cute.' Laila shrugged.

'Really? Then why did you send me to talk to him. You should go tell him about *cookie of the day*.'

'Yeah, let's freak all our customers out. No one will ever come here because the employees don't allow them to drink their coffee in peace.'

'You insist that we have a *cookie of the day* and a *cupcake of the day*. What's the point in us baking if we don't sell it?' Maahi asked.

'Did you seriously just ask me what the point of baking is? As a baker? As a baker under *my* training?'

Maahi threw her hands up in surrender. 'My bad. You're just confusing me by asking me to market my products and then not marketing your own.'

'Because we already freaked him out with one announcement. What did you do to him? Did you see the way he ran out of here—all hurried and hassled?'

'He left?' Maahi followed Laila's gaze to the door, and then checked his table. There was no sign of him.

'You look disappointed,' Laila observed.

'You're the one who thought he was cute.'

'Yes, but for you. I'll chew him and spit him out in a week and he wouldn't know what hit him,' Laila said.

Maahi shook her head, a bored look on her face. Laila spoke as if she was tough and heartless, but really, she wasn't. In fact, over the year they had been working together, Maahi had been more and more surprised to find how alike they were. Maybe not on the outside—with Laila in her sleek and minimal black, white and grey outfits and Maahi in her vivid colours and girlish attires. But they definitely shared a deeper connection, a result of their core similarities in nature.

Maahi was confused about Laila's love life. She acted like a player, but to Maahi, she seemed like someone who would easily get attached to another person and begin to care about them in no time. She never went on dates. She said she was concentrating on her classes because she needed to build a career for herself. Her parents were divorced and she lived with her mom, who she wanted to take care of. She wanted to be financially stable so that her mom could retire. She said she had no time for love, but Maahi saw through the 'tough' exterior she put up to repel possible 'fuckboys' that Laila kept warning her about. She once texted Maahi a definition of the term she found on the Internet.

A fuckboy is the type of guy who does shit that generally pisses the population of the earth off all the time. He will also lead girls on just for hook-ups, says he's really into you just to fuck you but doesn't want to deal with all the 'relationship bullshit'. He thinks about himself and himself only all the time, but pretends to be really nice. He also does really fucked-up shit and then complains about people who do the same old shit as him. Once a fuckboy always a fuckboy.

Maahi had been hurt before, and she could hardly claim to have recovered from her first love and first heartbreak, but this wasn't how she saw men at all. She doubted Laila saw them that way either, but she maintained that position, at least on the outside. She believed that by not caring about them, she denied them the power to hurt her. Maahi thought it was a good concept in theory, but real life didn't work that way.

Maahi hadn't thought about anyone since Kishan, which was two years ago. She kept telling herself to stop being scared and she knew she couldn't hide forever in fear of getting hurt. But the truth was that she simply didn't believe she would ever fall in love again.

'Those look good,' CJ commented on her cupcakes. Maahi turned to see their manager walking in from behind them.

'Fuck. You scared me. Where did you come from? Were you in the kitchen this whole time?' Laila asked.

'No. I just came in a minute ago. How's everything looking here?'

'Good,' Maahi said.

'Are you guys still trying to force your creations down people's throats?' CJ eyed the cupcakes and cookies laid out in the front, separated from the rest of their basic baked goods.

'No one comes here for those croissants or those pound cakes, CJ. You know that,' Laila said, pointing towards the display.

'You're right. They come here for the coffee. That's why we are called Cozy Coffee. This is a *coffee* shop, not a bakery.'

'Why can't it be both? It's not like we don't bake all our baked goods. If you want this place to be just another coffee shop, why are we baking our own cream puffs and brownies and everything? Why don't we just buy them to sell?' Laila argued. 'People love my cookies.'

'And my cupcakes,' Maahi added quietly and then shut up. She had been involved in way too many of these arguments.

'Yes!' Laila said. 'You're the only one who has a problem with our creativity.'

'I really don't. It's great that people like your baking; I do too. I'm just saying—let's not lose focus here, okay?' CJ said. He looked from Laila to Maahi and then back at Laila and clapped his hands together twice, saying, 'Now, let's get brewing.'

'Fine. But just so you know, we're making all of our toppings right here in the *coffee* shop from scratch, starting today. We're done using all of that packaged stuff—it brings down the quality of our food significantly. I'm changing the orders,' Laila said and walked away to the bathroom, not giving CJ a chance to respond.

'Okay then,' CJ muttered and wrapped a *cupcake of the day* in tissue paper before waving Maahi goodbye.

Maahi waved back. CJ's daily visits were short and sweet, just the way both Maahi and Laila preferred. He was easily recognizable in the neon-coloured turbans he donned. The first time Maahi had met him, it had been neon-pink, which she thought would be a tough act to follow. But in all the days Maahi had worked for him, she had never been disappointed. Except for the one time he wore a plain grey one, and Maahi thought for a second that he looked handsome. But he actually apologized to them, telling them he was in a rush and had to borrow a turban from his brother, promising he would be back in 'form' the next day.

'Is he gone?' Laila asked, returning from the bathroom. 'I'm done pretending to pee.'

'Yeah. He took one of my cupcakes.'

'That hypocrite. Wait, can I have one too? Those look delicious,' Laila said and helped herself. CJ never paid for the stuff he took because he owned the place. Laila never paid because, in her head, she believed that *she* owned the place. 'I'm glad we went too deep. This is heaven.'

'Thank you,' Maahi said, feeling proud of herself and the distance she had travelled in a year. That night, when she couldn't explain to her parents why she liked working at Cozy Coffee, why she would risk their precious reputation over serving coffee, she had discovered why. Watching Sarthak appreciate something she created from scratch, and then Laila, an actual baker, reinforcing the idea that she had actual talent, she had felt empowered. It had come as a blessing in a time when her self-worth was at an all-time low.

It was only slowly that she realized exactly how much she enjoyed baking, that it wasn't just the idea of it that appealed to her. Under the tutelage of Laila, who was herself learning a lot more at college and practising at the coffee shop, Maahi learned everything she knew about baking. The more she learned and baked, the better she got, becoming more and more passionate about it. She liked experimenting with new, unconventional ingredients. These experiments ended in disaster most times, which only made her more determined to try more things, to get to the ones that were just right.

※

When Maahi woke up the next morning, she heard voices in the living room. She got dressed for college and went to the kitchen to get breakfast, regretting it immediately. She would prefer skipping breakfast over talking to Sushanti aunty, who used to be their neighbour four years ago, but still refused to stop being a part of their lives. She behaved as if she were still a neighbour to everyone in the colony.

'Namaste, Aunty,' Maahi said, smiling sweetly. She didn't care, but her mom did, so pretences needed to be kept.

'Namaste, beta. How are you? How are your studies going?'

'I'm good. Everything's good.' Maahi served herself some upma from the kadhai on the stove and looked for ketchup in the fridge.

'Good, good. We were all so worried about you when you came back from Bangalore. See, you are so thin now. You looked so weak that in the beginning we thought you were sick. What happened to our chubby little Maahi? But good that you're back on track now. Your mom and I were just talking about how important education is.'

'Yeah?' Maahi sat down to eat, planning on gulping down her breakfast at top speed and getting the hell out of there as soon as possible.

'Yes. Girls nowadays are doing so many things. All career women. Look at your mom—she has such a good career and she also takes care of the family. She cooks and everything. But at least women are worth more than that now, profession-wise. They do both. At least she doesn't have to go to work and cook there too!' Sushanti aunty laughed.

Maahi concentrated on swallowing her food without choking.

'Oh, but it's not like that,' Ma said. 'I enjoy cooking, especially for my family.'

'I'm saying that only, no? For the family, yes, but why cook for strangers? What is the need?'

Maahi finished eating and brought her plate to the sink. 'You're so right, Aunty. Thank you so much for thinking about my well-being,' she said.

'Haan, beta. I only say this because I care about you. That's why I worry,' Sushanti aunty said, beaming.

Maahi contemplated asking her about her son, who had been made to resign from his position at work because of sexual harassment complaints about him, but decided she was above that. He seemed to have found another job without difficulty, and went around telling people that he quit his previous job because there was no scope for his talent in a small company like that, but one of Rohit's friends worked in the same company, so they knew the truth. She said bye to her mom and left.

Sarthak was leaving too, and offered to drop her to her college on his bike. He told Maahi how Sushanti aunty was praising him nonstop all morning. He seemed to think it was a ploy—just to raise expectations to a level that he eventually won't be able to match and then they could act regretful about how much potential the Kotharis' son had and how he ended up wasting it.

Her day at college didn't go as well as she'd hoped, but still better than her morning. She got seventy-one per cent on her tests, which she was fine with, but it wouldn't please her parents. She had made a few friends at college, so it was easier to get through her classes and was a huge help especially during exams when they studied together. But she couldn't wait for her classes to end so she could rush to the coffee shop and bake with Laila.

That day, Maahi got out of classes early and reached an hour before Laila. She got started on her lemon cupcakes, another experiment. The cupcake itself was easy; she just added lemon juice in her regular batter and beat it extra-long. Maahi used to think her cupcakes would be fluffier and generally better the longer she beat them. She had learned over time that beating the batter too much wasn't the best thing to do—because that resulted in bubbles. She remembered Laila's pursed lips when she had seen that especially bubbly batch of red velvet cupcakes Maahi once baked.

'What smells good?' Laila came in just as Maahi was preparing the frosting.

'*Cupcake of the day* in progress.' Maahi pointed at the tray she just pulled out of the oven. 'Lemon cupcakes with lemon Italian meringue frosting.'

'Wow, complex. How's that going? What did you put in it?' Laila stashed away the brown bag she was carrying, and peeked into Maahi's bowl.

'I started with sugar and water, cooked the syrup at 240. Then took lemon juice and lemon zest in another bowl, added egg whites to it, beat it for a while. Mixed the syrup in it and have been beating it ever since,' Maahi explained excitedly.

Laila took some frosting on a spoon and tasted it. 'Mmm, good. Keep at it—needs more beating.'

'I know. I've been on this forever. But does it taste okay? I was worried it might get too sour.'

'It has the right amount of lemony tang to it, don't worry,' Laila said. 'You finish this up. Mohan is getting off his shift in a minute, so I'm going to man the counter. Come out when you're done. I have elaborate plans for *cookie of the day* that I need to get down to.'

'Cool,' Maahi said. She wanted to ask Laila what she was planning to bake, but she had already left the kitchen. The highlight of Maahi's days, apart from baking, was getting to eat Laila's cookies. Sometimes she thought that they stuck to the *cookie of the day* and *cupcake of the day* tradition just so they got to bake and experiment, and also eat each other's creations.

Maahi finished with the frosting and decorated a dozen cupcakes. She sprinkled lemon zest on top and shredded rosemary leaves—the yellow and green looked lovely against white. She placed them on a display tray and brought them out to the counter. 'All done,' she said happily.

'Awesome. I'm going to put carrots and walnuts in my cookies today,' Laila announced.

'For real?'

'For real.' Laila smirked. 'You'll see. And by the way, the doctor is here again—the guy wearing the AIIMS identity card who didn't want your *cupcake of the day* yesterday. You could try selling him this one. He didn't go for the immensely sweet one, maybe he likes his cupcakes a bit sour.'

'I think I've embarrassed myself enough before him. I'm going to let him be,' Maahi said, glancing in his direction. He looked exactly like he did the day before, wearing the same white coat with black trousers. Maybe it was a different white coat, but she had no way to tell.

She pulled out the book she was reading. It was a Sylvia Plath title Laila worshipped and had forced on Maahi. There wasn't much to do at the coffee shop in the afternoon hours, once the lunch and late-lunch crowd had passed. They got a lot of mostly quiet time to read and catch up on their college work. Soon, the smell of Laila's cookies wafted towards her—it was odd, delightfully weird. She couldn't wait to try it. She looked up to find that man from yesterday at the counter.

'Hey, what can I get for you today?' she asked. She hoped he wouldn't recognize her, or at least pretend, just like she was trying to do.

'Hi. Is that today's *cupcake of the day*?' he asked, pointing at Maahi's lemon cupcakes.

'Yeah,' she said. 'I didn't bake them this time, so if you decide to get one, I promise you'll be safe.'

'Oh. I was hoping you baked them.'

'Really? Actually, I did.'

'But you just said you didn't,' he pointed out.

'Yesterday you didn't want one because I baked them so I was hoping you'd get one of these if I said I didn't bake them, but I did,' Maahi blurted. 'I realize I'm not very good at marketing my products.'

'Wow. So you just lied to me.'

'I was only kidding! I was about to say "JK, I did bake them" but then you said you actually did want me to have baked them and that threw me off!'

The man narrowed his eyes at her.

For a second, Maahi couldn't figure out if they were still kidding or if he was serious now. Then he shook his head gently, almost to himself and his lips twitched to one side in a hint of a smile.

'I'll take one of those,' he said.

'Are you sure?' Maahi asked.

'You *really* aren't good at marketing your products, are you?'

'Yes, I suck. I'm the worst.'

'I think you're pretty awesome,' he said, out of the blue.

Maahi paused. She looked at him, trying to figure out what that meant. He really was cute and now that he was standing, Maahi could see traces of the good body Laila and she had anticipated under that lab coat. The way he was looking at her made her want to sit down.

He let it linger for a moment before saying, 'I meant at marketing. That was sarcasm.'

Maahi laughed nervously. 'Got it. Do you want it here or to go?' she asked, printing out his receipt.

'Here, please.'

She picked up a pair of tongs and carefully placed one of her cupcakes on a square white plate before pushing it towards him. She tried not to look at him as he walked away, but found herself stealing glances. She told herself it was because she wanted to see what he thought of her cupcake, which was something she did whenever someone fell for her pitch.

He was busy on his phone, probably playing Clash of Clans again. Maahi smiled to herself. He took his first bite and three seconds later, Maahi found their eyes locked from across the coffee shop.

10

'Oh, you guys, so cute,' Laila said.

'No, we're not. Because there's no *we*. There's nothing and you need to stop,' Maahi said, as seriously as she could. It was after closing and they had dimmed the lights and closed the place down. They sat at the table by the window with their cupcakes, as was their daily ritual.

'Then why are you blushing?'

'I'm not.'

Laila raised one perfect eyebrow and went back to her cupcake, thin lips pursed. 'You killed it with this one, man. This is it—this right here is the real deal.'

'I read a recipe online, and thought about working on a variation. I think the green mango really works here. And the chilli.'

'No shit. I've never had a mango chilli cupcake before. How did you come so far? I didn't teach you any of this. Hell, I don't know how to do half of the things you're doing these days.'

'It's because you just want to *eat* the cupcakes, minus the work.'

'True. I like having you as my slave!' Laila laughed. 'Seriously though, that boy is cute. You need to let it happen.'

'There's nothing happening. And whatever's happening wouldn't have been happening if you hadn't stuck your little nose in my business in the first place.'

'Exactly. What was I supposed to do? You guys were talking for like, what, two weeks? He came in here every other day—it was clear that he was into you and you didn't even know his name. As your friend, it was my responsibility to butt in. Also, my little nose is very cute.'

'You're so proud of yourself, aren't you?' Maahi narrowed her eyes.

'Duh. And don't even pretend you don't like him. You guys text all day long. It's quite disgusting, if I'm completely honest with you.'

'You were just saying we're cute.'

'So cute it's disgusting. Keep up, Maahi!' Laila laughed.

Maahi and Siddhant had been texting each other for a week, courtesy Laila's meddling. What started as funny banter, graduated to shy flirting and was presently somewhere between long-thoughtful-conversations-about-weird-things and catching-up-on-each-other's-past phase. He came to the coffee shop if he got a chance before or after his work. He was a medical intern at AIIMS, and lived in Gurgaon near M.G. Road. His days were pretty crazy, with a lot of studying and practising. His internship hours were super hectic and he was always trying to juggle everything. That's the basic information Maahi had gathered about him in the past few weeks. They often found themselves talking about the most random things.

'Okay, let's leave. I need to be home soon, hopefully before Mom comes back from work. She's not feeling too well. I'm going to get home and cook dinner before she beats me to it.

She just doesn't listen; she needs to do everything,' Laila said, looking worried.

Maahi felt a pang of envy every time Laila talked about her mom. She felt bad for feeling that way, as if she was betraying her own mother. Also because Laila's parents got divorced when she was eleven and the struggles that she and her mom had faced ever since were way bigger than any of Maahi's problems with her family.

'I hope she feels better,' Maahi said as they got up and cleared the table.

⁕

The next day, Laila called in sick. She told Maahi that it was her mom who was sick, not her. CJ couldn't arrange for someone to cover for Laila, so Maahi was closing alone. He offered to stay back with her, but Maahi preferred to spend the rest of her shift without him.

'Hey there,' a familiar voice said.

Maahi looked up from the Hemingway book Laila had recommended and lent her. She skipped a heartbeat when she saw him, but hid it in a small smile. 'Hi, Siddhant.'

'How are you doing today?'

'Not that great, actually. Laila isn't here, so I'm holding fort all by my lonesome.' Maahi sighed exaggeratedly. She wondered if she looked as frazzled as she felt. She had blow-dried her hair—which was longer now and cut stylishly with side bangs—into loose waves and bordered her eyelids with brown liner that morning. Those were two additions to her usual wash-and-moisturize routine, which helped her confidence. The way Siddhant's gaze lingered on her helped too.

'Oh, that sucks.'

'Pretty much, yes. How was your day?'

'I got done with work earlier than expected. So I get to go home,' Siddhant said. 'Which must sound like bragging to you at this point.'

'It's not like you're even trying to hide your excitement. But I don't care. I'm just going to be over here, with my book. You go out there and live your life.'

'Could you be more dramatic?'

'I can, trust me, I can,' Maahi said. 'What can I get for you?'

'Do you even have to ask? What's today's special?'

'It's dark chocolate with peppermint. You know what? It's actually not that good. I wouldn't recommend it.'

'You're not getting any better at marketing.' Siddhant laughed. 'I'll still try one. And I'll take one of those coconut lime cupcakes from yesterday too, if you have any left.'

'We do, actually. Just a couple. That one was a hit!' Maahi said cheerfully.

'I haven't had breakfast or lunch today, so I'm glad I have room for these,' Siddhant said when she brought him the cupcakes. 'Looks delicious. I haven't slept in thirty hours. I need to go home and pass out, so I really shouldn't be having any sugar, but what the hell, let's throw caution to the wind.'

'Such a daredevil!' Maahi grinned. He left after a while, and even though Maahi wanted to spend more time with him, she could see how tired he was. She was sad to see him go, and when she realized it, she paused and wondered why. Maybe she was beginning to like him.

Maahi pushed that thought from her mind and got back to Hemingway. Laila was pulling her away from the dystopian YA novels she still adored and introducing her to more challenging literature. Time flew as the book demanded her sincere attention. Just as she was about to close the shop, she got a text from Siddhant.

> Siddhant: What's up?
> Maahi: About to close. You?
> Siddhant: Just woke up. Want to hang out?
> Maahi: Now?

Maahi regretted the second question mark as soon as she hit send.

> Siddhant: Yeah! Come play Mario Kart with us?
> Maahi: Who's us?
> Siddhant: Me and my roommates.

This was the first time Siddhant had asked to meet her anywhere. Maahi needed to go back to Vaishali, and didn't want to be late. Besides, she might have known him for about a month, but didn't *really* know him. She hadn't even seen him in anything other than his long, white lab coats. Between all the doubt, that thought excited her—seeing him in regular clothes.

She texted Laila to ask what she should do. Laila texted back within seconds: 'Oo. Go for it, girl!'

Maahi decided not to overthink it, and said yes. Siddhant texted her his address. She took her time closing, and then walking slowly to his place, as if waiting, hoping for a sign to make her turn around and go home. However, nothing of that sort happened, and before she knew it, she was at his door, and he was waving at her from his balcony. There was another guy with him, probably Siddhant's roommate. She got more nervous.

'Come on up,' Siddhant said and disappeared.

His smile reassured her, but not enough. She walked in and up two flights of stairs. He met her at the door, and greeted her with a small hug. It was the first time they had any kind of physical contact, and Maahi could feel his arm around her long after he released her.

He was wearing a navy-blue sweatshirt that had a strange, colourful Aztec pattern printed on grey in the front, with light blue washed-out jeans and a pair of grey sneakers. Maahi found it funny that their shoes almost matched. She liked seeing him in something other than his lab coat. He looked well rested too.

Siddhant led her into his apartment, and Maahi looked around, trying to estimate the amount of danger she would be in if they tried to hold her prisoner or something. She took one step into the living room. There was a girl lying senseless on the couch.

'That's Alia.'

'Is she ... alive?'

'She's fine. She hadn't slept in a long time and then she ate too much—she's basically passed out on food,' Siddhant explained.

'Is that a real thing?' Maahi asked.

'Yup,' Alia's muffled voice came from under the pillow. She remained unmoving, facedown, but raised two fingers and said, 'Hi.'

'Nice to meet you. I'm Maahi.'

'Welcome.'

Maahi didn't hear from Alia for the rest of the night. Siddhant introduced her to his other roommate, Eshaan, who was a short guy with square-rimmed glasses. He was from Assam, here for his medical studies. All three of them went to AIIMS, and were in their internship year of MBBS.

From the living room, she could see three doors, one on her right and two on the other side, so she assumed it was just the three of them living there. 'Where do your parents live?' Maahi asked Siddhant.

'They live here, in Delhi. It's easier for me to live with these guys because we can study together and our schedules are all over the place, so it makes sense to live with other med students. Although, my parents are both doctors too, so it's not like they don't understand,' he said. 'I don't want to be a bother, mostly. Their lives are pretty hectic as it is.'

'Your parents are both doctors?'

'Yep. And my elder brother,' Siddhant said.

'Yeah, so there was no pressure on Sid to become one,' Eshaan added.

Maahi laughed with them, but noticed something off with Siddhant's laughter. 'That must've been tough. But you've made it,' she said.

'Not yet. Med school's just the beginning. There's a long way to go, trust me. I haven't even started yet,' Siddhant said, staring at the blank TV screen, suddenly very serious.

Maahi turned towards Eshaan for support, but found him nodding at the coffee mug in his hand. Maybe he was thinking about his own career and the path ahead. Maahi got intimidated for a second, seeing how driven and ambitious these men were. Admittedly, she knew nothing about the struggles in a doctor's life and career, and found herself unqualified to comment. 'One step at a time,' she said quietly.

Maahi thought about her own life. She wished she had that kind of passion and vision for her career. Laila had graduated a couple of months ago—after the first six months of theory and practical training, she had interned at a five-star hotel for the last six months, which was a course requirement. She then took up a day job at a hotshot bakery. But the closest she got to baking there was handling the packaging of baked goods and desserts. Her job was mostly keeping track of stock levels, filling out inventory and managing production sheets. It was taking much of her time, and even though she was making money and the work environment was excellent, she wasn't enjoying her actual work. She had been working at Cozy Coffee less and less. Maahi still had about two years of college left, but she couldn't help but get nervous.

'Wow, quite a mood we've got going here, huh? One basically dead person on the couch, and then there's the two of us, sitting here all depressed about our lives.' Siddhant laughed. 'We really know how to entertain our guests.'

'We sure do!' Eshaan agreed. 'Didn't you say we were going to play Mario Kart?'

'Yeah, let's do it. Alia, you want to play?'

There was no sound from the lump under the pillows. They were all on the same L-shaped couch—Maahi between Alia and Siddhant, Eshaan on the other side of Siddhant. Eshaan set up the game and Siddhant taught Maahi the controls.

'Who do you want to be?' Eshaan asked Maahi.

'I don't know. I've never played this before. Which one should I pick?'

'Be Toad.'

'Yeah, Sid's right. Toad's awesome.'

Maahi couldn't figure out whether they were making fun of her or being serious. She picked Mario; it seemed like a safe bet. Siddhant chose Yoshi and Eshaan chose Toad. Maahi wanted to be Toad now, but didn't want to say anything.

They were playing on Nintendo Wii, a console she had no experience with. Sarthak had a PlayStation 3 at home, which she was familiar with, and she'd also played games on Rohit's Xbox. Even though Siddhant taught her the controls, she kept messing up and landing in ditches. Eshaan kept drifting and slipstreaming his cart expertly and Siddhant performed spectacular mid-air stunts and wheelies on his motorcycle.

'Your controller looks different from mine!'

'Yes, ma'am. Mine's the Nintendo GameCube controller—which is awesome!' Eshaan bragged.

'That's unfair,' Maahi complained.

'Your controller is easier, if that helps,' Siddhant said.

'Fuck you. Yours has a steering wheel, when you don't even have a cart! Who uses a steering wheel to ride a bike?'

'I gave you the classic controller, so I'm stuck with this! I was only trying to help you out because you're a beginner.'

'Beginner, my foot. I'm going to kick your ass,' Maahi said, not looking away from the TV screen.

'Whoa!' the guys hooted together.

Despite her promise and intention, no matter how hard she tried, Maahi couldn't kick anyone's ass. The rest of the evening was spent with the boys making fun of her, repeatedly beating her at each game. Maahi was terrible in the beginning, bumping into everything in her way, most times going out of her way to bump into things. She came twelfth in the first couple of rounds. Siddhant was nice enough to take the blame for it, saying he picked the wrong levels for a beginner, and Maahi told him that she knew he did that on purpose so she could come last, and he would come first—and that would be good for his ego.

Maahi stopped using the excuse of never having played the game before and concentrated very hard in the third round. She finished fifth, beating Eshaan, who came in seventh and Siddhant came first. She let herself go in the fourth and final round and finished tenth, while Eshaan came in third and Siddhant came in first, as was the trend, something that annoyed Maahi, but she felt strangely proud of at the same time.

'Oh, I didn't realize what time it was,' Maahi exclaimed, when she looked at her phone.

'You need to be home?' Siddhant asked.

'Yeah, it's getting late. I have to go all the way to Vaishali.'

'Oh, yeah, that's right. I'll walk you to the Metro station. You take M.G. Road, right?'

'Yeah,' Maahi said. She said her goodbyes to Eshaan and the unconscious Alia, and walked out with Siddhant. It had been a fun evening, despite her nervousness in the beginning. They talked about her poor performance at Mario Kart on their way to the Metro, and Maahi accused him of being an egotistical loser.

'Well, I think we could all see who the real loser there was. Quite clearly.' Siddhant laughed.

'You're so mean.'

'As if you're not!'

'I don't know why I'm even talking to you,' Maahi said, shaking her head and looking away.

'Come on! You know I'm only kidding. I'm not mean for real.' Siddhant put his arm around her back and touched her waist for a second.

Maahi laughed with him, trying to hide her blush.

'I had fun,' she said when they reached the station.

'Me too,' Siddhant said. 'Safe to assume we'll hang out again? Unless you're planning to never see my face again.'

'We'll see,' Maahi said, giving him a quick hug before leaving. They both knew they were going to see each other again soon.

Siddhant texted her later that night, asking if she had reached home safely. They chatted for hours. They had been texting before that too, but seeing each other outside of Cozy Coffee really opened the communication channels between them. Maahi went to sleep with a silly smile on her face, still feeling his slight touch on her waist.

11

'I don't know what! Everything was okay,' Maahi said, her elbows on the counter, her face in her hands.

'Something must have happened. Are you sure you didn't say anything stupid?' Laila asked. 'Maybe later on? Something that might've offended him?'

'No. I mean … I don't think so.' Maahi tried to go back to the conversations she had had with Siddhant. She didn't remember having said anything offensive to him or him reacting to something in a strange manner. As far as she could tell, everything was okay between them. Not just okay, things were actually going great. He was attentive, and interested in her, asking how her day was, talking about his own—Maahi thought it was on the way to becoming something special. It definitely seemed to have the potential to.

Until, all of a sudden, he stopped texting her first, and then he stopped texting her altogether. It reached a point where he was only responding to her texts, his responses stiff and precise. Maahi felt like she was talking to a wall. For the first couple of days, it really hurt. Realizing he wasn't into her, facing and accepting the rejection brought back her insecurities, making her feel like she wasn't good enough. Then they tried to evaluate why that happened. Why, if he was interested to begin with, did he stop being interested now?

'Well then, I don't know. Men are weird. Maybe he's just a fuckboy. Maybe this is his routine—giving attention to make sure you notice him and then pulling back,' Laila said. She was wearing a cloth headband that went from the base of her neck to the top of her forehead. It was grey with off-white flower patterns—quite unlike her usual style, but she made it look less girlish by pulling her hair back in a high ponytail. Her face was clear of all makeup except for a dull-red lipstick. That and her already perfect arched eyebrows gave her the edge she carried with her.

Maahi nodded. 'Maybe.'

'I'm sorry, love. I know you don't want to hear it. Hell, I don't want to say it. But I really don't know what's up. He seemed okay to me,' Laila said. She put an arm around Maahi and squeezed her.

Maahi let her head fall on the counter.

'Come on, man. Don't let him do this to you,' Laila said. 'You can't let this get to you. You're better than that, you know that, right? You know that.'

Maahi got off her stool and stretched her legs. 'I need to bake,' she said. 'Maybe that'll help.'

'Yes! What do you need?'

'Can I bake the cookies today? You take over the cupcakes?' Maahi asked. 'I just can't today … Siddhant, he used to come here for my cupcakes…'

'No. Maahi, you can't do this. I won't let you. You can't stop what you love doing for a guy you've known for what, six weeks?'

'Let it go, Laila. I just can't, today. It's not like I'm giving up on life. I need some time—a day. It's not that big a deal.'

Laila stood in front of her with her arms folded over her chest, studying her, as if mad at her for being sad. Maahi understood that Laila cared about her, but she hoped her friend would let her be a normal human being and *feel* for one day. She really liked Siddhant. She was developing feelings for him, and it hurt that he didn't feel the same about her.

'Okay?' Maahi asked.

'Yeah,' Laila said. 'As long as you're fine. I just don't like seeing you like this. It makes me sad, which pisses me off. Anyway, I was planning on almond meal coconut cookies with chocolate chips. Would you like to bake that?'

Maahi looked at her friend, so tiny and trying to be so tough. A small smile crept on her face. 'Only if you bake it with me.'

Maahi's mid-term exams were close, and she still had to figure out where to get notes from and what the syllabus for the tests was. She had been skipping classes recently. Not many—just a few, to work with Laila at the coffee shop, which they were slowly turning into a bakery, or at least they would've if CJ hadn't interfered. They had really grown passionate about baking and decorating cakes, and went for elaborate designs, spending multiple days on one cake.

A couple of customers, impressed by their cookies and cupcakes, had inquired if they baked custom cakes on order and Laila had lied through her teeth and said yes. Things escalated and they found themselves drowning in cake orders. Soon enough, CJ got a whiff of the situation and cakes were banned from Cozy Coffee. CJ wanted the place to simply sell coffee. It made sense to Maahi, but Laila didn't see it. Her logic was 'why settle for less when we can get more?' CJ's was 'less is more'. Maahi chose to stay out of it. Ten days of baking cakes had really put her behind on her coursework and Maahi was panicking.

She decided to meet her teacher later that day and ask him for guidance, book references and such. She sat through the third class of the day, trying to make sense of what they were being taught. She checked her phone once the class ended to find a text.

Laila: Your boy's here.
Maahi: He's not my boy.

She resumed her day normally. She had neither the time nor the energy to deal with that right now. She wondered why Laila was at the coffee shop that early. She herself was supposed to go there in two hours from then.

Maahi finished her work at college and took her time getting there. There was no way Siddhant would still be there, but she didn't want to take any chances. She wondered briefly why he had come by, and what he would've done if she'd been there, but tried not to think about it.

Still, when Maahi reached the coffee shop, she felt a weight at the pit of her stomach when she looked around and couldn't see Siddhant there. She liked seeing him around, had even become used to it, expectant of it. She reluctantly admitted to herself that she missed him.

Laila met her eye and read her feelings. She stuck out her lower lip at Maahi, a what-can-we-do expression. Laila even tousled her hair when she got behind the counter, which Maahi thought was weird because she wasn't exactly her child, even though it sometimes felt that way.

Late that night, when Maahi got off the Metro at Vaishali, she received a message from Siddhant: 'Hey'. On her walk to her house, Maahi contemplated whether she should respond to it or not, and if yes, what she should say. She reached home, changed, had dinner with her parents—Sarthak was out group studying with his friends—and got into bed before responding a well-thought-out, calculated text message: 'Hey'.

Siddhant responded within minutes: 'How are you?'

Maahi: Good.

Siddhant: What's going on?

Maahi: College, coffee shop, the usual.

Siddhant: Hmm. So listen, I realize I need to apologize for my behaviour earlier. There was just a lot of shit that I've been going through, still am, and I didn't know where this would fit in.

Maahi: Nah, it's alright. You don't owe me anything.

Siddhant: Maybe not, but you deserve better. And I'm sorry if I hurt you at any point. Trust me, that was never my intention.

Maahi wanted to trust him, but something held her back. Maybe it was the fear of getting hurt again, maybe it was Laila's voice repeating the definition of fuckboy in her head or maybe she just didn't want to hope again.

Siddhant: I understand if you don't want to talk to me anymore. But I would really appreciate another chance.

She didn't know how to respond. She thought about calling Laila up immediately, but decided against it. She had to follow her instincts on this one; no one else could give her an answer. Maahi thought back to the evening she had spent with Siddhant, playing Mario Kart with him and his roommate while his other roommate was passed out on the couch. She remembered how Siddhant smiled surreptitiously when she came last in the first couple of rounds. She remembered how he touched her waist while walking her to the Metro station. She could still feel his fingers there.

She hadn't seen him since that night. It had been over two weeks, and regardless of what had happened and how hurt she had been by his behaviour, when she thought about seeing him again, she felt excited. She texted him back: 'Okay'.

꽃

Siddhant dropped by the coffee shop to say hi late the next evening, just before closing. Maahi wanted to get under the counter and meet him on the other side, in the hope of a half hug, or any kind of physical reassurance of his presence. But she had to settle for his lopsided grin. The first thing Maahi noticed was how worn out he looked.

'Hey,' he said, stopping in front of the counter.
'You look so tired.'
'Oh, thanks. You see me and the first thing you say is "God, you look shitty". Nice!'

'*No*,' Maahi said. 'No. I didn't mean it like that. I was just saying, well, that you do look like you haven't slept in a while.'

'Because I haven't. The internship's been crazy and I have so much studying to do. There's time for little else, including sleep.'

'Showering too?' Laila asked from behind Maahi.

'You must be Laila. I'm Siddhant.' He offered her his hand. 'I've heard a lot about you.'

'Can't say the same.' Laila shook his hand.

Maahi laughed nervously. She was afraid Laila would scare Siddhant off. 'She's being mean for no reason. It's just her personality. Don't take it personally,' she said.

'That's alright. It's not as if you're any less mean!' Siddhant said.

'Ha!' Laila laughed loudly. 'See what happens when you turn against your friend? Now Sid and I are going to gang up against you.'

'Oh God. It's not like you both individually aren't enough pain for me already; I don't think I can handle the two of you together.'

'Nothing you can do. You chose this life.' Laila shrugged dramatically.

'No escape,' Siddhant added.

'I feel so attacked right now!' Maahi complained.

'Not for much longer. I'm going to bounce now. Are you coming?' Laila asked.

Maahi looked from her to Siddhant, who said, 'I would like to hang out with you for a bit, unless that's inconvenient?'

'No, she can stay,' Laila answered for Maahi, turning towards her. 'Don't stay out too late and text me when you get home, okay?'

'Yes, Mom.'

'Good girl. And it was nice to meet you, Sid.' Laila squeezed Maahi quickly and got her stuff to leave.

'Pleasure,' Siddhant said.

Laila left a silence behind her. Maahi and Siddhant looked at each other, smiled and looked away. Things had just begun to get awkward when Siddhant asked, 'What was today's cupcake?'

'drunken butter rum.'

'You're kidding!'

'Nope. For real,' Maahi said. 'And you missed it—it was quite a hit. We sold out!'

'I don't get to taste it? I can't believe this! Damn it—that sounds delicious.' In that moment, Siddhant looked like a child. Maahi wondered if he was pretending to care about her cupcakes or really did care about them, but his face left little doubt in her mind.

'I can bake you a fresh batch.'

'Really?' Siddhant's face lit up in a wide smile.

'You're such a child,' Maahi said. On impulse, she leaned over the counter and pressed his nose with her finger lightly.

'And you're so awesome,' Siddhant said, following her to the kitchen.

'You're just saying that because I'm baking cupcakes for you!' Maahi turned on the lights and gathered her baking gear. She laid down a counter mat and placed a large mixing bowl on it. She took out a set of measuring cups, whisks and spatulas, and laid out a cooling rack next to the oven. 'Can you hand me those baking sheets, from the top drawer?'

'This one?' Siddhant asked, showing her a set of three baking sheets of different sizes.

'The two bigger ones. Do you want to take some home with you? For Eshaan and Alia, assuming she's alive, of course.' Maahi smiled.

'Yeah, she survived somehow. Alive and well. I'm sure they'd love some cupcakes. Who wouldn't?'

'You're just being fake at this point. So obvious.'

'I'm not! I really do love cupcakes. *Your* cupcakes.' Siddhant brought the baking sheets to her and placed them on the counter. He stood against the granite platform, close to where Maahi was standing facing the counter on his right.

'You see—right there? You could've wrapped it up at "I love cupcakes"—honest, believable; but you had to take it further and ruin it.' Maahi laughed. She measured butter and sugar and began beating them.

'I'm being honest. It's not my fault you don't know how to take a compliment, or even recognize one.'

Maahi looked up from her mixing bowl at him.

'Why do you think I came here all the time? It's not like there's no other place I could get a cupcake in Delhi and Gurgaon. Hell, I wasn't even into cupcakes that much. It's these,' Siddhant motioned to her baking gear in general, 'that I've become addicted to. Although I guess you're right. It's not just the cupcakes, it's you too. You with your beautiful eyes. I come here for both.'

Maahi blushed and bent her head lower, busying herself with cracking eggs and adding them to the bowl, trying to hide herself from him, which was difficult with him standing less than two feet away.

'See? No idea how to take a compliment. And I really do admire the work you do. I mean, God, I could never do it. It's fascinating to see how your brain works, coming up with ideas, mixing up these crazy ingredients together. I can never forget the one that you made with pickle and ice cream. Or the one with Eggs Benedict on top—that one didn't even look like a cupcake! Where are you getting these? That crazy head of yours. You're not afraid to try anything. I know you don't want to hear it—but it's quite amazing.' Siddhant pushed the hair back from her face and tucked it behind her ear. 'Are you going to speak, like, ever?'

His fingers were still behind her ear. Maahi cleared her throat. 'Cupcake moulds,' she said, pulling open the cabinet on her left. 'Which ones do you want? You get to pick from these.'

Siddhant chuckled to himself. Maahi didn't look at him.

'I'll take the round ones. I don't really care about the shape though,' Siddhant said, tongue-in-cheek.

'You're terrible!'

'What? I'm just talking about the cupcakes. I only care about the taste. What did you think I was saying?'

'You *know* what,' Maahi said. She measured flour and added it to her mixing bowl, along with baking soda and salt.

'You've got a dirty mind. Appearances can be misleading, I'm learning.'

Maahi changed the topic. 'Now, tell me what kind you want. The drunken butter rum or some other kind? Let me see what we've got here ... I can do something with coffee, or green tea. I've got almonds, pistachios, honey butter, dates, sprinkles—I've got a lot of stuff. What do you want?' She felt warmed by his compliments and wasn't ashamed of almost bragging at this point.

'Surprise me.' The lopsided smile was in place.

'How about almond cupcakes with whipped almond buttercream frosting? Or, ooh, we could try coffee cupcakes with whipped chocolate frosting? Seeing the child that you are though, I'm almost game to try Oreo cupcakes with Oreo buttercream frosting.'

'Works for me. I love Oreos.'

'What a surprise,' Maahi said, shaking her head. 'I love having you as my child. I could totally get used to this.'

'Oh yeah? Don't challenge me—I can grow up real fast.' Siddhant was looking at her with fake seriousness.

'God, you're shameless, aren't you?'

'Don't pretend that you don't love it.'

'Seriously, stop,' Maahi said. 'Let me concentrate.'

Siddhant brought his finger to his lips and shut up. Maahi couldn't look away from the finger, and his lips, but forced herself to tear her eyes away. Siddhant behaved himself for the rest of the night. Maahi had mixed feelings about that. She was productive—the Oreo cupcakes came out great—but she missed his teasing eyes and cheesy lines.

When she was finished baking, they laid out the batch on the cooling rack, waiting to be decorated, and set to cleaning. The simple task of wiping down the counter and putting everything back where it belonged felt oddly satisfying. Siddhant helped her with it. They settled into a comfortable partnership—quiet and harmonious.

Maahi topped a dozen cupcakes with Oreo buttercream frosting and boxed them for Siddhant. She went out to the counter to get a paper bag for the box and Siddhant followed her, turning off the kitchen lights behind them. They walked towards the door together. When Maahi reached out for the doorknob, Siddhant held her hand and stopped her. She turned and looked up at him.

'I need a proper good night,' Siddhant said.

Maahi's chest fell and rose again, higher.

Siddhant rested both his hands on her waist and pulled her up into his arms. He bent towards her and Maahi rose on her toes to meet him. His open lips touched hers and they stayed there, very still, for a sweet, torturous moment before he let his lips close around hers. He pulled her closer and she found herself cocooned in his warm embrace as he kissed her.

Maahi rested her palm on his cheek, feeling his stubble, her fingers tracing his jaw, coming to rest at his chin. Siddhant's lips moved around hers and she responded, sucking on his lower lip. She dropped her mouth down to his chin, held it between her teeth lightly and bit. They laughed softly. Maahi hid her face under his neck. He kissed the top of her head.

Like every time he touched her, long after they had broken their embrace, walked out of the coffee shop and said their second, and much paler, goodbye at the Metro station, Maahi felt herself in Siddhant's arms. She could still feel his chest against her face. She could still feel his soft heartbeat, and taste his lips.

12

They didn't put a label on it. They didn't call it anything. They didn't talk about it at all. They took it one day at a time, one date at a time. Over the next few weeks, Maahi got caught up in preparation for her final semester and Siddhant with his. They managed to find time for each other, making sure they met at least twice a week. When it got harder for plans to work out, Siddhant dropped by the coffee shop for a hello and a cupcake. They enjoyed each other's company, talking to each other, sharing the events of their days with each other before falling asleep.

Just to be able to talk to Siddhant about her day was a huge blessing for Maahi. She was having a really hard time at college. Although she had submitted all her assignments on time, she was still behind on her preparation for exams. And it wasn't as if she couldn't sit down, get her shit together and do it. It was that she didn't want to.

When she looked at her syllabus, she felt lost. She questioned what she was doing. When she looked at her life from an outsider's perspective, she saw a girl trying to do something out of a misplaced sense of responsibility, to make her parents happy. She could keep doing it, continue her education, get a degree. But then what?

Does she continue living the farce and get a job in market research or economic consultancy and spend her life analysing credit and finance? When she looked at her future, at that life, she saw nothing but darkness. It wasn't for her. She wasn't meant for that.

She wanted to *create*. She wanted the satisfaction of putting together something from scratch, by starting with odd bits and pieces and ending up with a tangible end product, something she could see, smell, touch and taste. That's the person she was, not someone who sat at the office and punched numbers.

She continued to go to college, study business economics, score decent grades and keep her parents and the neighbourhood aunties happy. But it had an expiration date. The conversation she needed to have with her parents would be a tough one, possibly the toughest of her life. But if she kept quiet and continued what she was doing, she would have to have the same conversation three more semesters later. There was no escape. It made sense to her to save some time and tuition fee while she was at it.

Yet, something held her back. Maybe it was the fear of knowing she would have nothing to fall back on. No degree to find her a job if she ever needed support. Maybe it was the thought of seeing herself working at the coffee shop forever, eventually hating it, resenting it for being the thing that made her give up her safe degree. Maybe it was the thought that she would never be able to earn respect in her parents' eyes, being a twelfth-pass girl, making them the target of all sorts of questions and comments in their society and neighbourhood.

It saddened her to not be able to do what she wanted to the most—bake. Her parents had always assumed it was a hobby that would come to an end when she grew up and got a real job after college. But what if the meaning of growing up for her was the realization of what she really wanted to do with her life? And what if it didn't align with her parents' hopes and expectations?

She had to think it through before saying anything to them. They would ask questions—many, many questions—that she wouldn't have answers to if she went in unprepared. Maahi looked at her course books with a sigh. She really didn't want to study for her exams, but failing the semester would only put her parents in a worse mood and she couldn't have that on top of everything.

She knocked on Sarthak's door twice before pushing it open.

'What's up?' her brother slipped his headphones down to his neck and asked. He was sitting at his study table, several tabs open on the laptop in front of him.

'What do you want to do with your life?' Maahi asked, slumping down on the edge of his bed, next to his chair.

He rotated it towards her and laughed. 'What? What do you mean?'

'I mean after twelfth. Next year.'

'Career wise? I told you—mechanical engineering. I'm confused between aerospace and acoustical, but I'm not too worried about it yet. We'll see,' Sarthak said, shrugging.

'Ugh, I hate you,' Maahi moaned and fell back on his bed.

'What's up with you? Why all the drama?' Sarthak was laughing, which made Maahi madder.

'My *life*.'

'What does that mean?'

'I'm fucked. I'm fucked, I'm fucked,' Maahi kept repeating.

⌘

'Is everything okay?' Laila asked, setting her bag down on Sarthak's bed, next to Maahi's limp body. Laila sat down beside her and shook her. 'Maahi! What's going on with you?'

Maahi hadn't moved or said anything in a while. She just lay there quietly, and every time Sarthak asked her a question, she repeated 'I'm fucked' under her breath. Sarthak had tried to ignore her in the beginning, but got annoyed and concerned after the first hour or so. That's when he called Laila for help.

'I'm fucked,' Maahi said, opening her eyes.

'What? How? What happened?' Laila's perfect eyebrows burrowed together to form a small hill in the centre.

'I'm fucked, I'm fucked, I'm fucked.'

'Dude. Stop being weird,' Laila said.

'Seriously. You're scaring me now,' Sarthak added.

'I'm fuc—'

'Say it one more time and I swear to God I'm going to slap you across your stupid face,' Laila said. Maahi shut up. 'Now, be a normal person and tell me what's up. Did Sid do something?'

'Who's Sid?' Sarthak asked.

'Shh! He doesn't *know*,' Maahi said, sitting up.

'Well, if you don't speak I'm going to keep asking questions. So just tell us what's up,' Laila said.

Maahi took a long breath and released it, slumping down, her head bent in dejection. 'I don't know where to start, what to do, or if this is even possible or will forever stay a dream. But I feel like if I don't do it now, if *we* don't do this now, we'll never do it. So I'm going to ask you, and you don't have to feel any kind of pressure, because I'm planning to do what I love, what I want and I want you to do what you want too. Although, what you say more or less decides whether I get to do what I love and want or not. So, respond in one word, make it quick and painless.' Both Laila and Sarthak were looking at her with bored, annoyed but somewhat curious expressions. Maahi held Laila's eyes and asked, 'Will you open a bakery with me?'

'YAAS!' Laila jumped to her feet. 'Oh my God, *yes*! Of course. I've been thinking about this since forever, but you had your college and you're basically a kid—'

'Hey, I'm twenty-one. Almost twenty-two!'

'—and I didn't know if you were serious about baking as a career. But God, *yes*. Let's do it. I get to quit my job, we get to quit Cozy Coffee and bake in an actual bakery, with an actual *cookie of the day* and *cupcake of the day*, we'll have our own space, our own rules, there won't be anyone holding us back and we can experiment and do what we want. We'll have a cool logo and a cool name and T-shirts and caps and business cards. Oh, I thought you'd never ask!' When Laila's outburst of excitement simmered down, she sat on the bed and squeezed Maahi tight. 'You'll officially be my work wife.'

Maahi felt exhilarated and relieved and terrified. She hugged Laila back, thinking back to the first time she had met her, when Laila had tried to sell her the *cookie of the day*. She would never have imagined how her life would turn upside down, it all starting with that accidental meeting. When she tried to see what her future could be like, she didn't see darkness anymore. She saw hope.

'Umm, ladies? Someone needs to tell Ma and Papa,' Sarthak said and rotated his chair back to his computer screen, headphones on.

They broke their hug and looked at each other, eyes wide.

᯽

Maahi had expected Laila to be every parent's nightmare—with her constant cursing and no-fucks-given attitude—the first time she had introduced her to her family. She was pleasantly surprised to find that her parents loved Laila, who seemed like a capable, sorted young woman to them. They liked her enough to overlook her black, white and everything-in-between wardrobe and she was decent enough to watch her language around them.

So when they decided to tell her parents about their bakery, they agreed that it would be best if Laila was the one who led the conversation. But before they did that, they laid out the building blocks of their bakery. They assigned themselves roles—Laila was in charge of finding funding and space, and Maahi was taking care of creating the business plan and calculating start-up cost to begin with. They would take care of pricing, menu, purchasing appliances and equipment, design and marketing once they got to that stage.

They were in the pre-planning phase of their bakery, but even so, they created a PowerPoint presentation and brought a couple dozen assorted cupcakes and cookies with them as pacifier and proof of their talent. As always, Rohit's wide network of connections didn't let Maahi down. His uncle was in the culinary business in the outskirts of Delhi and had agreed to guide them. Anil uncle was acting as their mentor, helping out with the general directions and answering all their questions. They felt much safer with someone experienced on their team.

Laila also thought that asking her mother to come to their *meeting* would be a good idea. Her mom had accepted the fact that her daughter was a free spirit, a self-made, independent child who would anyway do whatever the hell she wanted to. She hadn't been overjoyed at the idea of Laila quitting her day job to work on this start-up, but she got on board when they assured her that Laila would keep at least one of her jobs until they got funding.

So on D-Day, they came armed with a presentation of their vision and mission, cookies and cupcakes and Laila's mom.

It was a Saturday night, and the Kothari family had invited Laila and her mother over for dinner, a plan orchestrated by Maahi. After dinner, they went back to the living room, where Maahi was bringing them dessert. Everyone took position—Laila's mom opposite Maahi's parents, Laila next to her. Sarthak sat back with a hidden grin, waiting for the drama. Maahi could almost see the popcorn bucket in his lap.

'Who is going to eat all of these? There are only so many of us!' Maahi's mother said when Maahi brought two trays, one filled with cupcakes and the other with cookies.

'I'm on it,' Sarthak said. Maahi glared at him. He picked up a cookie and retreated.

'Our daughters are so talented. I'm so proud,' Laila's mom opened.

'Yes, we simply adore their baking. Maahi brings these back from the coffee shop all the time,' Maahi's mom was quick to agree.

Maahi panicked and blurted out, 'Which reminds me—Ma, Papa, I have something to tell you. And I request you to please hear us out before you say anything. I know that you have certain expectations from me, and I want to keep you happy, but I don't know if I can do this any—'

'*Maahi*,' Laila said, firmly pulling her down and making her sit. She muttered, 'Stick to the script.'

'Right,' Maahi murmured. She looked down at her feet and sat like that the rest of the time as Laila explained the situation to her parents. She stole glances at her mom every few minutes. Her dad was quiet too, which scared Maahi.

Laila's mom shared her concerns, eventually explaining how she got over them and decided to give the kids a chance. Laila went through their plans for the business and projected timelines. She finished everything they had planned on saying, and asked Maahi's parents if they had any questions, neither of whom had spoken the entire time.

Maahi dared to look up, mostly out of nervousness. She tried to guess their response and was met with blank expressions.

'Are you saying you will drop out of college?' Papa asked.

'*Again*?' Ma added.

'Not if you don't want me to,' Maahi said, dejected. She had really hoped they would understand. But if staying in college meant they would be okay with her starting a business, she was willing to make that compromise.

'But Cookies + Cupcakes is not a side thing. It's their *main* thing,' Sarthak said. Maahi looked at him in surprise. 'I'm sure it'd need way more attention than a part-time job.'

'Sarthak's right,' Laila joined in. 'We're serious about this. This is going to be our career, and we're going to give it our everything. At least we plan to.'

It was in vain. They tried to convince them with everything they had, but her parents remained hell-bent on Maahi staying in college and finishing her education. Maahi made a point that even if she finished college and got a degree, it would just be a worthless piece of paper, as she didn't plan to do anything with it. The time she would spend pursuing that piece of paper would take precious time away from their start-up. Her parents said they would rather have her get that piece of paper than not.

The conversation went off-track when her parents kept arguing about her education instead of discussing the bakery. Laila and Sarthak kept trying for a long time, but Maahi became quiet. She accepted defeat. She saw the look in her father's eyes. He wasn't going to change his mind. Her mother didn't even try to listen to anything anyone was saying. She repeatedly voiced her concern over having a twelfth-pass daughter with no future. When she asked Laila's mom how she could get on board with their daughters' ridiculous whims, Maahi decided it was time for Laila and her mother to leave. She didn't want Ma to say anything to Laila's mom that would offend or hurt her.

When Laila squeezed her at the door, tears finally escaped Maahi's eyes. She stayed in Laila's arms for a minute to compose herself, wiped her tears and went back inside.

When she returned to the living room, they weren't there. Their bedroom door was closed. Maahi turned off the living room lights and went to her room, a lump in her throat.

Hours later, she heard a knock on her door. It was soft, but unmistakable. Her heartbeat fastened. Was it her mom, there to lay down more rules for her to follow? Or her dad, to tell her how she had been a disappointment to them? She contemplated ignoring it, pretending to be asleep, but at the same time, if they were there to tell her that she wasn't allowed this pointless pursuit, she'd rather not wait to find out. She got up and opened the door.

'Couldn't sleep?' Sarthak asked.

'What do you think?'

'Get dressed.'

Maahi didn't question him. In the cold November night, they rode to Gurgaon on his bike. Laila and Siddhant were waiting for them at the coffee shop. Maahi looked at Siddhant, who smiled at her, a smile of condolence. Laila looked dejected. No one said anything. Maahi didn't let anyone hug her; she was afraid she would break down. She walked right inside to do the only thing she could to help her get over some of her frustration. Laila took a step back and let her do the baking. Both Sarthak and Siddhant sat on either side of the counter, close to Maahi, yet keeping a safe distance.

They slowly began talking, mostly Laila talking to Siddhant, and then to Sarthak. Eventually, Sarthak and Siddhant started talking to each other. The circumstances under which they were meeting for the first time weren't ideal, but they did their best to cheer Maahi up, without actually talking to her or getting in her way.

Maahi was making banana walnut cupcakes with a simple cream cheese frosting. It was only once she started beating the eggs that she began to relax. She didn't talk much that night, but she was actively involved in the conversation, listening to everything, observing how her three favourite people interacted with each other.

She even smiled once, when she removed the baking sheets from the oven. She brought the golden-brown cupcakes to the cooling rack, taking in the heavenly aroma of the life she craved.

Part Four

13

Maahi went over their pitch presentation one more time, while Laila sat next to her and peeked in. She was overwhelmed by the time she reached the end of it. All this preparation, instead of adding confidence, made her nervous. The more content they put into their presentation, the more room they created for cross questioning. Being rejected those last few times did nothing to help her anxiety.

'What? Why do you have that look?' Laila asked.

'I don't know…'

'No. Don't even start second guessing at this point. We've been on this for six fucking months and I don't know how much longer I can take it. We need funding, *now*.'

'I've been on this with you for these six months too. Only I know how I've managed to manage this alongside my fourth semester. I understand your frustration and trust me, I share it. But do you really think we should add these slides about our possible competitors? We don't even have a space yet. How do we know these bakeries are going to be our competitors?' Maahi asked.

'Then what should we do? How is this pitch complete without talking about our competition? How do we show them what's unique about what we are offering if we don't compare it with others?' Laila asked. She ran her fingers through her short hair, starting at the base of her neck, going up. She pulled at the ends before releasing them.

'You're going to go bald if you keep doing that.'

'I don't care. As long as we have funding.'

'We will! If we stop pitching the entire business plan! Listen, I know we need to have a detailed business plan, but we need that *if* we are asked. Why can't we just have our vision, what we're offering, target market, revenue model, sales and marketing strategies, and financials in the pitch?' Maahi ticked off points on her fingers. She pointed to the OneNote file open on her laptop and said, 'We can always have other details—the competition, traction and validation, the use of funds and all of that in the actual business plan—when we know we have their interest and they're listening when we talk to them? If we mention all of this in the elevator pitch, they're going to get frustrated. They just want us to get to the point. What did Anil uncle say? Short and succinct. Remember?'

'Short and succinct,' Laila repeated. She looked at the computer screen. 'Short and succinct.'

'One page. We only have ten minutes.' Maahi deleted the unnecessary details from the pitch presentation and started moving the content around the page as Laila sat watching. 'And I read an article online that said a pitch should be able to stand alone without us presenting it. So we're going to have to remove these bullet points and finish these sentences.'

'I don't know how you're doing this,' Laila muttered.

'Sometimes I don't know either. But when you panic and go a bit loony, someone has to hold the fort. And in a two-people team, that responsibility inevitably falls on me.'

'Right. You have to step up—no other option.'

'Yep.' Maahi adjusted the font size and moved back to observe how it looked on the page. 'Looks good?'

'Not bad,' Laila said.

'Come on. I hate when you sound so low. Cheer up!'

'How? We've literally tried everything. Angel investors, venture capitalists, banks, equity investors—what else can we do?'

'Keep at it,' Maahi said. She put her laptop away and stretched her back. 'That's the only thing we can do. And not lose hope. The only two things we can do at this point.'

'I can't live on my Cozy Coffee and home-baking income forever, Maahi. I can't.'

'I can't either. Good thing we don't have to. It's going to happen.'

'Soon?' Laila asked. 'Because I really don't know how much longer I can take this. And it's kind of creeping me out how calm you are about this.'

'I'm really not calm. Not at all. I don't remember the last time I slept for more than a couple of hours. Siddhant was just saying last week that he's getting seriously concerned about my health. This is the only thing I think about. But I have faith. I don't know … I know it's going to happen. We have everything. We worked so hard on the business plan—the research, the plan itself—and it's at a point where there are no leaks, we just need someone whose vision aligns with ours, and we have everything else.'

Laila nodded, still looking sombre.

'Trust me on this, Laila. You have to. You can't lose hope. Hell, you're the one who came up with most of this in the first place! And before you say it—I know it hasn't worked yet. But it only has to work once. We've only learned and become better with every time we've been rejected. It's not all for nothing. Our business plan has improved several times from the first one we came up with, and it's all because of the feedback we've got along with the rejections.'

Laila sat with her legs folded under her in the middle of Maahi's bed, looking completely lost and out of place—in her grey tank top and black shorts, against the red-and-green floral bed sheet. Her curly hair was no longer tied in a bun on top of her head. She had got it cut down to just above her shoulders, tendrils of curls framing her face in layers. Maahi missed her bun phase, but thought the pixie suited her well.

It was in quite a contrast with Maahi's hair, which had grown significantly, reaching down to her waist. Laila's hair was much darker, almost a midnight black, compared to Maahi's coffee brown. Laila sometimes straightened her hair to make her look tougher, but it didn't work, neither did her colourless outfits.

Laila finally spoke. 'Ugh, I hate when you're right. Also, who the fuck asked you to grow up and become this career woman or whatever the fuck you're trying to pretend to be?'

Maahi laughed. 'Now you're just hating on me!'

'You deserve it.'

'Why!'

'Because you're the one who showed me this dream. You come in—the wide-eyed child all enthusiastic about baking and learning. I always planned to bake, sometimes even thought about setting up my own bakery, but not *right now*.' Laila narrowed her eyes. 'You with your experiments and shit. I had never had anyone to do all that with before and oh,

Maahi, why? You showed me this dream. I even quit my day job—and here we are, with nothing to show for it. It's still a dream, it's still far, far away.'

'You sound like a regretful wife, realizing you never should've married me. Never should've said yes when I proposed!' Maahi chuckled.

'Exactly! I never should've said yes!'

'Well, I, on the other hand, am glad you did.' Maahi pulled Laila to her in a bear hug. 'And I know it's going to happen for us. I know it. You think it's easy for me? Taking a stand, doing what I want, going against my parents' wishes, almost dropping out of college for the second time? You've seen all of it happen. You know how hard it's been. And that's exactly why we can't give up now. I can't afford to give up now.'

'Yeah,' Laila pulled away from Maahi and said. 'If you drop out now and our bakery plan fails, Aunty will probably send you back to college to study electrical engineering or shit like that. At least I have a bachelor's degree and my mom is on board with Cookies + Cupcakes. You're the twelfth pass loser with no fallback options.'

Maahi shook her head grimly. 'Thanks for pointing that out. It wasn't enough to just live it. Hearing it is always a pleasure.'

'You're welcome,' Laila replied cheekily.

Maahi was working on the design of their logo when Sarthak knocked on her door, later that evening. 'Come in,' she said, knowing full well that he would've even if she hadn't asked him to.

'Busy?' he asked, sitting down on her bean bag.

Maahi swung her chair around to face him, laptop in hand. She turned the screen to Sarthak. 'How does this look?'

'Meh.' Sarthak shrugged.

'Thanks. I've only been working on it for like, five hours.'

'It's going to represent your brand for as long as the brand exists, so yeah, let's *not* look at the big picture here.'

'You're so annoying,' Maahi sulked.

'Just because I'm right, I'm annoying. Why did you ask me if you didn't want to know?'

'God, stop lecturing me. Why are you here anyway?'

'You only have to tolerate me for one more month and you can't even handle that?' Sarthak said, his face sullen.

'Oh, the drama!' Maahi said, but she felt sad thinking about her brother moving away next month. Never having had the reputation of being serious about anything, Sarthak surprised everyone with his JEE results. Maahi always believed that if he got his shit together and concentrated on something he really wanted, there would be no stopping him. Plus, he had a natural talent for numbers. He got into IIT Mumbai for aerospace engineering, completely changing his position in their parents' and Sushanti aunty's eyes. In the process, Maahi looked like more of a failure. It still bothered her, but not as much. She had learned to develop thick skin. And she couldn't be prouder of her brother's success.

'It's true. You don't have time for me anymore.'

'I have time for nothing right now. Not until we get funding! And even less after that!'

'So you're just going to ignore me for the next few years? Is that what you're saying?' Sarthak asked. His face looked so deadpan, Maahi couldn't tell if he was kidding or serious.

'Of course not,' she said seriously. She put her laptop back on the desk and closed the lid. 'Is something up?'

'I heard that guy's back in town—Kishan. Your ex.'

'I heard too.'

'Did he try to talk to you?'

'Yes,' Maahi said quietly. 'I have nothing to say to him. It was a long time ago and it doesn't affect me anymore,' Maahi said. She was glad she meant it. 'But that's not what I'm asking you. I'm asking if something's up with you?'

Sarthak was quiet for a moment, and Maahi could tell there was definitely something on his mind. She noticed how tired his eyes looked, weary with dark shadows underneath them. He had shaved that morning, which made him look much younger, even though Maahi always saw him as a baby anyway. He pursed his lips and shook his head.

'What?' Maahi prodded, panicking a little inside. She was so used to seeing Sarthak upbeat that this person in front of her scared her.

'I broke up,' he said finally.

'You had a girlfriend?'

Sarthak glared at her.

'What? How was I supposed to know if you never told me?' Maahi asked, exasperated.

'You never asked.'

That made Maahi pause. She had been so caught up in their plans for Cookies + Cupcakes, her equation with her parents and her relationship with Siddhant that she hadn't been able to give any time or thought to her brother, with whom she was sharing a roof. Laila and she had set up a webpage and started marketing their brand digitally and selling their products to build a name, so when they weren't working on the pitch and business plan or weren't at their jobs, they baked from home to fill the orders. Maahi also had college, on top of that. She was taking advantage of the one month she had left before her final year at college began, but time was flying. There was too much to do. 'You're right,' she said. 'I'm sorry.'

'Nah, I could've told you. You told me about Siddhant.'

'Then why didn't you? Do you want to talk about it?'

'It wasn't anything serious; there was nothing to tell. She was in my coaching class for JEE. We had only been going out a few months, but I thought it could become something. It was different with her. But we had to end it,' Sarthak said. Maahi felt a punch in her chest when she saw how sad and wistful he looked.

'Why did it have to end?' she asked slowly. She walked over to him and sat next to him on the giant bean bag.

'She's going to Kharagpur. I didn't get in.' Sarthak snickered suddenly. 'All this time everyone's been saying they are so proud of me for getting into IIT-B, when I've been cursing myself for not getting into the college she got into.'

'Did she get into Bombay?'

Sarthak shook his head and got up. 'It doesn't matter. It wasn't that serious. We couldn't let it get serious because of precisely this reason. And then the JEE results came. We talked about long distance, but fuck that. That shit never works.' He gave her his hand.

Maahi took it and got up. 'Are you okay?'

Sarthak shrugged. 'It was only a few months, but I really felt something ... I could've really fallen for her, if I let myself. Maybe I did too. A little bit. I couldn't help it. And trust me, I tried.'

'Yeah,' Maahi said quietly. 'It doesn't work like that, does it? Can't really control it.'

'Yep.'

'But it will get better. You have to give it some time.'

Sarthak nodded. 'Want to go for a ride? I'm sick of being inside. There's nothing to do. All my friends have already started moving to their colleges and I don't want to see people from my coaching—they keep asking about her. And you've been so busy with your shit.'

'Let's go,' Maahi said. She cleared her throat. 'Also, umm, watch your language.'

⁂

Maahi flipped off the tube light and sat down at Siddhant's desk. They had plans to meet for dinner but he got stuck at the hospital. Neither of them wanted to cancel, so he asked her to go to his apartment and told her he would join her as soon as he could. He ended up getting delayed further. So, Maahi ordered food with Alia and Eshaan. After they ate, Maahi came to Siddhant's room to work on her logo while she waited for him.

There was so much work to be done for Cookies + Cupcakes. Maahi had taken over the design templates of the logo, menu, flyers and business cards. They were also planning on some promotional T-shirts and caps, but that was Phase II. Maahi pretended that she wasn't crumbling under the pressure of setting up a new business, but she wasn't doing so well. She usually had help from Laila, but Laila was in one of her freaking-out phases, so Maahi was allowing her some time off, away from all this. She had some of those too. At any point during these past few months, one person was always drowning in pressure and scepticism while the other carried the weight for both of them.

Just when she was struggling to keep her eyes open, she got a message.

> Siddhant: Still here. Doesn't look like they're going to let me off any time soon.
>
> Maahi: Should I wait up?
>
> Siddhant: No. Go to sleep. I might be able to join you in a couple of hours, but I can't promise anything.
>
> Maahi: That's okay. Have a good night.
>
> Siddhant: I'm really sorry. Sweet dreams.
>
> Maahi: No, please don't feel bad. I totally understand. You take care of yourself.
>
> Siddhant: I do feel bad. I haven't seen you in forever.
>
> Maahi: Finish your work and come home. I'll be here.
>
> Siddhant: The only thought that's keeping me sane right now. Seriously.

She had a smile on her face when she went to sleep that night. They had been seeing each other for almost a year, and even though they started slow, deciding not to read too much into it—be each other's companion, spend time together, share and be there for each other more than anything else—they had come to really depend on each other.

Maahi's thoughts went to Kishan. She barely thought about him, that too in passing, but ever since she'd heard he was in Delhi, she couldn't help but think about him. It reminded her of how she had changed completely over the last three years. From the wide-eyed teenager with rose-tinted glasses to someone who had a passion and ambition for something. She now tried to face challenges instead of being afraid.

And yet, she couldn't deny that she wasn't entirely fearless, not when it came to love and relationships. After things ended with Kishan, she had been very cautious. She wasn't ready to invest emotionally in another person. But over time, without trying, she had developed feelings for Siddhant. She saw people in relationships all around her, struggling, unhappy and frustrated. When she looked back at her relationship with Kishan, that's what she saw too. Maybe time had warped her memory and she had a skewed perception of how things really were. The thing she recalled most vividly was never feeling at peace with herself. Never feeling content.

When things started getting serious with Siddhant, she got scared. The last thing she wanted was to get into something that would add to her stress. But their relationship had grown in a way that gave her a certain amount of reassurance. Siddhant had only made her life easier. Apart from the incident after their first date—the Mario Kart night—when he had stopped talking to her for a while. She didn't think about that; they had come a long way from there.

Maahi liked sleeping in his bed; it smelled like him. She had told her parents she was staying over at Laila's because they needed to work. Which they did, but Laila was being useless, and Maahi was taking over. She sometimes wished she could tell her parents about Siddhant. She hated having to lie every time she had to come out to meet him. But she was already walking on thin ice with them. They had made a compromise that she would stay in college in exchange for their approval for the bakery. Until now, they only had a webpage and a title of home-bakers that they weren't exceptionally proud of. They had a long way to go. Maahi planned to drop out of college as soon as they secured funding. She feared her parents' reaction when that happened. On top of everything else, she couldn't tell them about Siddhant. At least not yet, when she and Siddhant didn't even know what they were doing and hadn't discussed a future.

For now, she was happy just being where she was. Even though he wasn't there, she could still feel closer to him. She missed him; they hadn't seen each other in over a week, but something was better than nothing. And this was definitely something.

14

'No, don't wake up. Go back to sleep,' Siddhant whispered in her ear.

Maahi turned her head to look at him, but couldn't see anything in the darkness. She felt his arm coil around her and rest at her waist as he lay down next to her on the bed. 'What time is it?' she asked.

'Four. Almost five. Go back to sleep,' Siddhant repeated.

He held her to him, her back against his chest. Maahi could feel the warmth of his skin. She snuggled in. They both fell asleep instantly.

The next time Maahi opened her eyes, she found them in the same position—Siddhant asleep behind her, still holding her.

She couldn't go back to sleep. She turned towards Siddhant, sideways, and looked at him, whatever she could see in the dark, the only light was the blue blinking one coming from the Internet router against the wall. His slanted forehead was partially covered with his messy hair. He clearly hadn't got a haircut in weeks. She wondered if all doctors had to work this hard, and if they all had trouble finding time to get haircuts. She didn't mind it. Siddhant was usually very organized and she liked moments like these when he wasn't trying to do anything. The unkempt long hair was more natural and endearing. It made him look younger, but that could also be because he was sleeping. He always looked younger when he was asleep. She was tempted to touch his hair, but resisted.

His long, thin face was covered in a stubble. Maahi could tell he hadn't shaved in two or three days. His beard made his nose look longer, more prominent, and his chin subtler. Maahi wished she could see his eyes—her favourite thing about him. His brow cast a shadow over his deep-set eyes, those intense eyes that she could never look away from, especially when he laughed, resulting in adorable crinkles in the corners.

His lips were slightly open. Maahi could hear his slow breathing. On impulse, she rested her weight on her elbow and leaned in to kiss him. She was careful not to disturb him; one small kiss was all she needed. She lingered just above his lips for a second, looking at him, and then let her lips touch his. She moved them gently, holding his between hers, pulling in, before releasing.

Maahi pulled away, but couldn't resist going in for just one more little kiss. This time, she didn't move at all. She rested her lips on top of his and held them together between hers, pausing for a moment. She could feel his breath on her face. She laid her hand on his chest for support, feeling his heartbeat under her palm.

This time, when she pulled away and lay down on her back, Siddhant moved with her. He rose and turned towards her, as if he was being pulled to her by some unknown force. His eyes were still closed. He rested his elbows on either side of her and kissed her mouth unhurriedly. He gave her several small kisses, moving back after each of them, just to lean right back in and kiss her again. His eyes were closed, Maahi suspected that he was still half asleep, but that didn't stop him.

His mouth slipped from her lips to her cheek and then her ear, leaving a trail of wet kisses. He hid his face in her hair and grunted. Maahi only heard the end of his sentence. '... smell so good.' He kept lying there, smelling her hair. He supported half of his weight on his elbows, half on her.

Siddhant rubbed his nose in her hair, his cheek grazing hers. The gentle scratches on her face sent shivers down her spine. His face still in her hair, Siddhant supported himself on one arm and slipped the other down her body—starting at her waist, moving down to her thigh, her knee, and further down to her ankle. He held the heel of her foot and moved it away, pushing her legs apart. His hand travelled back to her knee, held it and pushed it further away, making space for himself between her legs.

Maahi rested her hand on his shoulder and felt his muscle flex as he held her hand and pulled it up, next to her head. He finally lifted his face from her hair and looked at her. He leaned forward and kissed her before moving back to look at her. He came in to kiss her again. Pinning his one hand under her chin, with his thumb grazing her lower lip and the other holding her hand down, Siddhant kissed her passionately. His lips moved against hers, sucking, nibbling.

Maahi moaned. Her eyes shut and her spine arched back to receive his kisses. She could smell Siddhant's musky scent spread through her. His lips were soft, gentle yet persuasive. His tongue made its way into her mouth, coaxing her to open it further, let him in. They pulled back and caught a quick breath before their lips touched again. She opened her eyes to look at him, but his eyes were closed.

'Siddhant,' Maahi whispered.

'Mmm?' He continued kissing her. Maahi just shook her head. 'What is it?' he asked.

'Nothing. I just like your name.'

'Mmm,' Siddhant grunted and slipped from her lips to her neck. He nipped at it, causing Maahi to quiver under him. His fingers found the bare skin between her T-shirt and shorts. He placed his palm down on her stomach and slithered it unhurriedly to her lower back. He pulled her closer to himself, her stomach arched up to nestle softly against his.

Her hand finally free of his captivity, Maahi placed it on his chest, running it up to his shoulder, and then back. She reached down and pulled his T-shirt up, using both her hands. Siddhant rose up and helped her take it off. As soon as it was on the floor, Siddhant leaned in to kiss her again. Maahi ran her fingers freely on his back, feeling his smooth skin, his taut muscle.

'I haven't seen you in so long,' Siddhant muttered, releasing her lips to look into her eyes.

'I know.' Maahi touched his nose with hers.

'I missed you.'

Maahi wanted to say something, but she struggled with finding the right words to express her emotions.

Instead, she held the back of his neck and drew his face closer to hers. She kissed him, her one hand on his chest and the other playing with the hair at the base of his neck. Siddhant rose up on his knees, his body between her legs. He pushed them apart. Maahi raised her head from the pillow as she sat up, their mouths never breaking contact. Her long hair cascaded in the air, landing on the space-grey pillowcase in waves. Siddhant caught hold of a few strands and played with them.

She pushed him backwards by his chest, getting up and turning him over on his back. She straddled him and ran her fingers up his stomach, to his chest, stopping at his neck. Supporting herself on her knees, she bent forward to kiss him.

Siddhant reached for her T-shirt and pulled it off in one swift motion. Maahi kissed his chin and trailed her tongue over his jaw before circling it around his earlobe.

He groaned. 'You're killing me right now.'

Maahi didn't stop. Their bodies touched, and shared heat. Maahi placed her hands on each side of Siddhant's face and held it in place while she explored his mouth with hers. He welcomed it, he participated in it. They played with each other's lips. Maahi traced his lower lip with her tongue before sucking on it.

Siddhant held the back of her head in place as he kissed her. He slipped his other hand up her stomach and then around, reaching for the clasp of her bra. He unhooked it. Holding the straps in both hands, he helped her take it off, sliding his fingers down her arms in the process.

He looked at her with such intensity that Maahi's cheeks turned red. She bent, trying to hide herself in him. Her hair fell on his face, which he moved out of the way. 'Let me look at you,' he breathed.

Maahi shook her head, her lips grazing his chest.

'Tickles,' Siddhant said. Maahi did it again. 'You...' Siddhant held her eyes before letting his glide to her lips, her neck, all the way down to her stomach. He pushed her on her back and reached for the waist of her shorts. 'We won't be needing this,' he murmured, pulling on the pink ribbon that held her thin cotton shorts in place.

Siddhant's fingers touched every inch of her legs as he pulled her shorts off leisurely, teasing her. He bunched them in his fist before throwing them to the floor. He lay on top of her, resting his weight on her body, as he kissed her mouth. She could feel the rough fabric of his jeans against her hips.

Maahi pulled him towards her as they kissed. He pulled back slightly and looked at her. Their eyes met. A small smile appeared on Maahi's face. Siddhant kissed her forehead, and looked her in the eyes again. His fingers rubbed softly against her cheek as he examined her face, his eyes moving from her eyes to her cheek, to her lip and back to her eyes.

'You're so beautiful,' Siddhant murmured.

Maahi breathed harder, matching the rhythm of Siddhant's erratic breaths. Her eyes were darker, his eyebrows casting that mysterious shadow over them. He fumbled with the knob of his bedside table, looking for the box of condoms. His lips were parted slightly, blowing warm air on her face. Maahi reached for his zipper, her fingers unsteady.

Siddhant let his hand slide over her jaw, over her neck and pause at her breasts. He followed the movement with his mouth. Maahi arched her body back. Her eyes shut, her fingers digging in his shoulder as she felt his mouth on her. She gasped for air, her lips parting.

※

Maahi lay in bed with him for a long time. Siddhant had barely got a few hours of sleep, and went right back to sleep. Maahi was surprised he had even woken up in the first place. He had been up for over thirty-six hours before that. But that's the cost of following your passion, she reasoned. He loved what he did, and was working hard for it. She needed to get up and get back to her work too. They were meeting with prospective investors late in the day. She had to go over the pitch presentation with Laila and make sure she wasn't still freaking out.

Maahi slipped out of bed and into the bathroom. She took a quick shower and came out. She would ring Laila on her way so that they could meet up and revise their presentation thoroughly. Having done it over and over again, it was difficult to be as enthusiastic as they had been in the beginning. It was, however, important to remember that they might have done it tens of times but the investors were only hearing them the first time. It made Maahi nervous. A lot was riding on this.

When she came back to the room after her shower, Siddhant was lying on his stomach, his arms sprawled above his head. It reminded Maahi of the dead man outline. She sniggered and hunted for her clothes. She gathered them from around the room and quietly got dressed. Packing her laptop and charger in her handbag, Maahi looked around for anything else she left behind.

She wanted to say bye to Siddhant but didn't want to wake him up again. He'd barely been awake the last time. She smiled, wondering how he even managed to find the energy.

Just as she turned the doorknob, she heard his muffled voice, 'Maahi?'

'Shh, go to sleep,' she spoke softly. 'It's only seven.'

'Come back here.' Siddhant raised his head from his pillow and blinked.

Maahi dropped her handbag to the floor and went to him. She bent down to kiss him lightly on his cheek. She spoke softly, 'I'm going to go now. You get some rest, okay?'

As she moved away, Siddhant held her hand and pulled her back. 'Don't.'

Maahi sat down on the bed next to him and he pulled her face closer to him, holding her by the back of her neck. He rested her head on his shoulder and closed his eyes.

'Siddhant?' Maahi whispered when he didn't say anything. She was half sitting up, awkwardly, with her legs dangling over the bed, on the floor.

'Just don't go, Maahi.' That's all he said.

Maahi paused for a second, wondering what that meant. He was in a weird mood, and it wasn't just that he was sleepy or under rested. She kicked off her sneakers and snuggled under the covers with him. 'Is everything okay?' she asked after a minute.

Siddhant turned towards her. They lay on their sides, facing each other.

Maahi touched his face. 'You look sad.'

'I don't want you to leave.'

'I'm here.'

'No. Not just now. I ... don't want you to leave,' Siddhant repeated. His eyes reflected the sunlight coming in through the window.

Maahi's breath got caught in her throat. 'What does that mean?'

'Do you remember that time, right after the first time we hung out—our Mario Kart date?' Maahi nodded. Siddhant continued, 'Do you remember I was weird around you for a couple of weeks after that? I never told you why that was, did I? And I don't really expect you to understand ... and I'm also not saying that this is how I felt it was with you ... What I'm trying to say is that it wasn't about you. It was all me.'

'Tell me,' Maahi insisted. She wished he didn't look so forlorn. She didn't like seeing him like that.

'Growing up, I always faced a lot of pressure from home to work hard. I was never given an option to not top a class, not get into AIIMS, not be a doctor. And I'm not saying that that hasn't helped me get where I am. You know I love what I do. I'm grateful to my parents and my brother for pushing me so hard. But I can't say it wasn't tough. They all studied at AIIMS and work there now. My path was predetermined. I never had time for anything—to go out, have friends, anything other than studying.'

Maahi nodded, waiting for him to continue.

'I didn't get into AIIMS the first time around. I had to drop a year. And it might be unfair to say this, but it was because of a girl. Because I was seventeen and I fell in love and that took over my life. She was all I could think about. I wanted to spend all my time with her and when we weren't together, I was thinking about her. I guess it was good—it felt great at the time. My first experience of love. But that was exactly why I didn't get into AIIMS. Hell, I didn't even make it into any decent college through AIPMT.' Siddhant dropped his eyes to her neck and pursed his lips. 'I'm not proud of it, but I blamed it on her. It wasn't her fault. I was the only one responsible. But I still put the blame on her. And she left. At that time, I was glad that that's how it worked out—that *she* left *me*, not the other way around. Saved me the guilt of leaving her, at least. I took the whole year to myself, studying. This time, I didn't even apply for AIPMT. I knew I was going to get into AIIMS.'

'You did.'

'I did. It only got much more difficult after that. Getting in is a tiny anthill when compared to the mountain you have to climb in these five-and-a-half years. It was a conscious decision to not get involved in anything else, with anyone else. It was easy for the first four years; I was lucky I didn't meet anyone I liked. And then I met you.'

'You don't have to be so grim about it,' Maahi said, mostly to lighten things up.

Siddhant rested his palm on the side of her waist. 'I'm not. It's the best thing that happened to me in a long time.'

Maahi smiled, looking into his eyes. 'I'm glad.'

'It's the best thing that has *ever* happened to me.'

'Now *that's* just exaggeration. You never learn where to stop, do you?'

But Siddhant wasn't smiling. 'It's not funny. I could see that you were going to be trouble. I knew that from the very beginning. I liked talking to you and spending time with you so much that it scared me. I barely knew you, but I couldn't stop thinking about you. I started coming to the coffee shop even when I needed to be studying or catching up on sleep. And it really scared me, Maahi. You have no idea what you were doing to me.'

Maahi touched his face. Her fingers rested on his jaw, and her thumb rubbed his stubbly chin. 'And that's why you stopped talking to me. You didn't want me to come between you and your career,' she said quietly.

'Shitty as it sounds, yes. Trust me, it was hard. I had only been talking to you for a little over a month and you were taking over my thoughts already. If something went wrong, I didn't want to end up hating you for something that wasn't even your fault. I do that—I try to find something or someone to shift the blame on when the blame comes on me. That's the easiest way, I've found, in my life full of expectations that

I've tried my best to meet, but ended up failing sometimes, regardless.'

'I know all about that. My parents haven't exactly been pleased with me these last few years. But that's an unfair comparison. Growing up, the pressure on me wasn't half as bad as your. Not even close. I've only recently learned to disappoint my parents.'

'Oh, I've done that all my life,' Siddhant said, his eyes glazed.

'You've done so well. You're not a disappointment; you can never be. I feel so proud of you—even though I wasn't even a part of your journey for the most part,' Maahi said. 'When I think about the long hours you put in, the hard work you do, how much you study—I could never do that. Not everyone can do what you do, Siddhant. It's high time you start seeing that.'

He breathed out with a smile. 'I feel the same way about what you do! It takes major guts to deviate from viable career options, not once, but twice, and do what you really want to do. *I* could never do that. With so little support, just a dream … all for your passion. You're seriously talented. And I'm glad that you see that enough to take this leap.'

'Or I'm really stupid and am heading down a path to disaster.'

'Or that, yes.'

'You're so mean!' Maahi punched his shoulder lightly.

Siddhant clutched her hand. 'You know I'm only kidding. I think you're amazing. You changed everything. I was so caught up in the medical world, from school to hospital—my friends, my roommates, my family … It was so refreshing just talking to you. You were like a breath of fresh air to me. I wanted to talk to you after a long day. Sharing with you made me feel so much better. I was so much happier since the day I met you.

You're silly, and hilarious, and so talented and passionate. In all this time I have known you, you've always been there, you've always cared—from day one. I don't know how you even do that.'

'Come on, it's not like *you* don't care about *me*! You're always there for me too. You always listen to me, help me vent. You give me advice; I turn to you every time I have a crisis or panic attacks—which is plenty nowadays, trying to get Cookies + Cupcakes started.'

'Well, I—'

'I'm not finished!' Maahi cut him off. 'And you're a doctor, so that comes in handy for cuts and scrapes.'

'Yeah, a personal cardiologist at your service for first aid.'

'Exactly. How many people can boast of having that? Also, you're pretty hot, so that helps.'

'True.' Siddhant shrugged. 'Seems like you're all set.'

'Yep.' Maahi nodded fervently, relieved that he didn't look as sad or serious as he did earlier.

'I'm set too.'

'Right. Because I'm awesome.'

'Yes, you are,' Siddhant said quietly. 'And I don't want you to go. I want you to stay.'

Maahi paused. 'Forever?'

'If that's okay with you.'

Maahi sat up, turning away from him. She rested her elbows on her folded legs and covered her mouth with her hand.

Siddhant got up too. 'What is it?'

Maahi looked at him, her mouth still covered, her eyes wide.

Siddhant examined her face intently. His expression reflected confusion at first and then he pursed his lips. He nodded ever so slightly, looking away. His voice was low when he spoke. 'It's okay. I thought you felt the same way ... But okay.'

'No, it's not that!' Maahi said, removing her hands from her mouth to hold his face. 'I do feel the same way. It's just that ... I've known ... I don't know what to...' She shook her head, trying to clear it. 'You don't know how happy you make me.'

'Then what is it? I love you, Maahi. We have never said that to each other, and I think that's amazing because we never needed to. I always thought you knew, and just in case you didn't—I love you. And I want to spend the rest of my life with you. I can't imagine waking up and going through a day without you in my life. I just ... can't. It's not possible.'

'Siddhant...' Tears flowed down Maahi's cheek.

'No, please, don't. I can't...' Siddhant shook his head, his expression pained. 'I hate that I'm doing this to you. Please don't cry.'

Maahi got goosebumps. She was scared to take the leap. She was in love with him. She had known that for a while now. But the last time she had fallen for someone, it had ended up destroying her. She looked into Siddhant's eyes, so sincere and full of devotion, and she derived strength from them. 'These are happy tears ... mostly. I love you too. I thought you knew that, but just in case you didn't—I love you.'

'Hey, that's my line!'

Maahi sniffed and giggled. 'Sorry. But there's nothing you can do about that. Now that you've asked me to spend the rest of my life with you and all...'

'So, does that mean ... Is that a *yes*?'

She wiped the tears off her cheeks and narrowed her eyes at him. 'What do *you* think?'

'I think it's a yes,' Siddhant said, throwing a punch in the air, with a muttered *yes*.

Maahi laughed quietly, before Siddhant shut her up by kissing her. He held her by her shoulder and with his other hand, tilted her chin up. His mouth rested on hers and Maahi could feel his excitement in his warm breath. 'God, I love you so much,' he whispered before taking her lips captive.

15

Maahi and Laila sat in the waiting area, Maahi wearing a charcoal skirt suit and Laila dressed in a crisp white shirt with tapered black trousers. Maahi thought Laila looked like a runway model—sleek, skinny, dressed to kill, her curls stylishly messy, framing her perfectly made-up face. She wasn't kidding.

Maahi could barely keep the silly smile off her face and it was driving Laila crazy. She tried to stop herself, it was no fun being around Laila when she was in a bad mood, but every time her mind wandered to Siddhant, she couldn't help but smile stupidly. And her mind wandered to Siddhant a lot.

'Seriously, I'm going to punch you in the nose,' Laila said through gritted teeth.

'This is your fifth threat to me today. Why are you so violent?'

'Because you refuse to concentrate! I'm saying something to you. I made changes to this section—revenue model. You have to catch up.'

'I saw that. You already told me about it. Relax! It's a good day!' Maahi exclaimed.

'Don't tell me to relax. You stop relaxing and start taking this seriously. This is important,' Laila said. 'Have you looked over the changes in traction and validation?'

'In the business plan? Yes, I did. But aren't we here just to pitch?'

'They might ask us to show them the business plan too. Maahi, look alive!'

Maahi sighed. 'I'm going to go sit over there until we're asked to come in,' she said and walked over to the seat farthest from Laila. She sat opposite her, with ten feet worth of distance between them. She was in great spirits, but Laila was really starting to bring her down. She wasn't sure they could afford that. Nothing she could do or say seemed to improve Laila's mood, especially since she seemed so annoyed by Maahi.

She got a text.

Rohit: How's it going?

Maahi: We're waiting outside.

Rohit: All set?

Maahi: I guess… SO nervous!

Rohit: True. Uncle asked to tell you there's a typo in your updated pitch…

Maahi: WTF! Where?

Rohit: JK

Maahi: Don't joke about shit like that! Literally just gave me a heart attack!!

Rohit: I'm just bored

Maahi: Why, where's Ruchika?

Rohit: Waiting for her outside her house. She's taking foreverrrrrr

Maahi: So you're just passing time with me?
Rohit: Yep
Maahi: Loser.
Rohit: Kthnxbai she's here now
Maahi: Have fun.

Maahi slipped her cell phone back in her bag. They were at the offices of a consultancy company, to meet the CEO, Mr Jindal, who was known to angel invest in start-ups in the Delhi/NCR, and was an old acquaintance of Rohit's uncle and their mentor, Anil. He had shown interest in them and offered them fifteen minutes of his time. Laila insisted they get there an hour early, just in case Mr Jindal had more time and wanted to give it to them. Maahi thought Laila watched too many movies.

She looked at her from across the room, wondering why she was being so crazy lately. The role reversal was not only weird and unsettling, it was also taxing for Maahi. She was used to relying on Laila for support. She wasn't very good at holding up the fort by herself. She needed her partner, her best friend.

Maahi walked back and sat next to Laila. 'Do you want to show me the changes you made in the revenue model once again?' she asked quietly.

'Okay,' Laila said.

They went through their pitch deck again. They had a one-page version and a longer one with eight slides. They went through both. Over-preparing tended to overwhelm and stress Maahi, but she realized that Laila needed to do that in order to relax. And it was a good day for Maahi—her stress threshold was much higher that day.

'Maahi Kothari and Laila Kapoor?' the middle-aged woman at the reception called.

'That's us,' Maahi jumped up and said.

'Chill,' Laila whispered to her as they collected their things and rushed to the reception.

'I'm here to convey Mr Jindal's apologies. He has to be somewhere and won't be able to meet with you today,' the woman said. She was wearing a blue sari with black horizontal stripes. 'I'm really sorry, but something just came up.'

'What? But we have had this meeting scheduled for *ages*!' Maahi exclaimed, pressure bursting her calmness.

'Literally five weeks,' Laila added. 'Is there any way he can meet us? Even for just five minutes? We have a shorter version of the pitch prepared...'

'There is no need—' the receptionist began but Maahi cut her off.

'What the f—!'

'*Maahi!*' Laila pulled her back and kept a hand firmly in front of her to ensure distance from the receptionist. 'I'm sorry. I hope you understand that we're frustrated. We've been preparing for this meeting for a long time,' she explained.

'I understand,' the receptionist said, looking from Laila to Maahi. She turned back to Laila and said, 'As I was saying. There is no need for a pitch presentation, Mr Jindal says he definitely likes you and Cookies + Cupcakes. You presented this pitch to Bharat Bhardwaj, he said. Mr Bhardwaj recommended you to Mr Jindal.'

'Seriously?' Maahi and Laila cried together. Maahi's hand slipped from Laila's stomach to her side, clutching her hand.

'Yes. Mr Jindal would like to see the business plan sometime this week. We can schedule a meeting?'

'Oh my God, I love you!' Maahi screamed. 'I'm so sorry about being rude before. I can be a bitch sometimes but it's definitely my bad.'

'That's alright. How's Thursday around noon for you? Say 12.30 p.m.?'

'That's perfect!' Laila said, her hand still holding Maahi's tightly.

'Thank you so much!' Maahi said.

'Yes, thanks!'

'You're welcome. See you Thursday,' the receptionist said and left.

'Oh my God, oh my God, oh my God!' Laila squealed.

'Right?'

'It *is* a good day. You were right!'

'I told you,' Maahi said, as Laila smothered her in a tight hug.

'You did. I'm sorry for being such a bitch!'

'You promise to never be a bitch again?'

'Umm.' Laila pulled back and bit her lip.

'That's what I thought. Sorry about my little outburst earlier. I don't know what happened. She said Mr Jindal called off the meeting and I just couldn't deal. I need to find my chill. Do you want to go out for a movie or something? I need popcorn. Or we could—'

'But now we need to work harder than ever! We have Mr Jindal's attention. We have to make it count. We're proposing the business plan on Thursday! We have to go over it slide by slide and make sure we know everything through and through. There's no room for errors anymore.'

'Or we could ... do that, yeah. That's what I was going to suggest next,' Maahi said. She could see Laila's mind drifting to their presentation already. The presentation they had revised and re-revised at least twenty times in the past week. But Maahi didn't mind doing it twenty times more in the next couple of days. Judging by her sudden moment of panic earlier, she could do with more preparation. If Mr Jindal liked what they had to say on Thursday, Cookies + Cupcakes could become an actual thing. Just the thought gave Maahi chills. It definitely was a good day.

꽃

They worked on the presentation all day, dividing their roles clearly. They were each responsible for their own sections; splitting the responsibility made it easier for them to have more command over their content.

'Are you taking the first slide or am I?' Laila asked.

'The introduction? Vision and value proposition?'

'Yeah. Maybe I could begin with speaking about the general idea first—the introduction and then you can jump in with the vision?'

'Improv?' Maahi asked.

'God, no. Are you kidding me? We have to rehearse the whole thing. I'm not leaving anything to chance.'

'Right. Sorry I asked.'

'Do you want to do this one more time?' Laila asked.

'Sur—' There was a crash in the living room. Maahi went out to look. Sarthak was standing over shards of broken glass and water spread on the floor.

'Oops,' he said, looking at her walk in.

'What happened?' Maahi asked, going to the kitchen.

'What's going on?' Laila asked from the door.

'Bumped into the centre table. The glass slipped from my hand,' Sarthak explained, just as Maahi came back from the kitchen with a broom and dustpan. 'Give me. I'll take care of it,' Sarthak said.

'I got it; you'll cut yourself. Get out of the way,' Maahi said, picking up the bigger shards on the dustpan.

'Okay.'

'You can help us though. If you're not doing anything.

'Help you with what? I already came up with the name Cookies + Cupcakes for you. What else do you need from me?' Sarthak sighed loudly. 'I have to do everything around here.'

'Just pretend to be an investor and let us pitch it to you,' Maahi said. 'Tell us what you think.'

'That sounds dull.'

'Oh yeah? What are your colourful plans for the evening?' Laila intervened.

'Anything other than this.'

'Sarthak,' Maahi said pointedly.

'Ugh, fine. I'll hear out your pitch. If I had money to give you, I would've.'

'That's quite alright. We don't need your money. Actually, you know what, four years from now, when you graduate with your fancy degree from IIT Bombay and start making shitloads of money, and we still don't have investors, feel free to pitch in,' Laila said. 'Maahi, we need to take this pitch seriously. Sarthak might be our investor.'

'Seems like we need to take everything seriously, all the time,' Maahi muttered.

'If you don't have investors in four years, maybe it wouldn't be a good project for me to invest in,' Sarthak said.

'Yeah, well, we'll make you,' Laila said. 'Now let's go.'

Maahi finished clearing away the broken glass and they followed Laila to her room. Sarthak sat down on the bed and Maahi and Laila pulled up the first slide of the OneNote presentation on her laptop.

'Cookies + Cupcakes is—' Maahi began.

'Great name. Bravo,' Sarthak nodded.

'Shut up,' Laila said.

Maahi started over. 'We see Cookies + Cupcakes as a speciality bakery that will change the way Delhiites look at bakeries. We offer innovation and experimentation, we use ingredients that are unheard of, especially here in India. These unconventional ingredients could be anything—from cucumber martini to whiskey ganache to cola! Apart from the standard menu with our own recipes, we also provide the customer an opportunity to make their own! Laila, remember to print out the menus before the meeting,' Maahi said, and turned back to Sarthak. 'They can customize their own cupcakes on the spot, picking and choosing cupcake flavours and toppings from our list. For cookies, it's slightly different, because it takes time, we'll take orders in advance.'

'Of course, we will also act as consultants to help people choose the best combinations,' Laila said. 'We'll have algorithms to serve as virtual consultants on the website, which we believe is a great platform for Cookies + Cupcakes. Customers can take the two-minute *bake my cookie* slash *bake my cupcake* quiz and mark the flavours they like, the ones they have or haven't tried and other such questions. Our system will automatically generate a list of flavours based on the customers' choices and whether they are looking for something similar or want to experiment.'

'And is this website live now?' Sarthak asked.

'We're looking to outsource website development and management, once we have funding to get started. We have been baking from home and building a name for ourselves for the past one year. We have a Facebook page and a Pinterest profile and we've received a very encouraging response from our customers. We have tie-ups with three coffee shops in Delhi/NCR. They stock our products. We are planning to launch the website and the physical store around the same time. The website could be live for a week before the store, so that people can place their orders and we can have the orders for our first batch of customers ready and showcased,' Maahi said.

Laila pitched in, 'Our passion for baking and penchant for experimentation drove us to create Cookies + Cupcakes. I'm taking care of the cookies exclusively, and Maahi will be in charge of cupcakes. We, of course, have these boxes of samples for you, from our main menu.'

'And these boxes here have cupcakes of different flavours and a selection of toppings, if you'd like to try and experiment. Moving on to the market opportunity—Delhi is a city of food lovers. There is no specific demographic we are targeting, because everyone gets a cookie.' Maahi smiled, and continued, 'But if we had to guess, we believe the younger crowd would be more interested in Cookies + Cupcakes. We are looking for spaces in South Delhi, somewhere near the Hauz Khas, Greater Kailash area, places our demographic likes to visit.'

'Our customer would be—' Laila began, but was interrupted by a phone ringing. 'Whose is it?'

'It's mine,' Maahi said, pulling it out of her jeans' pocket. 'Unknown number.'

'Ignore it. Unless it's someone calling back about investment.'

'At nine on a Tuesday night?'

'Just take it,' Laila said, and turned towards Sarthak, raising her hand up. 'Pause.'

'Hello?' Maahi said into the phone.

'Maahi,' the voice from the other end said. Maahi skipped a heartbeat. She looked at Sarthak, who raised his eyebrows.

'Who is it?' Laila asked.

Maahi shook her head and hung up the phone. He sounded the same. Her name from his mouth took her back five years—the first time she had told him her name and he had repeated it. '*Maahi ... Beautiful.*' She still remembered that night. It still gave her chills.

She had heard Kishan was back in town, and he had tried to contact her through his cousin. Maahi's friend who had introduced them in the first place, whom she hadn't been in touch with in years. He had managed to get her number from somewhere. In theory, when Maahi thought of Kishan moving back to Delhi, it didn't affect her. Enough time had passed. But she still felt the air knocked out of her lungs when she heard him say her name.

'Maahi? What's up?' Laila asked.

Her phone rang again. Maahi stared at the number for a second, almost picking up again, but didn't. She turned her phone on silent and slipped it back into her pocket. 'Where were we?'

'Who was that?' Laila asked.

Maahi shrugged.

'What happened? Tell me. You don't look so good.'

'Nothing, Laila. I'm fine. Let's resume the presentation. We're still at—what—market opportunity?'

'Was that Kishan?' Sarthak asked. Both Maahi and Laila looked at him. 'It was, wasn't it?'

Maahi nodded.

'Kishan, the asshole ex-boyfriend Kishan?' Laila asked.

'Yes. What did he want?' Sarthak asked.

'I don't know. I didn't talk to him, as you both saw. Now can we please move on?' Maahi said, her face tight. 'I'm sorry. But please, I'd like to finish the presentation.'

And so they did. They followed their script, Maahi slipping once or twice, distracted but fighting it hard. They didn't talk about Kishan at all. Maahi didn't understand her reaction, and was in no mood to contemplate, so she tried not to dwell on it.

After they finished the presentation, they heard out Sarthak's comments—they were mostly compliments and, therefore, unproductive. He was sold at the idea as soon as they said Cookies + Cupcakes; he hadn't needed much more. He did say that bringing actual product samples and letting the investors customize their own cupcakes was inspired. He also thought that seeing the actual menu, flyers and business cards would further add to the charm of the bakery.

'I'll work on the menu more tonight,' Maahi said. 'I'm not sure about the colour template we're using. I'll try a few new things tonight and we can go over them tomorrow before getting them printed?'

'Sounds good,' Laila said. 'I'll get going then.'

'See you tomorrow.'

Laila watched Maahi keenly and said, 'Yes, good night. And good work; you were great, with everything. I'm proud of us.'

'Me too. Proud of you guys, I mean.' Sarthak chuckled to himself. 'I'm proud of myself too, generally, but not sure that's the kind of thing you're interested in.'

Laila glared at him.

'I'm going to bounce now. Good talk.'

After Sarthak left, Laila turned to Maahi. 'You okay?'

'Yep.'

Laila waited for a second, but when Maahi didn't say anything, she bent down and gave her a tight squeeze. 'I'll go then. Give me a call if you need anything, okay?'

'Yeah.'

Laila ruffled her hair and left. Maahi watched her walk away and her thoughts immediately went back to Kishan, as if they'd been waiting for her to be alone, to attack her. She took out her phone again. There were no more calls from him.

Maahi ran to the balcony of their third-floor apartment and peeked down. 'Laila, wait!' she yelled. Laila looked up, car keys in hand, lights blinking on her black i20. 'Hold on, just one second.'

Maahi went back in and shoved a toothbrush and some clothes in her handbag before running downstairs.

'Where are you going?' Sarthak called out from the living room.

'Siddhant's. Tell mom I'm staying at Laila's to prepare for Thursday's meeting.'

'You got it.'

Maahi called Siddhant from the car. He was home, but was on standby. He might have to go on call in the middle of the night. Maahi didn't care, as long as she got to see him; it was better than not seeing him at all. Just hearing his voice over the phone helped her relax.

'I'll try not to get irritated by your smile,' Laila said, looking ahead at the dark road as she drove.

'How generous. Thanks.' Maahi hadn't realized she had been smiling.

'Although I would say—that smile is dumb and stupid and annoying and it pisses me off. But. I'm glad that you're happy. Always liked that guy. Wasn't sure he had it in him to step up and actually propose. I like being surprised every once in a while.'

'He didn't *really* propose.'

'He did, for all practical purposes. Did you want an American rom-com with a ring and champagne and roses?' Laila laughed, shaking her head. 'No, sweetheart. You'll get a long and possibly fruitless battle with both your parents just to get permission to marry each other. So let's call this an engagement.'

16

They were in the most difficult and crucial slide of their pitch presentation deck. The asking-for-money part. They delivered the first eight slides well and the response from Mr Jindal and his two associates sitting in on the meeting seemed favourable. They had discussed all their hopes and plans enthusiastically. It was time to ask for the funds that would actually make it happen.

'This is a specialty service bakery, and we're planning for a sit-down space. Any and all scaling-up in the future will be in terms of opening more branches, not expanding the services themselves. We will be open to ideas and exploring more, as long as we stick to the core vision. After all, we're all about experimentation—that's how this started. But we would like to experiment within the realms of cookies and cupcakes,' Maahi wrapped up her part.

Laila was taking the lead on the financials. She began, 'As Maahi said, we're looking to invite people into our bakery, so we'll need commercial sit-down space, apart from a commercial kitchen space. The start-up cost—which includes: 1) the projected cost for such a space in South Delhi—we're considering Hauz Khas Village for calculation purposes 2) the one-time cost of equipment and appliances like refrigerator and ovens and smaller items such as pans and utensils, and 3) seed money to live on while the business gets established—is enclosed in the folders in front of you.'

Maahi began talking about the competition as their potential investors flipped through their files. After they finished presenting, they were asked to wait while Mr Jindal discussed it with his colleagues.

'So?' Maahi asked Laila when they came out to the waiting area.

'I think that went well. Don't you?'

'Yeah. I screwed up a bit when talking about the revenue model. Thanks for taking over there.'

'Nah, it's all good. I'm pretty sure they didn't notice. They looked impressed, right?' Laila was shaking her legs, probably involuntarily, in anxiety.

'Let's sit down,' Maahi said and pulled Laila to the chairs against the wall. 'Mr Jindal seems kind enough. Can't you just tell how smart he is, just by looking at him? If he does decide to invest in us, I think he'd be a good mentor, like Anil uncle. Both of them have invested in a restaurant before, so that's kind of similar to a bakery.'

'Mr Jindal has done a whole bunch of stuff. The other man is his lawyer-slash-friend. Who's the woman?'

Mr Jindal was a charming, tall, slightly overweight man in his late forties. He had smiling eyes that calmed Maahi's nerves, but she didn't let them mislead her—he was a clever businessman and definitely not as easily impressed as his body language suggested. His lawyer friend was older than him, Maahi guessed mid-fifties. There had also been a younger woman in the room with them. 'Didn't she introduce herself as Harshita Jindal? I assumed she was his daughter. Or somehow related to him. I don't know. He might be too young to have a daughter that old.'

'Yeah, she seems about your age. I'm guessing twenty-three? Twenty-four, maybe.'

Just as they talked about her, Harshita came out, walking towards them. They stood up and met her midway.

'Hey,' Harshita said. 'So, we discussed the business plan, and we're definitely interested in working with you girls, with a few alterations. Would you like to come back in to discuss?'

'Sure,' Maahi said. She clutched Laila's hand and pulled at it when Harshita turned around. Laila squeezed her hand back, as they followed Harshita into the conference room.

'Please sit,' Mr Jindal said, looking up as they entered. He pointed to the boxes of cookies and cupcakes and said, 'I am impressed. We all are. Such talented young women. And quite a solid business plan, I must say. Has anyone been mentoring you?'

'Thank you, sir. Mr Anil Shukla has been guiding us and we've done our research and used that to develop these plans,' Laila said.

'Ah, Anil Shukla. I haven't seen him in ages. He's an old friend.'

'He speaks very highly of you.'

Mr Jindal guffawed. 'You don't have to lie to me. I'm sure that bastard has some indecent stories to tell!'

'Seems like he has kept your secrets, sir.' Maahi smiled and added, 'We look forward to your mentorship. If there are certain things that could be done better using a different approach, we're definitely open to discussing them.'

'Good. We do have some suggestions. Let me share them with you quickly. First, we would like to start off with a counter service model, as opposed to a sit-down bakery. This would cut down cost significantly—to begin with, a smaller space would cost less, and we'd need less help for cleaning and management of the eating space and such. Think about it. It wouldn't have a sizable negative impact on the sales. Second, think less Hauz Khas Village and more … newer areas—the ones that are on their way. Like Meherchand, or Shahpurjat. Greater Kailash is dead, so let's not even go there. Third, we would like to take the website more seriously. As seriously as the physical store. As you said, your market is the younger crowd. They're Internet savvy, and would definitely appreciate being able to order online. Which brings me to my fourth point, home delivery. I see sense in investing in that as opposed to sitting space—a far more lucrative model. And my final point, Maahi—you mentioned that you would drop out of college?' Mr Jindal looked at her.

'Yes. That would help me direct all my energy towards this venture without distraction,' Maahi said.

'While that intention is commendable, we would like you to stay in college and finish your bachelor's. There's no replacement for education and this course in business economics can only help you with starting up a business, won't you say?'

Maahi fidgeted under his gaze. 'Yes, sir.'

'It's all about time management. I'm sure you'll live,' Mr Jindal said. 'So, yes. Those are our suggestions and concerns.'

Maahi and Laila looked at each other when he stopped talking.

'You don't have to decide immediately. Get back to us when you're ready,' Mr Jindal said.

'You can get in touch with me. If this works out, I'll be your point of contact,' Harshita said. 'You can direct all questions and concerns to me too. I'd be happy to answer them.'

'Thank you,' Laila said. 'I think Maahi and I will need a couple of days to think this through, if that's okay with you?'

'Sure. Take your time,' Harshita said.

They thanked everyone for their time and interest, collected their presentation materials and left. As they walked out of the building, Maahi turned to Laila and asked slowly, 'So … how important is the sit-down space to you?'

'Honestly?' Laila said, meeting her eyes. 'I don't give a fuck. Like, seriously, I just care about our cookies and cupcakes and people eating them. I don't care about it looking like a sit-down restaurant. A counter service model serves the purpose perfectly.'

'*Right*,' Maahi said, excitedly. 'I don't care about it either. Also, I'm cool with Shahpurjat.'

'Same. I love that locality—so many young artists and gorgeous boutiques. It's definitely becoming the new place to be.'

'I can see Cookies + Cupcakes working there.'

'For sure,' Laila was quick to agree. 'Which leaves moving up website and home delivery on our list of priorities. Fine by me.'

'Same. But they want me to stay in college,' Maahi groaned.

'Big deal. They do have a good point there. You keep seeing the course as a distraction instead of learning.'

'Because all I want to do is bake.'

'And to be able to do that, you have to make this compromise.'

Maahi sighed. 'I guess.'

'Added advantage: it'll keep your parents happy.'

'True. Do you think it'll look bad if we turned back around and told them we're in, right now? Why did we ask for time anyway?' Maahi stopped walking.

'I didn't know how you felt about their conditions and we couldn't possibly discuss in front of them!'

'Then let's go back.'

'Are you serious? Won't that look unprofessional?' Laila looked at Maahi.

Maahi's eyes were wide with excitement. She smiled and shrugged. 'We're kind of ... *enthusiastic*. So what? They're going to find that out sooner or later.'

'Better sooner! No fucks given.'

'Exactly! Laila, oh my God, this is finally happening. I can't believe this is finally happening for us. This is like a dream. Is this for real? For real, for real?'

'For real, for real,' Laila repeated, clearly thrilled too. Her dark eyes were shining with happiness. Maahi also detected a tinge of tears.

Maahi jumped on her and pulled her in a hug, tightening her arms around her. 'This is so so so exciting. I told you it was going to happen. Oh, Laila, I'm so happy.' Maahi pulled back and looked at her. 'I can't tell you how glad I am for that day I walked into Cozy Coffee and saw the help wanted sign. You have no idea how grateful I am to have met you. You literally changed my life.'

Laila grinned. 'No, I didn't. You did. You're here because of everything you have done since that day you saw the wanted sign at Cozy Coffee.'

'Fine, say whatever you want. I know it was you who made all the difference to me. And I love you, and I can't imagine my life without you, and I would've married you if I hadn't already said yes to Siddhant.'

'Umm, that's quite alright, love. I'm not into you like that.'

'We're spending our lives with each other regardless, so deal with it.' Maahi laughed and cried a little, hugging Laila again, almost suffocating her.

'Dammit.'

୶

Maahi could barely wait to tell her parents, but she somehow managed to make it home without bursting out of happiness. She didn't want to do it over the phone. She'd gone to AIIMS first, met Siddhant for a second and shared the good news in person. He told her he was proud of her, and that made Maahi feel proud of herself.

Warm and giddy in exhilaration, Maahi climbed up the stairs. Someone had left an open polythene with fruit peels in the corner, which made the whole staircase smell like bananas. That would've annoyed Maahi generally, but she just giggled. It took her a few attempts to insert the key in the lock; her fingers were unsteady with excitement.

'Yo. You drunk or something?' Sarthak asked, appearing on the other side of the metal mesh door screen. He opened it for her.

'Kind of.' Maahi giggled, walking in. 'Well, no, not drunk. But I'm definitely in high spirits. We got funding, Sarthak. We did it. We got funding.'

'WHOA. That's AWESOME!' Sarthak turned around

immediately and called out, 'Ma, Papa—MAAHI GOT FUNDING!'

'Thanks. I wanted *you* to be the one to tell them. Exactly how I imagined it.' Maahi glared at him, but followed him inside anyway. Ma was in the kitchen, making dinner, Papa was sitting at the dining table.

'Oops, sorry,' Sarthak said sheepishly.

'What did you say?' Papa asked when he saw them.

'They got funding!' Sarthak said again.

'Dude. You've got to stop doing that! But, yes, Papa—we got funding! We had a second meeting with an investor and they were really impressed with us,' Maahi said, hopping on her feet, her face lit with joy. She looked from her dad to mom.

'What did they think of the business plan?' Papa asked. His moustache rose slightly on one end, suggesting a lopsided smile. That told her that he was happy, probably even proud, but he was never overtly expressive so that was the best she was going to get. She would take that. He wasn't comfortable with expressing emotions, so he chose to engage her in technicalities, showing interest in the business, which was motivating for Maahi. It made her feel like a grown-up.

'We've made a couple of changes to the business plan—we didn't have to but they recommended it, and it made total sense, so we agreed. They have agreed to provide us the initial capital and seed fund. We might look into another round of funding after that, if needed,' Maahi explained.

'What is their investment against? Ownership percentage?'

'We're furnishing the details right now. But yes, they want share in the company. Laila and I will have the higher percentage, but Mr Jindal is also looking for a certain percentage of shares.'

'What is the next step from here?' Papa asked. His eyes weren't in their usual state of silent amusement. Maahi could see that he was enthused too, but not in an obvious way like Maahi and Sarthak.

'We're in touch with an accountant, who will review our business plan, dig up more hidden expenses, I'm sure. Once we have the final numbers, we're ready to go. Mr Jindal is really keen on the website, so we'll find a developer and get started on that immediately. I'm taking care of the design and pricing and menu, etc. Laila is going to look for a place and pick out appliances and equipment. We need to get a permit, hire a couple of employees, start digital and social media marketing … Oh, there's so much work to be done!' Maahi felt nervous just thinking about it.

'You'll be fine. You've spent time on this plan; I'm sure you know what you're doing by now,' Papa said.

Maahi grinned wide. 'Thank you, Papa. This means so much to me. Thank you for letting me do this.'

'Must feel like a dream turning into reality, eh?' Sarthak said, picking up a sliced cucumber from the salad bowl on the dining table.

'Yep. I'm still quite dazed.'

'Understandable,' Sarthak said, looking around. 'Where's Ma, though? I'm hungry.'

Just then they heard their mom talk animatedly on the phone '… yes, yes. Thank you. It's all God's grace. We were worried too, but they worked very hard…'

'Bragging to the neighbours,' Papa said, smiling.

'I'll finish making dinner. What was she cooking?' Maahi said, going to the kitchen. She checked the pots on the stove. 'Aloo methi ki sabzi and moong ki daal. The daal is done, sabzi needs a few more minutes. Sarthak, can you set the table? I'll get started on the rotis.'

When Ma was done calling and telling all the women in the neighbourhood the news, she came back and hugged Maahi. She had tears in her eyes. They sat down and had dinner together, both sniffing their way through it. Maahi looked around the dinner table and felt overjoyed. Getting her parents to believe in her again was a huge load off her shoulders.

Sarthak concentrated mostly on the food. Maahi felt sad when she thought about him leaving for Mumbai in a few weeks. She wondered how many such dinners they would have as a family after that. Would he come back after graduating or move to some other city? If she ever found the courage to tell her parents about Siddhant, they might get married and she would move out. She wanted to hold off on that. She liked when her parents didn't think of her as a disappointment and wanted to bask in that for as long as she could.

※

Her phone rang right when she got into bed. Siddhant was going to be at the hospital till late, and she hadn't been expecting him to call. Laila, who had exhausted herself with all the excitement and anxiety, had gone to sleep early; and Maahi was home, so it couldn't be her parents or Sarthak. These were literally the only people who ever called her.

Maahi pushed away the comforter reluctantly and got up. Her phone was plugged in to charge at her desk. It was an unknown number. An unknown number she knew.

She turned her phone on silent and went back to bed. She was about to get under the covers when she paused. She asked herself why, after all these years, she was still so vehemently unwilling to talk to Kishan. Every time she thought of him, she thought about how far back in the past it was, how unaffected she was by his existence. Then what was she afraid of?

She texted Rohit.

Maahi: You home?

Rohit: Just reached. Sup?

Maahi: Want to take a walk?

Rohit: Cool. I'll meet you outside in 10

Maahi put on jeans and replaced her worn-out T-shirt for one without holes and climbed down the stairs. She saw Rohit's tall frame making its way towards her five minutes later. He bent down and gave her a hug.

'Goddammit, why the hell do you look and smell like that in the middle of the night,' Maahi exclaimed.

'You're in a good mood.'

'I'm just saying—you're just walking in Vaishali Sector 4 with me. This is no runway.'

'My hotness is a curse. What can I do?' Rohit flashed her a perfect smile, displaying his perfect teeth.

'Shut up and listen to me.'

'Yes, ma'am.'

Under sodium street lamps throwing a dirty yellow light on them, they walked on the deserted roads lined with parked cars serving as roofs for stray dogs. 'So, Kishan's been calling me.'

'What the fuck does he want?'

'I have no idea. I haven't taken any of his calls, and I'm trying to figure out why.'

'Isn't that clear? Because he's your ex. Past.' Rohit looked annoyed, even slightly disgusted. He hated Kishan for what the breakup had done to Maahi.

She was touched. 'I'm going to call him back,' she said.

'What the fuck!'

'Stop cursing! I had been afraid to talk to him because I didn't want him to see what a failure I was. I've changed a lot and I'm working really hard for something I really wanted to do, but it wasn't concrete. There was nothing to certify any of this. If I talked to him and he asked about what I was doing, I would have to tell him that I dropped out of college, ran back home, worked at a stupid app developing company and then a coffee shop, joined a college I want to drop out of, a second time, was trying to open a bakery, but nothing had happened. But now it has. There's evidence now.'

'So now that you have funding, you just want to show off,' Rohit said, looking down at her.

'I wouldn't put it like that, but yes.'

'How would you put it?'

'Umm ... well, there exists a constant need to *win the breakup*, to one-up the ex, and you may argue that it's childish, but can't challenge its existence,' Maahi said wisely, proud of herself.

'One, that's ridiculous. And two, do you think you've won the breakup? Do you even know what he's doing?'

'I'm not saying I've won it. But I'm definitely not afraid of talking to him anymore. I don't know what Kishan is doing, but I'm not doing too bad.'

Rohit thought for a moment. 'If we have to stick with your stupid theory, yeah, I see it. You're by no means losing the breakup.'

'Yep. So can I call him?'

Rohit shrugged. 'Your mind seems made. Thank you for inviting me to watch though. Thoughtful.'

'You're welcome.' She pulled out her phone. They turned a corner and Maahi stopped under the street lamp. There were two new missed calls from Kishan.

Maahi called the number, looking up at Rohit, who rolled his eyes.

Kishan picked up the call after the second ring. 'Maahi?'

'Hi.'

'Hi. How are you?'

'I'm good. How are you?' Maahi asked. Her heart suddenly beat faster and her fingers shook. She didn't really understand why.

'I'm fine,' Kishan said, then paused. 'I moved back to Delhi recently. Just wanted to touch base and see how you were doing.'

'I heard. And yeah, I'm doing well.'

'Great. That's great. I heard you dropped out of college?'

'Yep,' Maahi said shortly. She was surprised to find that she didn't feel the need to defend herself in front of him. Her success would speak for itself.

Kishan waited for a moment, then said, 'I quit Accenture too. It got too stressful for me. I mean, it was stressful to begin with, as you know. But then it got worse. I also wanted to come back to Delhi, so I started looking for something else. I'm with Bank of America now, in Gurgaon.'

'Oh, nice. Good for you.'

'Yeah, I'm liking it. It's great to be home and around people I've known all my life. How is everything with you—how's your family?'

'Everyone's good. Sarthak got into IIT Bombay. He starts soon,' Maahi said proudly. She knew she didn't have the skillset it took to crack JEE, but her brother doing it was as good as she herself doing it. It gave her bragging rights.

'Oh, that's great!' Kishan said.

They both became quiet.

'What?' Rohit mouthed.

Maahi shrugged. She tried to figure out why he had called her, what he wanted from her, but came up with nothing. A part of her needed an apology from him, for what he had done years ago. She knew it was irrational, but it infuriated her that he hadn't said a simple sorry in all these years.

'What's he saying?' Rohit whispered.

Maahi placed her hand over the speaker and said, 'Awkward silence.'

Kishan spoke just then. 'So, listen. Let's catch up properly?'

'Umm…'

'Would you like to meet for coffee sometime?'

Maahi took a minute, looked away from Rohit, and then said, 'Sure. Why not?'

Part Five

17

'But why?' Laila asked. Maahi was sitting with her in her study. They were looking over their options of website developers they were considering. She pointed to the screen and said, 'Ooh, I like their work. Did you see the health and beauty website they created? That was cute.'

'A bit too white and pink, but we can brief them. Which reminds me, I'm working on the brief right now. Could you check out a few websites and let me know if you have any ideas, something specific you'd like to have on our site? Email me your notes,' Maahi said. She opened a few other tabs. 'I like this guy too. He's only done a couple of sites, but he's talented. Can we trust that he'd be able to handle our project though?'

'If he has talent, why not? We could give him a chance. We're only just starting out too, but someone believed in us.'

'True. Okay, I'm putting him on our list. Let's look for one or two more and we can start talking to them and see what works out.'

'Cool,' Laila said, opening more links from the list Maahi had researched and put together. 'You didn't answer my question—why did you say yes to meeting him?'

Maahi sighed. 'Let's just let this go, please? It's not like we made any solid plans. I didn't want to say no, because then he would've thought I'm not over him, or I would've had to make an excuse and all that's just too messy.'

'Also, you wanted to see him.'

'No!'

'Fool yourself, don't try to fool me.' Laila glared at Maahi.

'Fine. I do, a little bit. But it's only because I want to get it out of the way. He's back here, so it's inevitable that we'll bump into each other, somewhere, sometime, so—'

'Not true. You have zero mutual friends.'

Maahi resumed, ignoring Laila's interruption, '—why not just do it and move on? That way, it'll be less awkward when we bump into each other.'

'You mean *if*. The chances are very slim. Also, you just want to see him because you want to see him—you're curious. Hey, I'm not judging you. It's normal and completely fine. But stop making excuses,' Laila said. She pointed at the screen. 'This one's not bad.'

'I like it too. And I guess I do want to see him…' Maahi admitted slowly. 'Is that bad? Does that make me a bad person? What with things going so well with Siddhant and all.'

'Oh, relax. You're probably just going to meet for coffee or something. That's hardly cheating.'

'It's because I haven't seen him since the night we broke up, and we haven't talked about the breakup—not that I want to—but, I don't know. I don't know why I want to see him. I just do.'

'That's alright. These things are twisted and complicated and we can't really rationalize them. There's no simple explanation. Don't overthink it,' Laila said. 'Maybe you just want him to see how awesome you are.'

'I used to be fat.' Maahi curled her lip.

'Oh, please. You weren't exactly fat; I've seen your pictures. Maybe like five Kgs overweight, if that. And you lost that real quick. It's amazing how much working for your passion changes a person. You don't even realize how much exercise your mind and body are getting, how mentally and physically active you get when you're immersed in doing what you love. Running around, meeting new people, facing rejection, trying harder, making shit happen. I'm proud of how much you've grown,' Laila said, nodding her approval, before saying, 'I don't know what's going to happen once the bakery is open and things settle down a bit though. You might become fat for real.'

'I look forward to the day things settle down. It's going to take a long time for us to even break even, let alone start making profit.'

'But it's all going to be worth it. I'm really enjoying actually starting work, instead of going over the plan over and over and over again. God, that was driving me nuts.'

'Yeah, I was worried about your sanity for a bit there.'

'Sorry about that,' Laila said sheepishly. 'It did make you step up and take charge though.'

'Thanks for that. There was no other way I would've learned.'

'You're welcome.'

They continued working on the research for the website. When they had enough to go on, they parted ways. Laila was working with a broker and they had a few leads on commercial spaces in Meherchand and Shahpurjat. They were going to take a look. The broker seemed very confident about one of the spaces, which got Maahi and Laila excited. They were thrilled to watch their dream take shape.

Maahi went back home and wrote emails to all four website developers they had shortlisted, introducing themselves and asking for quotes. She then started working on the menu. It was her favourite part. They already had a standard menu. She now wanted to polish it and give all items witty, quirky names. She also needed to look at pricing. They were offering a discount in the first week, and Maahi needed to calculate how that would affect their sales and profit.

She went from one website to another, looking at their menus, trying to get ideas. A couple of hours later, she somehow found herself on a middle-aged Russian's twitter page. He had been baking and selling pot brownies in the shape of marijuana leaves for a living for twenty years and called his food truck a speciality bakery.

'Maahi!' She heard her mom call from the kitchen.

'Coming!' Maahi closed the tab and looked back at her list. She wasn't getting anywhere with the names. She needed someone to bounce ideas off. She had tried calling Siddhant earlier but he hadn't taken her call. 'Is Sarthak home?' she asked, walking into the kitchen.

'I don't know. I haven't seen him in a while. He might be in his room with headphones on. Listen, Sushanti aunty and her family are coming for dinner tonight. I'm making chicken tikka masala, achari paranthas and pulao. Is that okay?' Ma asked, adding salt to wheat flour.

'Sounds good to me. Let me take care of this,' Maahi said, taking the pot from her. 'What have you put in this already?'

'Just flour, salt and ghee. Do you think we should make raita too?'

'Why not? I can make it. Boondi or cucumber? Ooh, wait, I can make it with potatoes and amchur and hing and everything. Really spruce it up! Where's the achar masala for this?' Maahi pointed at the pot she was kneading the dough in. Ma passed over the bottle to her.

'Okay, you make the raita. Anything else?'

'I'll cut some salad. Nothing fancy; we don't want to distract people from your yummy chicken. Can we make jeera rice instead of pulao? Pulao might be a bit much.'

'Okay,' Ma said, washing the chicken. 'Can you bake some cupcakes too? Sushanti aunty said she wanted to taste.'

Maahi snorted. 'Yeah, right. I've been baking for so long and she never wanted to try any. Now that we're opening the bakery, she wants me to bake some for her so she doesn't have to pay for it.'

'Maahi, be nice.'

'Fine, I'll bake. I was just saying.'

Maahi finished with the paranthas and salad, and got started with the raita when her phone rang. She put down the boiled potatoes she was peeling and went to her room. It was Kishan.

'Hey,' she said into the phone.

'Hi. What's up?'

'Just helping Ma in the kitchen. We are having guests over for dinner.'

'Ah. Do you have some time to meet up before that?' Kishan asked.

Maahi looked at the round clock on her wall. It had a giant owl with huge eyes on it, which was quite scary at night, especially because of the radium. It was almost six. They were expecting Sushanti aunty around eight, which by Indian time would mean somewhere around nine thirty.

'Okay,' she said.

They decided to meet at a CCD close to her place. Maahi finished making the raita and got dressed. She told Ma she would be back in an hour. She had no intention of spending more time than that with Kishan, and he knew she had to get home for the dinner, so she had a legit excuse to take off in case things got awkward.

Maahi walked to the coffee shop with a weird feeling in her stomach. She didn't have a chance to ponder over it; she was there before she knew it. To her surprise, Kishan was there already, waiting for her. He got up as she pushed open the glass door. He walked to her and gave her a hug. Used to hugging Siddhant and Sarthak, both taller than Kishan, Maahi felt awkward when she rose on her toes and her face didn't completely disappear in his chest. She had never noticed that before.

She was disoriented for a brief moment—he smelled and felt so different from what she remembered, still somehow familiar. She pulled back. 'Hi,' she said, looking up at him. He still had that U-shaped beard enclosing his face, but it was thicker than before. It wasn't long, just about a centimetre, but more evenly distributed; he had a moustache too. Maahi could see that he put a lot of effort into grooming his facial hair. He was wearing a white shirt, untucked, with olive-khaki pants and Oxford shoes. His hair looked thinner and he might've gained a little weight—his face looked fuller, even under the beard—but other than that, he looked the same. Same dark eyes, looking at her the same way as always.

'Hey. It's so nice to see you,' Kishan said.

'Same,' Maahi said. She walked over to the table where he had been sitting and put her handbag down.

'I just got a coffee. What do you want?' he asked.
'I'll get it,' Maahi said, picking up her bag again.
'No. Tell me—I'll get it.'
'It's okay. I'll—'
'Come on. Don't be a stranger,' Kishan cut her off.
Maahi sighed. 'Fine, a masala chai would be good.'
'Seriously?'
'Yeah.'
Kishan raised an eyebrow and laughed. 'Anything else?'
'No, thank you.'

As he walked to the counter, Maahi wondered what was so wrong with masala chai. She enjoyed the flavours and combination of cloves, ginger and cardamom. And what did he mean by 'don't be a stranger'? They essentially were strangers at this point.

Kishan walked back and sat opposite her. He smiled. He seemed very confident, which made Maahi nervous, for some reason. It was as if he didn't feel the need to make a first impression, or behave a certain way. All of the things she was feeling. He was as he had always been with her.

'So, how's everything going? You look amazing,' he said.

'Thank you.' Maahi blushed against her will. 'Everything's great.'

'Yeah? I heard you're into baking and stuff now.'

'Yes.'

'Nice. How's that going?' Kishan asked. He sat with his legs apart, leaning forward, his elbows resting on his knees. The same way he sat the last time she had seen him.

'Quite good. We're opening a speciality bakery in South Delhi. We have funding and are looking for a space right now.

There's a lot going on. Hopefully everything will fall into place soon,' Maahi explained.

'That's great! Can't believe you bake! Show me your hand—do you burn your fingers a lot?' Kishan laughed, pulling her hand into his, turning it over to inspect.

'No. I'm actually quite good. I didn't know how organized I was until I started baking. I've learned a lot about myself. Like, I had no idea how particular I am—to the point where I think I have OCD. I have to get everything exactly right,' Maahi said. She felt the need to defend herself and her work, which agitated her.

'Quite the perfectionist, huh? Meticulous and *disciplined*. I like that.'

Maahi didn't like the way Kishan stressed the word 'disciplined' and looked at her teasingly. A waiter brought her tea and she thanked him, glad about the distraction. She wanted to finish her tea quickly so she could leave.

Kishan looked uncertain for a second, and then said, 'Look, I don't mean to come across as an asshole. It's just really easy to go back to how things were with us, talk to you the way I always did, because even with all these years of distance between us, we were once closer to each other than anyone else. Having known you like that, I'm sorry but I can't pretend to be a stranger.'

'I didn't say anything,' Maahi said. 'I never asked you to be a stranger.'

'Yeah. I can see that you're not very comfortable, so I thought I should say something. Anyway, forget I brought it up.'

'Okay.'

Kishan met her eyes. He was studying her face, as if to find answers. Maahi looked away. He was exactly the same as before. For a second, she let herself wonder how things would've been if they hadn't broken up. She would've been in her last year of engineering, her parents and neighbourhood aunties would be happy, she would be protected from the outside world, with a stable career ahead of her. She might even have been happy. For a long time, she had thought that all she needed to be happy was to be with Kishan.

'You must be wondering why I asked to meet you,' he said. Maahi looked at him. 'I just ... the way things ended ... I can't tell you how horrible I felt when I left your hostel that night. I was an asshole. I was trying to settle into this new life, with new friends, colleagues.' Kishan shook his head. 'Even now, when I try to think about that time—it's all a blur. It was my first job, first time I was earning, living away from home. I was changing and unintentionally, I was trying to change you too. I was new to all that and you were even younger ... I shouldn't have done that. I'm really sorry.'

Maahi shrugged. Not knowing what to say, she picked up her cup and took a sip.

'I began to feel like we weren't right for each other. I was constantly struggling with the relationship, and that night, when you asked me if I wanted the relationship ... I wasn't sure. We should've talked about it. And I'm sorry I didn't. I'm sorry I let you go so easily. I didn't know what I was doing.'

Despite herself, despite all the years, Maahi's eyes filled with tears. She tried to compose herself. She couldn't let him see how much he had hurt her, and how he was still affecting her. She sipped her tea and sniffed softly. 'And there was that girl, Payal.'

'It wasn't like that!'

Maahi met his eye. 'There was never anything between you two?'

'Well ... after we broke up, for a very brief period of time.'

'I knew it.'

'There was nothing between us when we were together—trust me,' Kishan said.

'Don't lie to me. It was happening right in front of me.' Maahi gritted her teeth.

'I'm not lying. Maybe there was a ... chemistry. But we didn't act on it until you were gone.'

That stung. He made sure she was gone before anything happened. Or that's what he wanted her to believe.

'Say something,' Kishan said.

Maahi looked up at him. She remembered how badly she had needed him to say something that night, how his silence had felt like a stab in the stomach. 'It's okay,' she said, clearing her throat. 'It doesn't matter anymore.'

'Of course it does. Don't even pretend that it doesn't affect you. I know you, I can read you.'

Maahi despised that. 'Talking about this reminded me of that night, that's all. Now you have apologized, it was a long time ago and we can all let it go.'

'But I can't. I need to make sure we're okay. I have to know that you've forgiven me.'

'I have.'

'No, you haven't,' Kishan said, peering into her eyes. 'It's important to me.'

'But why?' Maahi asked, trying to make sense of the situation. Why, all of a sudden, was she so important to him?

'Because I never stopped loving you.'

Maahi set her cup down slowly and gulped the tea. Her throat went dry.

'I couldn't,' Kishan said. He leaned forward and took her hand again. 'What we had was real. And I shouldn't have let you go. I realized that immediately, but I didn't know what to do about it. For a long time, I thought it was best for us to not be together. We were too different and you'd be happier without me. But it's not true—we're not different! We know each other so well. It'll never be the same with anyone else.'

Maahi pulled her hand back. 'I'm in love with someone. I have a fiancé.'

'Really?'

'Yes. I have to go. Please don't contact me again.' Maahi picked up her bag and got up. She walked away before Kishan could stop her.

'Wait,' Kishan called. He came after her as she walked out of the coffee shop, acutely aware of all heads turning to look at them. 'So that's your reason?'

'Do you need a stronger one? I'm in love with someone. I'm going to marry him,' Maahi said, trying to impress the gravity of the situation upon him.

'You don't want to talk to me because you have a fiancé? Not because you hate me for what happened between us? How things ended? Not because you're still angry, because it still affects you? It still matters?' Kishan held her shoulder to stop her and asked.

'No, because it's not about you anymore.' Maahi hated that he assumed he still affected her enough to play a role in deciding what she did or didn't do in her life. She jerked his hand away and said, 'Don't create a scene.'

'Fool yourself all you want, but I know.'

'Look, I don't have a problem talking to you. We can be friends. Just as long as we're just that, and you don't try to start something.'

'Start something? It never ended between us—not for me. And I know it didn't for you either. We loved each other so much. It doesn't end overnight.'

'It's been three fucking years!' Maahi exclaimed. She started walking away from him.

'Then why are you still so angry? Why are you running away, Maahi?' Kishan called from behind her. 'Because you know you still love me too?'

She didn't turn.

⚘

When Maahi got home, Sushanti aunty and her family were already there. They had started dinner. They asked her to join, but she said she'd eat later. She went to the kitchen to bake, listening to the conversation at the dining table, which didn't help her mood at all.

'Beta, we heard about your bakery,' Sushanti aunty called after a while. 'We were just telling your parents how proud we are.'

'Thanks, Aunty,' Maahi said.

'We can't wait to taste some of those cupcakes.'

Maahi stopped whipping the batter. She went to the living room and said, 'You'll have to wait for the bakery to open. I just realized we don't have all the ingredients I need.'

'We don't?' Ma asked.

'No. Sorry, Ma.' Maahi hated to see her mom's face drop. But she really didn't want to give Sushanti aunty what she wanted. 'We do have Laila's cookies. I'll warm some of those up and serve them with ice cream and other toppings for dessert. If that's fine with everyone.'

'Oh, we were looking forward to your world-famous cupcakes, but what can we do?' Sushanti aunty said bleakly.

Maahi felt petty in her small victory. She went back into the kitchen and pulled her phone out. She called Siddhant, and when he didn't take her call, she texted him.

Maahi: Where TF are you?

She started working on the cookie sundaes, her fingers unsteady. She got a response from Siddhant a little later.

Siddhant: At the hospital. What's up?

Maahi: Why TF are you never there when I need you?

Siddhant: Aww, I'm sorry. You know I can't really do anything about it. What's wrong?

Maahi: Nothing. I just fucking need you sometimes but you're never there.

Siddhant: You're scaring me now. Is everything okay?

Maahi: Yes! Is it too much to ask for to talk to my own boyfriend? No, wait. My FIANCÉ. Just for one minute???

Siddhant: I'll call you as soon as I can.

Maahi: Don't bother. I don't want to talk to you right now.

Siddhant: Sorry you feel that way. Wish I could say that this is going to end soon, but this is my profession. Thought you knew that from the beginning.

Maahi: Yeah, thanks for reminding me.

Maahi dropped the tray she was holding. She was shaking uncontrollably.

'Is everything okay?' Ma called from the dining table.

'Yes,' Maahi called back, picking up the tray and placing the dessert bowls on them. 'Sarthak, can you carry these out?' she asked weakly.

Later that night, Maahi felt terrible about the way she had behaved with Siddhant. She wanted to hear his voice so badly, her throat felt constricted every time she thought about him and their fight. It wasn't really a fight; she had blown up on him for no reason. It was totally uncalled for.

Her phone vibrated and she picked it up immediately. She had kept it close to her pillow, anticipating Siddhant's call.

It wasn't him. It was a text from Kishan. 'I don't want to be your friend. I want you back.'

Maahi deleted it. 'I'm sorry', she texted Siddhant and put her phone away, trying to sleep.

18

Maahi woke up late the next morning and grabbed her phone immediately. She didn't have a text from Siddhant waiting for her, but there was a missed call, which made her feel a little better. She looked at the time and realized she was running late to meet the broker.

Just then, her phone rang. It was Laila. 'Are you on your way?' From the background noise, Maahi could tell that Laila was on the road. She threw away the comforter and jumped out of bed.

'Are we meeting at ten thirty?' Maahi asked.

'Yes. Where are you?'

'Oh shit. I'm so sorry I slept in. I literally just woke up when you called…'

'Maahi, what the fuck! It's ten! What if I hadn't called?' Laila asked, her frustration evident in her tone.

'No, I woke up *before* you called. I was—'

'Okay, let's not do this right now. We have to see five, possibly six spaces today. The broker already has appointments. Could you please hurry up?'

'Yeah, I'm sorry. It'll take me an hour,' Maahi said, calculating the time in her head.

Laila snorted. 'There's no way you're getting here in an hour. The second appointment is at eleven ... I don't think you'll be able to make it to that either. Meet us at the third place. I'll text you all the addresses.'

'Okay.'

Maahi ran to the bathroom. She skipped the shower and got dressed quickly. She shoved everything she needed into her bag and ran out of the door. 'Sarthak!' she called from the living room. If she took the Metro, it would take her an hour on the train itself, plus walking to and from the station. There was no response. She peeked into his room; he wasn't there. No one seemed to be home.

'Fuck,' she muttered, running out. She locked the door behind her and ran to Vaishali Metro station. The sun was shining bright, but she didn't go back to get her sunglasses or a scarf. She preferred facing the sun's wrath compared to Laila's.

When Maahi got off the Metro, it was 11.18 a.m. She called Laila, but her call went unanswered. The third appointment was at noon, so Maahi walked towards the second one, hoping they would still be there. She pulled up the address on Google Maps and walked hurriedly to it.

'Oh, there she is,' Laila said, coming out of the rectangular 10×15 shop space Maahi found herself in front of.

'Hey, I'm so sorry I'm late,' Maahi said, walking to them.

'You made it just in time. We were about to leave. Maahi, this is Rajesh—he's showing us the spaces,' Laila said, turning to the thin, dark man in a plaid shirt.

'Hi.'

'Hello. Nice to meet you,' Rajesh said. 'Do you want to see the space too?'

They went inside. It was a small rectangular space with a

garage door at the front. It had basic concrete flooring, and the walls were painted white over the plaster of Paris. Maahi looked at Laila.

'We have to really envision it. The good thing is that this space faces the streets on two sides. We could install glass walls or large windows on both these sides,' Laila said, pointing to the front and side walls. 'We'll obviously need to do something with the floor.'

'A carpet might be the easiest solution, I think. Cheapest too,' Maahi suggested. 'We can use our theme colours and really liven up the place.'

'Yeah, that's what I thought. We could contrast it with the wall ... Let's see. I'm not very keen on the location though. Shall we check out the next spot?'

'Let's. Isn't that one in Shahpurjat?'

'Yep. It's the ideal location, right in the middle of boutiques and restaurants. It'll be a bit more expensive than Meherchand, but I can see it being a viable revenue model.'

They spent the rest of the day looking at spaces. Rajesh was able to fix a few more appointments, which they squeezed into their schedule for the day. They saw eight spaces in total, three of which they shortlisted. The next step would be to create a positives and negatives comparison list and present it to Mr Jindal.

'We need to move fast on this. All of these spaces are available for immediate possession. They're not going to stay on the market for long,' Laila said as they walked to the parking lot.

'I'll work on the list tonight. Can you fix a meeting with Harshita? Maybe we can come out here with her and finalize this?' Maahi suggested.

'Yeah, I'll see if she can meet tomorrow,' Laila said. 'Which one do you like best?'

'I like the fourth one we saw—the little one on the ground floor with one door, next to that bridal boutique.'

'I like that too. What about the one we saw before that?'

'It's on the first floor. Kind of out-of-sight. I feel like, with food, it has to be right in people's faces, for impulse shopping,' Maahi said. They reached Laila's car and Laila beeped open the doors.

'You're right. It has a little balcony though. We could put a couple of tables there. Let's see what Harshita slash Mr Jindal thinks,' Laila said. 'Which way are you going?'

'Could you drop me by AIIMS?'

'Sure. You're meeting Siddhant?' They got in the car and Laila backed out of the parking lot.

'Yeah,' Maahi said. She texted Siddhant.

> Maahi: Are you at work?
>
> Siddhant: Yeah. What's up?
>
> Maahi: Can I come over to see you for a sec?
>
> Siddhant: Now??
>
> Maahi: In 20 minutes. I'm in Shahpurjat.
>
> Siddhant: Cool.
>
> Maahi: Great. See you soon.
>
> Siddhant: See ya. :)

Maahi and Laila discussed the pros and cons for each of their shortlisted shop spaces on the way and Maahi made notes on her phone, to make her job easier when she created a OneNote presentation for Harshita. Maahi contemplated telling Laila about the incident with Kishan the previous night, but by the time they were done discussing business, they were close to AIIMS. She saved it for another time.

When she reached the hospital, she texted Siddhant.

> Maahi: I'm here. Where are you?
> Siddhant: Wait where we met last time. Give me 10 mins?
> Maahi: Sure. :*

She waited in the lounge where they had met a few weeks ago. A part of her wanted to tell him about what happened with Kishan at CCD. She was deliberating over it when she saw Siddhant walk towards her. He was wearing his white lab coat and a smile. She watched him come to her and felt guiltier about her angry texts from before.

'Hey,' Maahi said softly as he greeted her with a hug.

'Hey there,' Siddhant said. 'How are you doing?'

'I'm fine. How are you?'

'Meh. Surviving. We've had three traumas already today.'

'Oh, that sucks,' Maahi said, as he led her by her elbow to a metal seat against the wall.

'Sure does. But it's just how it is. Some days are more taxing than others.' Siddhant shrugged. 'How's your day been so far?'

'It's been alright. I woke up late—accidentally slept in. God, was Laila mad! We were seeing commercial spaces for the bakery today and I missed the first one, almost missed the second one too.'

'That doesn't sound like you,' Siddhant pointed out, looking at her closely.

'You mean the me who has OCD?'

'I know you like saying that, and you do exhibit some of the symptoms, but you don't *actually* have that.'

'Yes, Doctor.' Maahi grinned sheepishly.

Siddhant laughed. 'You're silly.'

Maahi laughed too, and then paused. 'I'm sorry about last night. I shouldn't have taken out my frustration about other things on you like that.'

'It's okay. I know you have a lot on your plate right now.'

'That doesn't justify using you as a punching bag. I do want to see you more, but right now with our crazy schedules, it's difficult. I need to be an adult about it,' Maahi said. She pursed her lips.

'You can use me whatever way you want,' Siddhant said sincerely, then burst out laughing.

'Stop! I'm serious. I feel bad.'

'Well, I guess it'll be easier if we didn't have to sneak around ... or we lived together.'

'As in...' Maahi gulped.

'If you're ready to tell your parents about us, why not? I've kind of made up my mind to spend my life with you—I see no reason to wait.' Siddhant touched her face lightly, looking her in the eye. 'I hate not seeing you for days at a time.'

'Me too.' Her voice was meek.

'But you need more time?'

'Just a little bit. They're only now coming on board with the bakery and everything. I don't want to stretch it too thin,' Maahi said, and then rushed to explain. 'I love you, Siddhant. And there's nothing I want more than to be with you.'

'I know. I love you too.' He took her hand between his and kissed it. 'Whenever you're ready.'

They talked for another few minutes before Siddhant was called. He hugged her one last time and she apologized again. She was glad she had stopped by to see him. The agitation she'd been feeling ever since meeting Kishan began to dissipate.

She kept Kishan off her mind as much as she could. Things were finally going well for her, and she didn't want to risk messing any of it up by even thinking about him and what he'd said. She wasn't mad at him anymore. She might've been, to begin with, but she simply stopped caring after a certain point.

꩜

A week went by, engrossed in work. They were able to convince Harshita about the space Maahi liked. Laila organized refurbishing and decorating of the space while Maahi worked with the designers on the website, the menu and flyers. They were also working on the design for Cookies + Cupcakes merchandise.

'Let's meet early tomorrow morning to get the appliances and equipment for the bakery?' Laila asked over phone.

'We're ready to install appliances?' Maahi asked.

'Yeah, we're done with painting and cleaning. We can get started with setting up the kitchen while the work continues in the front.'

'Yeah, makes sense.'

'I really like the layout. Simple front window and a conventional shop-esque counter, kitchen at the back behind the counter. Perfect,' Laila said.

'I can't wait to start baking in that kitchen!' Maahi said, excitedly.

'Yes! I'm excited too. We can start testing out the appliances as soon as we get them installed. It'll also give us a sense of what else we need—in case we missed something in our list.'

They decided to meet the next day to shop for the kitchen. Maahi called Siddhant, but he didn't pick up. They hadn't met since the day she had dropped by the hospital to see him. She tried to find time to call him, but either he was really busy, or simply careless, because she didn't feel like he was putting in the same amount of effort.

It made Maahi think about Kishan, who had done something similar to her in the past. But he was there, asking for another chance, willing to work with her on whatever needed to be done to fix things between them. The thought made her angrier at Siddhant.

Kishan called Maahi every day. She ignored it most times, but she had taken a couple of his calls, in weak moments when she'd needed someone to talk to and Siddhant wasn't available as usual and Laila was too involved in work. It was easy to talk to him, because she felt like he knew her well enough to understand what she was talking about, where she was coming from.

Later that evening, when Maahi was looking over the new designs their developer sent her, she got a call from Kishan. She took it on impulse, reasoning that she needed a break. In reality, she wanted to talk to him. He asked her to come out to meet him and she agreed. She knew what he wanted from her, and she didn't want the same thing. She couldn't explain how he was able to pull her back so easily.

They went for a movie and ended up talking through it. So much had happened in their lives since they were last close—they had a lot to catch up on. Maahi found herself laughing at his jokes and having a good time with him. She was reminded of why she'd fallen in love with him in the first place, five years ago.

Kishan put his hand on her waist as they walked out of the theatre. Maahi reflected on how easy it was for them to fall back into their same comfort zone, pick up where they left off, before she pulled away.

'I don't want you to take the Metro home. Let me drive you,' Kishan offered.

'No, I'll be fine taking an—'

'Please. I'll feel bad. It's not far—let me take you.'

'Okay,' Maahi relented. She got into the car with him. The radio started playing the old Shah Rukh Khan song '*Badshah-O-Badshah*'. 'Oh, I love this song!'

'Me too.' They sang along as Kishan drove out of the parking lot, both off key and horrible in general.

Maahi laughed when the song ended. 'How ridiculous! I don't know why I love it so much.'

'Because, sometimes, things that appear ridiculous at first are actually fabulous.' Kishan smirked. He pulled over on the side, one block away from her house. 'Like us.'

'What do you mean?'

'The idea of us, together. It seemed so ridiculous to you when I first proposed it. But now that we've had a chance to talk and spend some time together—I'm sure you can't deny that we have something. It's still there.'

'Kishan—'

'No, hear me out. Don't be so quick to discard a notion simply because you're too afraid to consider it,' Kishan said. 'You told me that you have a fiancé. That's why you can't be with me. But who is this guy? Does he know you the way I do? Is this like an arranged-marriage type of situation? If your parents want you to get married, I'm down for that. You don't have to marry this stranger.'

'He's not a stranger! I *love* him,' Maahi said sternly.

'The same way you loved me?'

Maahi paused. She looked out of the window at the little kids in dirty vests drawing shapes on the side of the roads with sticks. They were parked outside the corner grocery store, which had been there for as long as her memory went. She waved back at the shopkeeper, Manoj uncle, as she said quietly, 'No. It's different. But just because it's different doesn't mean it's any lesser.'

'And your parents like him too?' Kishan asked. She studied his persistent eyes. He was not letting it go.

'They don't know about him yet.'

'Then how is he your fiancé?'

'Because he asked me to spend the rest of my life with him and I said yes!' Maahi exclaimed. 'I'll tell my parents soon.'

Kishan didn't break eye contact even for a second. Maahi felt something in her chest she hadn't felt in a long time; something only Kishan could make her feel. 'Don't you think it could be that you haven't told your parents because you're not sure?'

'No. Listen, I've got to go. Thank you for driving me here.' Maahi tried to open the door but it was locked.

'Please don't run away like that. Just talk to me.' Kishan put a hand on her cheek and turned her face to him. 'I know you want this too. If not, why did you come out with me today? Think about it. Think about us and how great we are together. I let you go once and I'm not going to do that again.'

Their faces were close to each other. Maahi felt his warm breath on her lips. She looked away from his eyes, her gaze dropping to his lips. Those lips that she had kissed uncountable times. The ones that had touched every inch of her. A shiver washed over her body like a wave when she remembered.

'Give me one last chance,' Kishan whispered, his thumb grazing her cheek.

'Kishan…'

'Shh. Don't say anything right now. You're only hurting me more.'

His thumb burned her cheek, as she looked into his eyes, breathing softly. Kishan examined her face intently. Through her glazed eyes, Maahi saw tears shine in his. She shook her head slightly.

Kishan leaned in and kissed her lips, holding her face in place with his hands. His lips moved against hers and paused. She caught her breath. He pulled back and looked at her again. 'Perfect, like always,' he said, before leaning back into the kiss.

Maahi couldn't move. She felt his lips on hers, soft and warm and wet and oh so familiar. He smelled the same, tasted the same. He kissed the same too. Maahi was overwhelmed with memories. He was the first guy she kissed. She was overpowered by the flood of memories—each kiss that they'd shared—and found herself incapable of movement.

Kishan pulled away, her face still in his hands. He met her eyes and said, 'If you'd let me, I would like to wake up to your face every day, for the rest of my life,' he said.

'I have to go,' Maahi breathed.

'No—'

'Please,' she begged.

'At least tell me you'll think about it.'

'Kishan—'

'Promise me. Please?'

She nodded slowly. Her lower lip quivered.

'Sweet dreams,' Kishan said as Maahi got out of his car and shut the door behind her.

She climbed up the stairs with wobbly feet, trying to make sense of what had just happened. She felt transported back a few years. It had been so easy to go back and pretend that all these years they'd been apart never happened and he'd never abandoned her. That man, he held a power over her that she was unable to comprehend. It made no sense. A few phone calls and a couple of meetings—that was all it took for him to pull her all the way back to the beginning.

How could she let this happen? She was in love with Siddhant. This was wrong. How would he feel when he found out? Her jaw hurt from clamping her teeth together to stop herself from breaking down.

Maahi pulled out her phone, desperate to tell someone, share her guilt before it crushed her.

> Maahi: I did something bad…
>
> Rohit: Uh-oh. What?
>
> Maahi: Kissed Kishan.
>
> Rohit: Wtf! NO!!!
>
> Rohit: NO. You're kidding, right?!
>
> Rohit: Are you SERIOUS?!?!
>
> Rohit: YOU CAN'T BE SERIOUS!!!!!

Maahi turned off her phone and slipped it under her pillow before falling face first into bed. She was in no mood to be judged.

That night, when Maahi went to bed, she didn't sleep until the break of dawn. Her eyes kept filling with hated tears, ruing the years they had lost. The wasted time they would never get back. She missed him for all the years she had forced herself to not miss him. She forgot about the horrible things they went through when they were together. All she could remember were the good times. All she could think about was how much she missed those days and how much she wanted them back.

19

Maahi had five missed calls from Laila. As she looked at it, her phone buzzed again; it was Laila again. She really needed a break—just one day off, away from everything, to find her balance, make sense of what was happening to her. But apparently, that was way too much to ask for.

She sat on her bed for a long time after she woke up. Her brain stopped operating; she wasn't thinking anymore, she was simply sitting there, glancing at her phone every time it lit up. Laila kept calling. She had several texts from several people.

> Kishan: Good morning. :*
>
> Laila: Hey, is your phone off?
>
> Laila: Pick up!
>
> Laila: Not again, Maahi. Swear to god…
>
> Rohit: Hey, you okay?
>
> Laila: Ugh, if you're still sleeping, trust me I'm going to kill you
>
> Laila: WTF DUDE
>
> Sarthak: You home? Laila Di called

Laila: Where TF are you

Rohit: You know you can talk to me…

Kishan: Just wanted to let you know… I'm thinking about you, baby!

She thought about how Siddhant never called her anything except *Maahi*. He would say her name with different inflections. After a while, she thought maybe she was waiting for him to call her, or send her a text message. And then she started waiting for it. It didn't happen.

Maahi spent the whole day in bed. She figured no one was home, since no heads peeked in through her door. Siddhant didn't text her, Kishan didn't text her again, Laila's calls and texts eventually ceased. She got a couple of calls from Sarthak too, and she tried to remember the last time she'd seen him. He had to leave for Mumbai in a week and was busy meeting his friends before that.

Feeling worse than ever, she sat there, contemplating her next steps. Was she really still in love with Kishan? He certainly seemed to believe so. She couldn't deny that she felt something when she was with him, when he kissed her. Her face grew hot, remembering the kiss. Would she never stop loving him? *Should* she? Maybe they were meant to be together. Maybe she was trying to build something with Siddhant forcefully, something that wasn't there.

The more she thought about it, the deeper she pushed herself into depression. She loved Siddhant, she really did. She could picture spending her life with him, but did she really ever love him the way she had loved Kishan? The innocent, selfless way, worshipping the ground he walked on, wanting nothing more than having him in her life, needing him like air? Can you ever love someone the same way you did when you were seventeen? They say a girl never forgets her first love. She was finding that to be true.

Exhausting herself, she finally gave up and lay down on the bed. She put a pillow over her head and called Laila. It was five in the evening, she knew Laila would be pissed at her, but she needed her right now; she needed her advice. She couldn't do it alone anymore.

'Maahi, what the fuck!' Laila screamed on the phone.

'Hey, I'm sorry…' Maahi said slowly.

'Where have you been? Are you okay? I was just on my way over. I called Sarthak, but he didn't know where you were either.' Laila's voice was shrill, loud enough to be heard clearly even over the noise of traffic.

'I've been at home. I don't … I don't really know where to begin…'

'What? What are you saying, Maahi? We had to check out the equipment today. I was forced to do all of that alone. I have short-listed a bunch of appliances. I'll send you the details. Could you please, please look them over so we can finalize and place the orders?'

'Laila, I don't think I can,' Maahi said, her voice cracking. 'I don't feel so good—I don't know what's happening.'

'What happened? Are you sick?' Laila asked. The noise from behind her was subtler and Laila wasn't panting. Maahi guessed she had stopped walking and found a quieter place to talk.

'No, I just need a couple of days off. There's so much happening…'

'Are you kidding me? Get your shit together. I'm begging you.'

'I only need one or two days…'

'Do you realize how much work this is? How can you expect me to do this alone?'

Tears overflowed Maahi's eyes. 'I don't … I'm not expecting you to do it alone. I just need a day to breathe. There's so much—I met Kishan last night and I'm so confused—'

'Okay, stop,' Laila cut her off. 'I literally don't have any time for this right now. You and your childish games … Ugh. Maahi, what is this?'

They were both quiet for a moment. Maahi wanted to talk to her, to tell her, but she knew Laila was in the middle of a thousand things, things she should've been in the middle of with her. She felt guilty about that. Laila spoke before she could say anything.

'You know why I didn't ask you to open this bakery with me?' Laila said slowly. 'I had had this idea for the longest time, but I never brought it up. It was because I wasn't sure you were ready. I don't blame you for that—you're young and still trying to figure things out. We all are. I didn't want to get you into something you would regret, or something that might come in the way of your personal development. But then you brought it up. You said you wanted this. You were passionate about it and I bought it. Maybe I just saw what I wanted to see. You weren't ready.'

Maahi sobbed quietly, her hand on the speaker.

Laila sighed, and then continued, 'I love you, Maahi. You know I do. But I don't think you see how important this is to me. If you can't do this, there's still time to back out. We haven't used much of the funds yet, we've only paid rent for the space, and the website designers. Actually, the accountant and some other expenses ... But it's better to stop now than later, with more of it down the drain. We might find ourselves in a situation where there's no out. There's one now, and I'm offering it to you.'

Maahi sniffed and cleared her throat. She removed her hand from the speaker and said, 'You're offering me an exit from Cookies + Cupcakes?'

'Yes.'

'But ... this is my dream.'

Laila breathed out. Maahi could picture a mixture of a smile and a snort on her face. 'You *think* it is. Think harder. Take some time.'

Maahi thought about it for a second and nodded, then realized she was on the phone. 'Okay,' she said bleakly. 'I'm sorry.'

'Nah. You take care and call me if you need me, okay? You don't have to make this decision alone.'

'Thank you.'

They hung up. Maahi got off the bed, only to sit on the floor and cry, her whole life a mess. When she couldn't handle it anymore, she went to the bathroom and stood under the shower. She expected to feel better, somehow lighter when she stepped out, but wasn't gratified.

> Maahi: I need to see you.
>
> Siddhant: Come over tonight?
>
> Maahi: No, this can't wait.
>
> Siddhant: Are you okay?
>
> Maahi: No, I need to talk to you. Please, this one time, just say yes.

Siddhant: Okay, let me see what I can do. Where do you want to meet?

Maahi: Can you come over?

Siddhant: What about your parents?

Maahi: No one's home. And I don't care.

Siddhant: I'll come as soon as I can. Is everything alright?

Maahi: I don't know.

Maahi slumped down on her bed and lay down, her wet hair on the bed sheet. She was in her navy sweatpants and a white T-shirt that had turned greyish over washes. She had got that T-shirt back when she was in high school. It had an image of Darth Vader printed on its front and no matter how much her mom hated it, Maahi couldn't throw it out. She hadn't even seen *Star Wars*.

Siddhant was there sooner than she had expected. He must've left immediately after her texts. Maahi got up and checked her reflection in the mirror. The old T-shirt hung loose on her skinny shoulders, her eyes were hollow, with dark shadows underneath, and her half-dried hair was a tangled mess. She pushed it away from her face and went out to open the door for Siddhant.

She smiled as she said hi, a vacant smile that didn't reach her eyes.

'Hey. What's going on?' Siddhant asked, entering.

'Come with me,' Maahi said, holding his hand and pulling him to her room. 'Sit down, I need to talk to you.'

Siddhant let her guide him and sat down at the edge of her bed. He looked up at her, his eyes searching. He didn't look so well either. His eyes were sunk in, missing their usual gleam. His hair and beard were in a mess again. Maahi touched a strand falling over his eyes and pushed it back, letting her fingers linger in his hair.

'What is it?' he asked.

Maahi pulled her hand back and sat down next to him on the bed. She sighed and closed her eyes, trying to form words, somehow construct sentences that would aptly deliver how she was feeling. And, maybe, in the process decipher what she was actually feeling.

'You're really scaring me now. Has something happened?' Siddhant asked. Turning towards her, he held both her hands in his. 'Maahi, talk to me.'

She sniffed and looked away. 'I told you about Kishan, right?'

'The asshole ex-boyfriend? Yes.'

'He's not an asshole! He's only human. He was dealing with some things back then and fucked up.'

'O—*kay*,' Siddhant said, confusion evident on his face. 'I know only what you've told me, and the way you've told me.'

'Right. But I was wrong. I judged him wrong—arrived at conclusions about him that aren't true. I shouldn't have done that.'

'And this is relevant because…?'

'He's here. He's in Delhi,' Maahi said. She gulped and looked up at him, trying to find the courage. She did what she tended to do in situations of stress and panic, and blabbered, words stumbling over each other to escape her lips. 'Kishan moved back to Delhi some time ago. He tried to get in touch with me, but I hated him! I didn't give him a chance to talk to me at all. Then he kept trying and I thought, fine, I'll just talk to him generally once and that will be it. Only, it wasn't. We started talking, and I finally started seeing how things happened from his perspective. I always framed him as the bad guy when it wasn't completely his fault. It was the circumstances.'

Siddhant was still holding her hand. His fingers tightened and loosened their grip on hers.

'I started talking to him again. He's a good guy, Siddhant. I judged him unfairly. I was in love with him for such a long time ... long after we'd broken up. These things don't just go away. When I met him again, I realized that things were exactly the same as before. I had only learned to live without him. I hadn't stopped caring about him ... He's not a bad person.'

'Okay. Now that we've established that your ex-boyfriend is a good guy, will you tell me why we're talking about him?' Siddhant asked.

Maahi looked around the room, her eyes darting from one object to another, not finding a resting place. She shook her head and said sullenly, her voice barely a whisper, 'You haven't been around.'

They paused in that moment, looking at each other, as Siddhant's face changed, going from confusion to comprehension to disbelief to impassiveness. It only took a second. Maahi saw it happen, and something caught in her throat. He released her hand and turned away.

'It was one kiss. He kissed me, and I didn't kiss him back,' Maahi rushed to explain, then added quietly, 'but I didn't stop it either.'

'And it's my fault.'

'It's not your fault! I'm just saying that you haven't been around. Which is true—you haven't. With so much going on with the bakery and my parents and everything, I've been so stressed and worn out and I try to turn to you but you're never there. But then I feel bad about turning to you in the first place and I want to talk to you about it, but you said your career is so important to you and you don't want anything to distract you. I don't want to be what that girl was for you...'

'Maahi, don't,' Siddhant said sternly. 'I've never seen you as a distraction.'

'You have! You told me yourself! When we first started seeing each other—after that Mario Kart date. You told me your primary focus is your work.'

'And I meant it. I have quite literally been working on my career ever since I was born. I had only known you for a few weeks. How can there be a comparison? And I still somehow found my way back to you. Those few weeks away from you were enough for me to realize how much I needed you in my life.'

'But what about since then? You've been so busy. You've always put your work before me!' Maahi cried, her frustration flowing.

'I've just started off. I don't know what you expected this would be like, but this is the reality. I can't stop being a doctor. I can't help my schedule. I knew what I was getting into. And I thought *you* did too,' Siddhant snapped.

'I understand the life you've chosen. I'm not *stupid*.'

'Then stop trying to blame me for what you did!'

'I'm not blaming you for anything. I'm trying to talk to you, have a conversation with you, tell you that I've needed you several times over the past few weeks and you've never been there,' Maahi said. Tears were flowing down her cheeks now, seeing Siddhant's distress and knowing she was the one responsible. Yet, for some reason, fighting it.

'You think *I* haven't needed you? You think when I get home after one rough day after another, I don't wish you were there? You've been busy too—but I don't hold that against you. I admire that you're so driven and hardworking, and I want nothing more than to see you succeed. But that doesn't mean I don't miss you. Just because I don't go around crying about it—'

'That's mean!'

'No. I'm telling you how I feel. I love you and I miss you and I care about you, and I want to spend time with you. Why do you think I've been telling you that we should talk to our parents all along? Because I was sure. I was ready. But I can see now that you weren't. You kept saying it's because you needed time to set up your business, but I can see the real reason why you were holding it off,' Siddhant said. He got up and ran his hands through his hair. 'It's because of this guy … Kishan.'

'No! No, it's not like that. It's because I didn't want to stir things at home. They're okay after such a long time. You have to trust me,' Maahi said restlessly.

'You'd understand how that's a little hard for me to do right now.'

'But I'm telling you the truth. And we don't have time to get married right now anyway. And I'm only twenty-three!'

'And I'm twenty-six. I never intended to get married so early either. But I just … I thought when it's real, I'd *know*. With you, I thought I knew. I'm sorry you felt pressured. I was simply suggesting telling our parents and getting engaged, so we could stop sneaking around.' Siddhant sighed. 'Anyway. None of that matters anymore.'

'What does that mean?' Maahi asked, scared to find out.

'Do you have to ask?'

'I never meant to hurt you, Siddhant. You have to believe me. That kiss ... I understand if you never forgive me. But you have to trust me—I never intended for it to happen. I would never intentionally hurt you. I'm so confused. Meeting Kishan, there are all these feelings rushing back—it makes me wonder if I always had feelings for him, maybe I was trying so hard to supress them, I fooled even myself. We've known each other so well, we're so familiar. I don't know what to think of any of this. And then there's you.' Maahi paused. She got up and stood in front of him. He looked straight ahead, his jaw clenched. Maahi touched it lightly and said, 'I love you so much ... but—'

'I have to go,' Siddhant said suddenly. He looked away from the wall he was staring at and took a step back.

Maahi took a step further. 'Siddhant, please ... I'm really sorry...'

'I can't do this.'

'Please, listen to me—let me explain.'

'I think I've heard enough,' Siddhant said. He looked at her. 'I can't stand here and listen to you tell me why you love me, *but*. I refuse to do that.'

Maahi wiped her tears and gasped for air. 'I never meant—'

'I don't have time for this!' Siddhant suddenly lost control and snapped. 'I should've never let it come to this ... never should've gotten into this...' He looked away from Maahi and shook his head.

'Don't say that!' Maahi cried. 'What we have—'

'We have *nothing*. That's what we have right now. You made sure of it.'

'But I love you!'

Siddhant snorted and turned away, but not before Maahi saw his clenched jaw shivering ever so slightly and his bloodshot eyes, dark and vacant, releasing a single drop of tear. He wiped it away angrily and opened the door to walk out.

For a second, as she watched his back disappear behind the door, Maahi's heart sank. She saw him walk away, and it struck her. She might never see him again. He would never want to talk to her after what she'd done. When Siddhant walked out that door, he was walking out of her life. She felt crippled with the pain in her gut. She bent inwards, holding her arms together, clutching tightly against her stomach, trying to physically salve her pain.

20

Maahi heard her mom's voice in the living room. She quickly pushed her hair back and ran her palms through her face before rushing out. Papa was sitting on the couch, taking off his shoes and Ma was by the dining table, a glass of water in her hand. Siddhant, who was by the door that connected Maahi's room to the living room, paused midstride.

'Who is...' Ma looked from Siddhant to Maahi, and asked, 'Is this your friend?'

Maahi sniffed and tried to compose herself. Her voice cracked as she smiled and said, 'Yes, Ma, Papa, this is Siddhant. Siddhant, my parents.'

Siddhant looked baffled for a moment, then said, nodding, 'Namaste Uncle, Aunty.'

'Namaste beta. *You're* Siddhant! Maahi talks about you,' Ma said.

'Really?'

'Yes. You're the one who studies at AIIMS, right?'

'Yeah.' Siddhant shrugged and added, 'Well, I don't study there anymore. I finished my MBBS, now I'm practising.'

'We weren't updated,' Papa said, laughing. 'Congrats, beta.'

'Your parents must be so proud,' Ma said.

Siddhant looked at Maahi, who stared back at him. They were both hurting; it was evident in their eyes. They somehow found themselves in this social situation, pretending to be friends, talking about his career and his parents' approval—both of which were sensitive topics for him. He nodded. 'I need to get going,' he said evenly to her parents. 'It was nice to meet you.'

'Oh, why don't you have dinner with us? I am making kadhi,' Ma said.

'That sounds delicious, Aunty, but I really should go,' Siddhant said.

'Okay. But you have to stay for dinner next time.'

'Next time,' Siddhant said meekly. He attempted a smile and walked towards the door. Maahi knew there would be no *next time*, and it killed her. It was only when she saw what she was losing that she realized how much she loved him, how much he meant to her. She couldn't stand to watch his back disappear once again.

'Siddhant, stop.' Maahi walked to him and held his forearm. He looked at her in confusion. She turned to Papa. 'Siddhant isn't just a friend. I'm in love with him.'

The stillness in the air was palpable.

Maahi breathed out. 'I love him,' she said. 'I didn't intend for it to happen like this, but I've been meaning to introduce him to you for some time now.'

Papa looked from Maahi to Siddhant, his face inscrutable. Ma put her glass down on the dining table and stared at them too, her mouth agape. Maahi waited. Neither of her parents said anything.

'Why are you doing this? What's the point?' Siddhant asked, his eyes narrow, brow knit in confusion. He looked at her parents and then back at Maahi, before turning around and leaving.

Maahi's hand stayed still in the air, where his arm had been. She didn't turn to watch him walk away. She wasn't sure she was capable of handling it. After he left, she walked over to the dining table and pulled a chair, placing it opposite Papa. She knew what was coming. She didn't have the energy to face it, but she knew she had no other option. So she sat down and waited for it.

Ma spoke first. 'What was that all about?' She hesitated and asked, 'Are you saying that he's your *boyfriend*?'

Maahi smiled sadly at the way Ma said *boyfriend*, as if it was a dirty word. She couldn't say yes. She just sat there, blinking away her tears.

'Since when has this been going on?' Papa asked.

Maahi stared fixedly at her lap and said, 'Over a year. Feels much longer.'

'When did this start? Where?' Ma asked.

'When I was working at Cozy Coffee.'

'So this is what you've been doing all along? Behind our back?'

'Ma—'

'We trusted you. We let you work at that place because you insisted. You know we never approved of you working at a coffee shop,' Papa said, his voice growing louder. 'Is this why you wanted to continue working there even after you joined college?'

'Did you want to drop out of college because of him?' Ma asked, gasping.

'No,' Maahi said mildly. 'I wanted to work at the coffee shop because I was learning how to bake, with Laila, and I really, really wanted to continue doing that. I wanted to drop out of college the second time because I didn't want to study business economics. There was no point wasting time and money—'

'I was willing to pay for it! All you had to do was stay in college and get your education!' Papa thundered. He got up and took a step towards Maahi.

Ma went to him and stood between them. She turned to Maahi and asked, 'We trusted you, when you've been doing this all along ... Who else knows? What if someone from the colony—'

'So *what*? What if someone from the colony found out? I don't *want* to keep it a secret. It shouldn't be a secret. I should be able to talk to my own parents about the man I'm in love with and want to marry!' Maahi cried. She got up too.

'MAAHI!' both her parents yelled together.

'WHAT? What is wrong with loving someone? He's a really good person. If you would just give him a chance, you'd like him. He's loving and caring and understanding. He's smart and funny and he makes me happy!' She struggled for breath as she said, '*Why* is it so bad? Give me one reason why—'

'Don't talk to your father like that!' Ma screamed.

'Fine! I'm sorry. I'm sorry I even tried.'

'What is that supposed—' Papa started, but Maahi cut him off.

'It means I'm sorry I thought, for one second, that you would be open-minded enough to consider this. I thought maybe, for one second, you could stop thinking about the neighbours and the distant relatives who anyway don't give a shit about us. But you care more about them than your own daughter. And you have no idea how sad I feel saying this, but it's true. It's always been true.' Maahi had backed up against the wall and was huffing angrily, her whole body shaking.

Sarthak walked in through the living room door, unplugging his earphones. He paused and looked around, sensing the atmosphere immediately. 'What's … ?'

'Maahi has a boyfriend!' Ma said. 'Did you know about—?'

'Yes, I have a boyfriend and I love him, and I tried to be an adult and tell my parents about him. I was stupid enough to expect them to be adults too.'

'Maahi!' Ma cried.

'Fine, I'll shut up. No one's listening to me anyway. In a couple of years, you'll be okay with marrying me to some random man I've never met before. Our ideals might not match, we might want different things in life, we probably won't even get along, but we would find all of that out *after* we're already married. And because I'm supposed to be a *good girl*, I'll spend the rest of my life trying to make it work, *pretending* to be happy. Because that's more important than me *actually* being happy. No one gives a shit about *that*.' Maahi snickered. She muttered dejectedly, 'Everything is great as long as the neighbours and the extended family think our life is perfect. As long as it *looks* like we're happy.'

No one said a word. Papa had been quiet for a while. Ma looked frazzled, but out of words. Sarthak took a step towards Maahi, but she walked right past him to her bedroom. She got her bag and walked out of the house.

Sarthak followed her as she ran down the stairs. 'Maahi, wait! Where are you going?'

'I don't know!'

'Hold on! You need to relax!'

'Don't fucking tell me what to do!' Maahi jerked her arm off his grip. 'Just because you don't have the strength to fight for what you want doesn't mean I have to be the same way. This house is fucking insane. Living here is torture and I can't stay quiet any longer.'

'What does that mean? What did I ever do to you?'

Sarthak looked so shocked and so obviously hurt that it tore at Maahi's chest. That didn't stop her though. She said, 'You didn't do anything to me, but look at what you're doing to yourself! You're not fighting for the girl you're so obviously in love with. Do you know how rare that is? How difficult it is to find someone you feel that way about?'

'Maahi, I didn't get into—'

'So what? Does that mean you have to sever all ties? You can't even try long distance? You could transfer to her college next year, or maybe she could transfer to yours—I don't know! You can at least *try* to figure it out!'

'I don't ... We don't...'

But Maahi had already walked away. She half ran, half stumbled to the Metro station and got on the train. She was glad that Vaishali was the last station and all trains went in the same direction from there. She didn't have it in her to make that decision at the moment.

༄

Maahi found herself in a dark room. She pulled the main shutter in the front all the way down and stood in the darkness, facing the empty space. Turning on the flash on her cell phone, she searched for the light switch. She found it all the way at the back, and flicked it on. She thought how it was the ideal location for the switch to be. It would be on the back wall, the one behind the counter.

Of course, there was no counter. There might never be one. She imagined it anyway. Customers would walk in from the front door—there was little space, two steps in there would be the wide display of their cookies and cupcakes. Lights overhead would shine on them and make them look even more delicious.

The way she envisioned it, there would be a lot of small mirrors around, wall decals in the shape of cookies and cupcakes. Their theme colours were turquoise and a subtle metallic gold. The walls would be painted turquoise, contrasted by the gold carpet, mirrors on the wall, overhead hanging lamps and a few tall stools in the corner. Their boxes would be in the same colour combination, just like the menu, flyers, coupons, business cards, website and everything else. It would be very tastefully done—subtle but not boring. All of it would have a very bohemian chic feel to it.

The piece Maahi was most excited about was a large mirror she had found at an antique store in Chandni Chowk. It was large and square, with a dust-gold metal frame in intricate design. She fell in love with the frame as soon as she laid eyes on it. She could picture it on the wall behind the counter. She wondered if Laila would love it as much as she did.

Maahi was in charge of the interior décor. To cut cost, they hadn't wanted to hire a decorator, and Maahi had wanted to do this from the start. She had looked at hundreds of stores online, found thousands of ideas on the Internet. She had gone around Delhi to find pieces that would be just the right amount of classy and subdued.

She walked into the back of the shop, where they would install their kitchen. It smelled sterile, and looked bland, empty of all appliances and equipment. The kitchen area was exactly the same size as the customer section—not very big at all. Just big enough.

Maahi could see herself there. She imagined where everything would go—the fridge, the oven, the appliances and equipment. She organized the drawers in her head. Even the thought of buying measuring cups and spoons excited her.

And it might never happen.

Laila had given up on her, disappointed. She was possibly the person who had shown most faith in her, and now she had given up too. Maahi didn't blame her. She simply accepted the fact that she wasn't good enough. She didn't have what it took to start something and see it through. She was a quitter. She dropped out of Christ, she quit Fourth Eye Apps, she almost dropped out of DU, she quit Cozy Coffee and now she was letting Cookies + Cupcakes, her dream, go.

And for what? She didn't resent quitting her two jobs—those were just placeholders—they brought her closer to her dream and she was only too glad to let them go. But she dropped out of Christ and messed up Cookies + Cupcakes over a guy. The same guy.

The more she thought about it, the more furious she got. Not at Kishan, at herself. She was the one letting it happen, over and over again. For once, she needed to stick to something and see it through.

Laila, her closest friend, was disappointed in her and contemplating shutting down Cookies + Cupcakes. She had fought with her parents. She had the best brother a girl could ask for and she had treated him cruelly. She hurt and drove away the man who loved her and cared about her. He might never forgive her or talk to her again.

All because she let the one guy who'd ruined her life once do it again. She quit even trying to understand how he still held that kind of power over her. How he could just waltz right back into her life and turn everything upside down. It terrified her.

Maahi felt like she had no command over her own life anymore. It was spiralling out of control, hurting everyone who cared for her in its wake.

She pulled out her phone. There was no missed call or text message. Because no one gave a fuck anymore. She called Kishan.

'Hey!'

'Kishan,' Maahi said quietly.

'Yeah, What's up?'

'I was thinking about you.'

'Aww, I was just thinking about you too!' Kishan said, chuckling. It infuriated her—how carefree he could be, how easy everything was for him, how he never had to work for anything in his life—got everything he wanted, including her.

'I don't want to see you ever again,' Maahi said through gritted teeth.

'*What?* Are you serious?'

'Yes, I am.'

'What the fuck, Maahi! Where is this even coming from?' Kishan asked, annoyance evident in his tone.

'The same place it should've come from the first time you tried to get back in touch with me. You're a fucking asshole, and you know it. You don't accept me for who I am, don't want to let me be comfortable in my own skin and I don't know if you know this—but you don't give a fuck about me. If you did, you wouldn't have hurt me in the first place. But you did. Do you realize the condition I was in after you left me? Do you have any idea what it took from me? How long it took me to recover?'

'I already said sorry about that. I don't know what else—'

'You said sorry, and that undid what happened, magically made it disappear?'

'No. But we can put it behind us and move on. It's in the past. We're both adults here.' Kishan sighed and added, 'At least I thought we are.'

'Shut the fuck up, Kishan! Just *stop*. Stop trying to make me seem childish when your brain isn't developed enough to even begin to understand the gravity of the situation. No, you *can't* just walk back into my life. We *can't* just pretend that all these years in between haven't passed, and pick up where we left off. Because that's *not* how it works.' Maahi breathed hard, her chest heaving. She was hot and cold at the same time, her forehead sweating, and gooseflesh rising on her arms.

Kishan was yelling on the phone. 'Where the fuck do you get off saying shit like that—'

Maahi was done. She hung up, disoriented, looking for support. She slid against the kitchen wall and slipped down to the floor. Folding her legs in front of her, she rested her aching head on her knees. There was no light in the kitchen and she was grateful for that. She closed her eyes and felt tears wet her cheek. This one time, she let them flow. There was no one around to see them. She didn't need to pretend.

21

Maahi heard a clatter on the front door and jumped up in alarm. Her head swam and she leaned against the wall for a second for support. Unable to see in the darkness of the unfurnished kitchen, she grappled with the doorknob, eventually pushing it open. She closed her eyes against the bright lights in the outer room. When she opened them again, she found herself standing in front of Sarthak and Laila—their faces pale and hair windblown.

'*What the fuck is the matter with you?*' Laila yelled and ran to her. She pulled Maahi into her arms and squeezed her tight. 'What are you *doing* here? Why are you such an asshole? Do you have any idea how worried we were?'

Maahi broke down in Laila's arms.

'Don't you fucking cry! I can't be mad at you if you cry.'

Maahi cried harder. Laila rocked her back and forth in her arms. 'I'm sorry. I'm so sorry,' Maahi said, her voice muffled against Laila's neck. 'I fucked everything up. It was going good and then I fucked it up like I fuck everything up.'

'Shh. Stop it,' Laila said, pulling back.

'I know you don't want to work with me anymore because I'm irresponsible and stupid and childish.'

'You *can* be difficult to work with. A little—'

'But I really want this, Laila. I really, really want this. More than anything else in the world. I don't even have anything else. I fucked everything up, pissed off everyone I know and now I'm all alone and I don't care. All I want is this. I've been sitting here, looking at this space and all it can be ... so much. We're so close. All that we have envisioned is so close to coming alive. How can we let it go? I can't. I can't, Laila.' Maahi shuffled on her feet. She threw her arms around restlessly, pointing to the walls. 'Did I show you the pictures of the pattern I've selected for the walls? You'll love it. It's so beautiful. This is the perfect little place. We can really make it something amazing.'

'I know,' Laila said, looking around too. She added, 'And I don't want to give up either.'

'Are you *serious*?'

'Yes. We haven't come this far for nothing. But, you have to really take it seriously this time. This is no joke.'

Maahi shook her head fervently. 'Yes. It's no joke and I'll take it seriously. I'll do everything that needs to be done and more. I'll look at the list of appliances tonight and I'll go with you tomorrow to order whatever needs to be ordered.'

'Relax. There's no rush. I'm sorry I blew up on you. I've been frustrated recently, and it's not your fault. I shouldn't have talked to you that way. I didn't realize you would take it that seriously,' Laila said sincerely. Her lips were dry and her face looked small, half covered with her curls falling over her cheeks. Under the overhead light, she almost looked younger than Maahi.

'But you *were* serious.'

'Yeah. For a second there, I seriously wondered if we could pull this off.'

Maahi nodded. 'It's my fault. I should've helped you out more in the field. You've been doing everything, running around ... I feel so bad. Why didn't you tell me?'

Laila shrugged. 'I thought I could do it by myself. Until it stressed me out too much and I couldn't take it for a second there. But it doesn't matter. Why didn't *you* fucking tell me about Kishan?'

'Kishan? How do you know?' Maahi asked, looking at Sarthak, who was standing next to the shutter, leaning against the wall, looking down into his phone. He looked so sad, his face so small, Maahi felt a tug in her chest.

'Siddhant called me, trying to find out where you were,' Laila said. 'I was still pissed at you, so I didn't pay attention. But then Sarthak called me too, asking if you were with me. We must've called you like a hundred times. Don't you fucking go disappearing on us like that again!'

'I didn't plan to. I lost track of time after I called Kishan and yelled at him. It was the weirdest thing. I fell asleep,' Maahi said. 'Guess I just kind of gave up. I was thinking about how badly I wanted Cookies + Cupcakes to happen, and stopped caring about everything else.'

'Hold up. One, Cookies + Cupcakes is our baby and we're *not* killing it. It's going to happen. I'm going to make you work extra hard, and you're going to cry and whine, but you're going to do it. You're so young and talented and I'd hate to see you lose focus. That's why I was pissed at you—because you weren't caring about the right things. And if you don't put in the work in the beginning, you'd never be able to keep up once we launch and things start going crazy. I've worked with start-ups before, and I've seen people mess up,'

Laila said. 'You're *not* going to mess up—not on my watch. Baking is one thing, setting up a bakery is a completely different ball game.'

'I'm not going to mess up. I promise.'

'I know you won't. Now wait, did you say you yelled at Kishan?'

'Yes,' Maahi said. A smile crept up on her face. 'I don't know what got into me. I was just *done*, you know? Suddenly, I was done with him and his bullshit and couldn't stand it anymore.'

'So you asked him to fuck off?'

'More or less.'

'Not good enough.' Laila curled her lips. 'Did you use the actual words?'

'I said *fuck* a lot. And I called him an asshole. I think at one point I did ask him to shut the fuck up. Does all of that add up and make a *fuck off*?'

Laila nodded. 'You make me proud.'

Maahi giggled. 'I feel so much better already. I don't need him.'

'*Of course* you don't! You don't need anyone. You're a strong, independent, ambitious woman. You can take care of yourself. If a relationship is making your life worse instead of better, you're in the wrong one.'

'I might've been in the right one … with Siddhant. But I don't think he will ever talk to me again.'

'He called me to check up on you. He definitely still cares,' Laila said.

'Enough to forget that I almost broke up with him over my ex? I don't think he can forgive or forget that I kissed my ex and tried to blame it on him. I've been so shitty with him recently … Like you said, if a relationship is making your life worse... I'm definitely making his life worse. I don't think he should be with me.'

'You don't mean that!'

'It's true. I'm always annoyed and treat him badly for no reason. He deserves so much better...' Maahi said sadly.

'Shut up. If you're going to whine, I'm out of here. Actually, let's get out of here anyway. What are we doing in here? It's so hot,' Laila said, pulling the neck of her top up and fanning herself.

'Ready to leave?' Sarthak asked. His face was taut.

Maahi could tell he was trying really hard to be impassive and appear as if he didn't care. 'I'm sorry,' she said. 'I'm really, really sorry. That was not only uncalled for, it was mean to the point of being cruel. I didn't need to take out my anger on you.'

Sarthak pursed his lips.

'I feel really bad. You have perfect reasoning for doing what you're doing. It makes total sense,' Maahi continued.

Sarthak finally looked at her. 'Nah. You were right. I talked to her...'

'*And?*'

'We're going to try to be friends. See where it goes.'

'That's awesome! I hope you don't get hurt, but I mean, hey, if not her, someone else is going to hurt you. You can't run away from that forever. Shit happens.'

'That's a very positive outlook on life.' Sarthak chuckled.

'No, I'm serious. If you have to get hurt, why not by someone who's actually worth it?'

'Makes sense to me,' Laila said. 'Look at her—our girl Maahi growing up!'

Maahi ignored her and looked up at Sarthak. 'So, we're cool?' she asked.

'Yep.'

'Hug it out?'

'Nope.'

'Fist bump?'

'Meh,' Sarthak said and reluctantly offered her his fist. Maahi bumped it with hers.

Laila cleared her throat. 'If your sibling PDA is done, can we go? This place is a sauna. Maahi—air conditioning—first on the list.'

'Got it.' Maahi gave her a thumbs up. She bent down to pull up the shutter. 'How furious are Ma and Papa?'

'Very. But I think I was able to turn them a little,' Sarthak said, bending down with her. He got hold of the handles of the shutter. 'I got this.'

'Really? What do you mean?'

'After you left, Ma went on and on about how disrespectful you were and how dare you and all that. Papa wasn't saying much. I just sat there quietly. And when Ma asked me how it came to this, and how could you go behind their backs and lie to them, I told her that maybe you didn't tell her because you knew this is how they would react. And you weren't wrong. I would've done the same thing. I told her that we sometimes feel like we can't talk to our own parents, even when we need help.'

'Shit. What did she say?' Maahi asked. They got under the half pulled-up shutter and stepped out. 'Oh God, I feel so bad.'

'What I said wasn't half as bad as you, but I guess both of us in the same day, with the difference in the tone ... I don't know ... They didn't say anything to me.' Siddhant shrugged. 'But I've got to say—I'm loving the role reversal. You the trouble child and me, the good one. It was odd at first, but I'm getting used to it. Keep letting them down!'

'Ha! Don't get used to it. I'm going to be awesome.' Maahi smirked.

'Guys,' Laila said, coming out of the shop. It was around three in the morning, and the area was deserted. The warm July air hit them, a light breeze flowing. It was odd to see Shahpurjat like that—a place that was always bursting with people.

Maahi turned towards Laila and followed her gaze. 'Siddhant?' she mouthed.

He looked confused for a second, as if trying to find them, and then walked towards them. Maahi was standing with Laila and Sarthak on each side. Siddhant stopped in front of her. They all looked at each other awkwardly. Maahi met Siddhant's eyes and held them.

'Umm,' Laila said, clearing her throat. 'So, we're going to bounce then?'

'Yeah.' Sarthak's face turned red as he said, 'I'm going to hang out in the parking lot. Just … you know, update me on the situation? Like if you're coming home with me or what? Let me know when you know.'

'I'll keep you company,' Laila said, and they walked away.

Maahi and Siddhant didn't pay any attention to them. They kept looking at each other. Maahi was so happy to see him. She didn't care why he was there, maybe he just wanted to fight with her, but she was glad that he was there regardless. She felt horrible about how things went down between them, and was glad for a chance to talk to him, maybe try to explain.

'You're okay?' Siddhant asked slowly.

'I'm really sorry,' Maahi said.

'I was worried about you.'

'Why? I'm such an asshole. You shouldn't care about me.'

'Can't help it.'

'I feel so bad about everything. I understand if you can never forgive me, and don't ever want to see me again. Why are you even here? You shouldn't talk to me.' Maahi looked up at him, wanting to touch his face, somehow holding back.

'Because I have a question I need to ask you. I couldn't ... I need to know.'

'What is it?'

'Do you love him? That guy ... your ex-boyfriend? Is that what you were trying to tell me when you told me about him and what happened between you guys last night?' Siddhant's face was distorted, crumbling. Maahi could see how much he was hurting because of her.

'No. I was confused. I was all over the place, saying all kinds of things ... I don't even know why I was saying any of that.'

'So you don't love him.'

'I don't!' Maahi said.

'Then what was *that* about? All the things you said you felt for him?'

'I can be an idiot sometimes. He came back and he was saying all these things to me. A smarter girl wouldn't have fallen into the trap so easily. I don't know how, even after all these years, he still holds a power over me. And I mistook that for love, or *something*. I thought it was something special.'

Siddhant nodded. After a quiet moment, he said, 'No. I can't say that I understand.'

'I don't either. But talk to me. Maybe I can help.'

'I don't understand how whatever was going on between you two made you forget about us. I thought we loved each other.'

'I thought so too. I still think so. I do love you, Siddhant,' Maahi said. She looked at him, remembering their first date—

the night they'd played Mario Kart. How excited she was, wondering how it would turn out, what it would become. It was good for a while. But all they'd done in a long time was fight. Whatever they had hadn't been able to survive the strain of two hectic schedules and that's not how it should have been. 'You're kind and caring and funny. I love spending time with you. But frankly ... we don't have any.'

Siddhant rubbed his face with his palms, and looked away.

'It shouldn't be so hard.' Maahi sighed and looked at her feet. 'We shouldn't have to struggle so much, right from the beginning. I love you, Siddhant. I made a mistake with Kishan, and I will understand if you hate me forever for it. All I've ever done is make your life difficult. I see that now.'

'Would you stop making assumptions about how *I* feel?'

'I don't want to get in the way of your career. I don't want to be the person who adds to your stress, instead of making it easier. I can never forgive myself for being that person.'

'Maahi—'

'No! Listen to me. I can't come in the way of something you've been working on all your life. You would resent me for it and I can't handle that. I want you to be happy, and you'd never be happy with me. I don't know why you've come here right now—is it because of some sort of obligation you feel towards me? You don't have to. You didn't do anything wrong. I was the one who fucked up.'

Siddhant was looking away from her, staring at the closed shops. Maahi pulled his arm and turned him to her. She held back tears as she said, 'It's not your fault. Don't worry about me. I'll be okay. I have my bakery. I'll keep busy. I can take care of myself. You don't have to be with me out of some misplaced sense of obligation.'

Siddhant didn't look at her for a while. She stood next to him and stared at the shops too. She wondered if he was going to leave. She was giving him an out, and the last time she had done that with someone, he had taken it. This time, she wanted him to take it. With everything going on with Cookies + Cupcakes, things were only going to get harder for them. And she wasn't so sure they would be able to survive it. If they didn't end it now, they would only add more torturous months before the inevitable end. And that would close all doors for any kind of friendship between them. She didn't want that. They had to end it before they reached a point of no return.

'Are you done deciding how I feel? Can I speak now, with your permission?' Siddhant asked slowly, still staring at the houses.

'Yes,' Maahi said meekly.

'You have no idea how much I love you, how badly I want to be with you. When you told me about Kishan today … do you have any idea how that made me feel? You kept undermining what we have, when I think what we have is the best thing that ever happened to me.' Siddhant slowly turned to look at her. 'Just thinking about that guy kissing you … it feels … it's unbearable. I honestly can't even think about it. And the thought that you chose someone else over me, while you were with me—'

'I didn't! I know it's difficult for you to trust me right now, but believe me, I didn't choose anyone over you. Whatever's going wrong between us doesn't have anything to do with Kishan. It might've triggered the realization, but it's always been there.'

Siddhant hooked his finger under her chin and studied her face. His own face looked pained in the light coming from their unfurnished shop. 'Yes. It has always been there. I wanted to be with you enough to ignore it, but it's still very much there. I'm so caught up in my work and you in yours. I don't know how we ever thought this was going to work.'

Maahi's voice broke when she tried to speak. 'Because we were in love and we thought we would win against all odds.'

'Maybe under different circumstances...'

Maahi nodded fervently, trying to hold back tears. 'Maybe.'

They were quiet for a while, as they stood next to each other, staring at the shops. It wasn't as dark as it was before; the sun was on the horizon. They had ended it, and it was for the best, but neither of them moved. With every second, her determination weakened. She imagined how easy it would be just to *be*. With him, in this moment, forever.

But real life didn't work like that. In a few months, once things settled down a bit, they might start talking again. They might become friends, or maybe even something more. Or they might never talk to or see each other again—this might be the last time. Her stomach hurt just thinking about it.

'Are you okay?' Siddhant asked. He came closer to her and wrapped one long arm around her. He sighed again, whispering, 'Maahi.'

Maahi bent towards him and rested her head against his shoulder. She looked up at him and smiled sadly.

'What is it?' Siddhant asked.

'It's the way you say my name...' Maahi thought about how he never called her anything other than her name. And how much she didn't mind. 'I never needed any terms of endearment from you. Just my name from your lips sounds like a love song. Even now...'

Siddhant's fingers grazed the back of her neck. 'I'm sorry that it worked out this way…'

'Me too.'

'I'm going to go now. You'll be okay?'

Maahi nodded.

Siddhant planted a small kiss on her forehead and left. Maahi watched him walk away, feeling a tug on her heart, watching his back recede. She sniffed and looked away.

Maahi turned back to her shop. She pulled down the shutter and locked it. She walked to the parking lot, where Sarthak and Laila were waiting for her. Maahi laughed. This was all she needed. It wouldn't be that bad. She could see her life around her—the people she loved, the thing that mattered most.

Epilogue

'It's unfair that you get to do this and I don't,' Laila said, staring sadly at the assortment of cupcakes on display. Maahi had used bright, solid colours, each cupcake had a unique design, all a riot of colours mixed together, reflecting the festival she made them for. 'I'm so jealous.'

'Holi isn't the festival for your cookies,' Maahi said, appreciating the display, breathing in the smell of the fresh batch she had set on the cooling rack back in the kitchen. 'Try something for Diwali.'

'I'm going to. I'm calling dibs on Diwali.'

'Okay.' Maahi laughed. 'I'm kind of nervous.'

'Oh, you'll be fine. Your parents have performed much better than expected. We've proved ourselves. You're good.'

'We've proved ourselves with the first shop. What if they don't like this one? How can I not be nervous?'

'Because all of this is awesome?' Laila said, looking around. It was the opening of their second shop, this one in Hauz Khas Village. Cookies + Cupcakes had been featured in *Vogue*, in their City Directory segment, which had significantly boosted their image. They had been really persistent with social media and digital marketing. Exciting things were happening and they couldn't be happier with where they were.

They kept the design of the second shop consistent with the first one in Shahpurjat. The turquoise they had picked for the walls came out lovelier than it looked on the palette. Along with the gold, it really livened up the place. They were especially happy with all their stationery and their website. The designer had exceeded expectations. They hired a baker to help them in the kitchen and a young girl for the counter. She reminded Maahi of herself, when she'd first started working at Cozy Coffee.

'I guess you're right. I wish Sarthak was here—he could've come in handy. He's good at handling awkward social situations, by being even awkwarder and making a fool of himself,' Maahi said. Sarthak was in Mumbai, in his second semester. Last time she checked, he was still friends with that girl he liked. They were *close friends*.

'Yeah, he's good at that. But I can cover for him, just for today,' Laila offered. 'Dammit! I hate that you're going to get all the compliments today. Let me run to the kitchen and bring out a box of cookies for everyone real quick,' Laila said, rushing inside. She brought a tray and placed it on the counter.

'Great. Now, if they hate my cupcakes, we've got a solid backup option.'

'They're going to love it,' Laila assured her.

Maahi looked out of the bakery. There was no sign of her parents yet. 'I bumped into Siddhant today.'

'Yeah? First time since breaking up?' Laila asked.

'Yep. We hadn't even talked or texted since that day, what, eight months ago?'

'How did it go?'

Maahi thought back to the surprised expression on his face, which had changed into a familiar warm smile in a second, spreading warmth inside her too. 'Not bad.' She grinned.

Laila raised an eyebrow at her.

'Oh God,' Maahi whispered, watching her parents coming towards the store. 'This is going to be something, isn't it?'

'We'll get through this. It has the potential to be quite a horror story, but we'll make it.' Laila put a hand around Maahi's shoulder and squeezed her. They burst out laughing.

Acknowledgements

Over the years, writing acknowledgements for my books has become an opportunity for self-reflection. The names in these lists tend to change dramatically each time, some of it is because I live like a friggin' nomad, relocating every few years, and the rest I attribute to growing up. When I say growing up, I mean losing people on the way, keeping the important ones close and making new friends!

Disclaimer: I'm only naming the people who at least read my books, because the alternative is stupid. I'm not going to thank you for not reading any of my books ever, duh. Unless you're family—then I'd have to put up with your defiance.

My constants: my parents, for letting me do my thing, even when it included moving 7,000 miles away from home. The rest of my family—my brother, Nishant Malay, and all of my many cousins (and their secret boyfriends/girlfriends—welcome to the family, btw). Deep Bhaiya, Bhabhi, TD, Avi, Shan, Chutru, Mohit, Sumi, Mona, Mili, Shreya and Tutu—I love each and every one of you!

When I finished writing the second draft of this book, I needed feedback. A lot of my dear friends offered to be my test readers and I forced the rest of them. Laura Duarte Gomez, for being my first reader and your not-baseless-anymore support. Robert Tanner, your literary swag continues to shine bright. Ashish Shrestha, I still hate you, but thanks. Tejal Shah, for being the elder sister I never had. David Torrone for, like, being who you are, I guess. Julie Goldberg, for making the book have more Mario Kart – the world will thank you. Alka Singh, for the constant support. Ava Mailloux, for the best-est review ever! Lauren Gary for making me calm the eff down every time I freaked out. Lauren's mom for being interested enough in that 'weird Indian girl' to read my manuscript. You guys are bomb.

My agent extraordinaire Anish Chandy, for staying on this journey with me, as I continue to be a pain in your neck. Ananth Padmanabhan, CEO of HarperCollins India and the sender of beautiful flowers and champagne and good vibes. My editor, Manasi Subramaniam, for putting up with my crazy schedule. This is the first time we're working together, but you're already kinda fed up of me, aren't you? Prerna Gill, for the final cleaning and polishing of the manuscript, which I know couldn't have been easy at all. Amrita Talwar, my publicist, the superstar. I'm writing this before we start promoting the book, but I'm sure it'll be awesome!

You, the reader, for being so warm and kind and always pushing me to work harder for you. Your love and support mean everything to me. Yeah, I'm cheesy like that.

And Guruji, Sri Sri Paramhansa Yogananda, for the positivity and faith you offer.